WATER
ON THE
MOON

WATER
ON THE
MOON

A NOVEL

JEAN P MOORE

SHE WRITES PRESS

Published 2014
Printed in the United States of America
ISBN: 978-1-938314-61-2
Library of Congress Control Number: 2013953912

For information, address:
She Writes Press
1563 Solano Ave #546
Berkeley, CA 94707

For Steve

All who joy would win
Must share it—Happiness was born a twin.

—George Gordon Byron, *Don Juan*

Contents

Running on Empty

*A*t seven thirty in the morning, on October 9, 2009, Lidia Raven, divorced mother of two, lingered in bed enjoying a no-school day at Greenwich High School. She had looked forward to this day, a little reprieve from the frantic morning ritual of getting her seventeen-year-old twins, Carly and Clarisse, out the door and off to school. Of late, senioritis had kicked in and claimed her otherwise conscientious daughters. But on this morning, while she lay happily reading her novel—just as Julian the protagonist was about to sleep with the Irish singer—she heard a plane's engine sputtering in the distance. Moments later Lidia became aware of a humming noise getting louder, much louder. *That's close, way too close,* she thought, tossing aside the covers, her book tumbling to the floor. "My God, it's going to hit," she said out loud, her feet on the floor before she had willed her body to move. Fear ignited an adrenaline surge that sent her sprinting up the stairs to the girls' bedroom. Standing between both beds, she pulled the quilts away, shaking the sleep from both until, startled, they lay staring up at their frenzied mother.

"Downstairs, now!" she screamed, pulling them to the landing and practically pushing them to the bottom, where she then shoved both in the closet under the stairs, a space barely large enough to hold them. Opal, their usually sensible black Lab, began barking hysterically, having been roused from her morning snooze. Lidia reached out and dragged Opal in by the collar. In this cramped space Lidia opened her arms like wings and wrapped them around her whimpering girls, Opal beside them. "What's happening?" the girls cried. "Mom!"

"Shhh," was Lidia's only response, certain the end was at hand, no time for anything but to comfort, to be calm; no time to think, only to pray, *Dear God, please don't let them suffer.* She felt waves of panic needing to be stifled, dread to be endured—until she thought her heart would burst; she felt regret for all that would not be—for her girls—her magnificent girls. How could this be happening? Lidia heard the thunderous noise and felt the vibration rattle her skull and every bone. Then she braced herself for the end of their mortal lives.

The plane she knew had been hurtling toward them struck with unearthly force. The trio and their dog were slammed against the wall, but the staircase held even as roof, walls, beams, and plaster crashed all around them. In an instant their life-saving little closet under the stairs was buried in their home's rubble, but they had miraculously survived. The closet was intact.

Lidia heard her daughters crying inconsolably, but she could not stop herself from laughing. They were alive. The worst thing imaginable had not happened. Her daughters had not been blown to oblivion. Squeezing them to her and thanking God out loud, she then unwrapped herself from her daughters, moving to touch them, to feel arms and legs, assuring herself they were alive. Alive.

"Mom, stop," cried Carly. "Why are you laughing? Are you okay? What's the matter with you?"

"What's happening to us?" asked Clarisse, her voice quaking.

"We're okay," she said, in disbelief, reaching out to feel for each of her girls, and Opal too. It couldn't have been more than nine in the morning, but the rubble surrounding them blocked out all but small slivers of light.

Lidia took a deep breath before trying to calm her daughters. "It was a plane, a plane hit the house," she explained, summoning all her strength to sound in control, her voice low but shaky.

"How will we get out?" asked Clarisse. "How can we get help?"

Just then, Opal, who had been quivering on the floor, roused herself and began digging below one of the slivers of light.

"We just have to be calm until help comes. The neighbors have called for help by now. I'm sure of it." She took one daughter under each arm and reached up to stroke their long dark hair, rocking them gently from side to side. Surely they would be saved. They hadn't survived the crash above only to die entombed below. Surely no god would be that cruel.

"I'm certain the neighbors have called for help—Mrs. Beltran, for sure."

Their house on a cul-de-sac on Apple Way in Greenwich had once been the only house on the street, but now they were in the middle of a neighborhood with much newer center hall colonials and only a few remaining white shingle farmhouses. The Ravens' nearest neighbor and long-time family friend, Mrs. Beltran, lived in one of the older homes.

No sooner had she uttered these encouraging words than Lidia heard muffled voices.

"Do you hear that, girls? Someone is out there. Do you hear them?"

The three wriggled toward Opal, trying to concentrate on the voices.

When the first muffled sounds became recognizable words, the trapped party screamed with relief.

"Oh my God," said Clarisse. "It's Mrs. B."

"Are you in there? Lidia? Carly, Clarisse, can you hear me?"

"Yes!" they all screamed in unison.

"Help is coming. Just wait. Don't worry, okay?"

Carly and Clarisse huddled against their mother. Believing now they would be rescued, their panic gave way to shorter and softer cries and then to silence. As they sat and waited for help, Lidia's relief at having survived the crash ebbed as a new fear rose. Her body stiffened. She felt the girls tense up, sensitive to her every move. She tried to relax but could not stop thinking about the plane, no doubt now lodged somewhere in the house, that would surely at some point explode, creating unbearable heat and sucking out all the oxygen. How could they escape that fate? Had they come this far only to die after all? Her heart began to race again. She could not utter a word or make a sound to awaken fear in her now calm girls, but her thoughts soon turned to escape—how would they escape? An urge to begin clawing their way out overtook her when the beam from a flashlight shone directly into the place where they were crouched.

"We're in here!" Carly cried out.

"Help us," said Clarisse.

With that, both girls scrambled out from under their mother and onto their knees, screaming encouragement to their would-be rescuers. "We're here, we're here! Help us, please."

They heard muffled voices in response, calling back to them and tapping on the wreckage above.

Within minutes, the digging began. At first it sounded as though handheld shovels were trying to move through the mountain of rubble. Then it seemed an earthmover must have been slowly and carefully removing the debris around them.

In the frenzy of activity that followed, they were freed, wrapped in blankets, checked for injuries by the EMS, and proclaimed whole, but just the same requiring an ambulance ride to the hospital for good measure. Amid flashing lights and with the whole neighborhood turned out to watch, Mrs. Beltran was the first to greet them, near collapse with relief. All three were strapped into gurneys, about to be lifted into the back of the emergency vehicle waiting for them.

"Wait," said Lidia, lifting up on her elbows. "Our dog. What about Opal?"

"It's okay, Lidia, dear. I've got her. She's right here." Lidia glanced down to see Opal near her gurney but staying close to their trusted neighbor.

"Of course, Mrs. B. You've got her. Thank you," said Lidia, relieved. As the girls were lifted into the ambulance, Lidia began to lie back down, but no—again she hoisted herself up, this time to take a long look at the devastation, the pile of broken boards, pulverized plaster, the ruthlessly strewn bits of furniture and personal belongings that had constituted her family's home for four generations.

The first sensation to emerge after numbness was nausea. "Will they make sure no one touches anything?" Lidia asked. "I have to get back here, soon, to see what can be salvaged."

"Your property is now an investigation site, Ma'am. Don't worry. The police will go over all this with you," a handsome young medic said, hoisting Lidia into the ambulance.

Lidia, somewhat assured, couldn't help wondering about little things—family photos of the property from the 1930s, before construction had started, for one. She had particularly loved looking at the images of empty fields and acre upon acre of apple orchards. Her grandfather had built this house, and it was the house where her father had been born, where Lidia had grown up and then lived with her ex-husband until the divorce three years earlier, where they'd raised their girls.

Owen had remodeled the downstairs before she'd gotten pregnant with Carly and Clarisse. Hoping to start a family, the couple had combined several rooms to form a large master bedroom, the likes of which their architect had assured them would form a comfortable suite, including a bathroom with his and her sinks, a small but quite serviceable reading room/office, large walk-in closets, and a sweeping view of the sloping backyard that led to what had once been her family's orchards. All of this remodeling would pay off handsomely, he said, in increased resale value when one day they went to sell, neither of them knowing then what the future would hold for them. While the work downstairs was underway, Lidia and Owen applied themselves to turning their old room upstairs into a nursery, efforts that required some rethinking once they found out they were expecting not one but two bundles of joy.

Now she looked at the ruins. Instead of her home, the once beautiful two-story white shingle farmhouse with its historic preservation plaque on the door, there was a mountain of debris, the tail of a small plane protruding from the general vicinity of where the girls' bedroom had been, that side of the house demolished beyond recognition, the rest still feebly standing. Lidia shuddered. Her girls. But they were safe. They were all safe. A miracle.

"The pilot," said Lidia suddenly, aware that at least one other life had been gravely endangered, or worse. "Is he . . .?"

"She," said the medic, who was now monitoring Lidia's blood pressure, as the ambulance doors were closed behind them. "She didn't make it. Only one fatality—there was no one else. You and your daughters are very lucky, Ma'am."

"Yes, we are. That poor woman," said Lidia. Images she didn't want to conjure up flashed through her mind. She began shaking uncontrollably, knowing the pilot was lying dead in the wreckage—*in our home*, Lidia thought as the ambulance drove away.

———◆———

It was three o'clock in the afternoon before Polly Niven came to pick up the Ravens from the hospital. They'd been there for nearly five hours, and Polly had been in the waiting room for nearly as long, ever since she first got the call from Lidia, who explained what had happened. Polly, after retrieving Opal from Mrs. Beltran, came to get the Raven girls, as she called them, in her old but recently purchased 1998 Subaru Forester. She had Opal in the way back.

"Let them through. My word," exclaimed Polly, whose short cropped white hair was shining in the fall afternoon sunlight. There was but a short distance between the hospital exit and Polly's car, but the crush of reporters was blocking the path of the fleeing party. With each step, Polly's long pale blue flannel skirt billowed around her legs and over her black leather boots, heightening the impression that a whirlwind was about to be unleashed if those obstructing her did not stand down. Her long slender fingers adjusted the delicate and intricately hammered silver belt she'd once bargained vigorously for in Kathmandu. The belt now slung low on her slim waist over her matching blue tunic, adding to the illusion of Polly's youth, dispelled not so much by her white hair as by the fine wrinkles on her face going both horizontally and vertically, forming a kind of grid under her eyes extending down onto her high cheeks bones. Even so, no one ever guessed her true age.

"The only thing hard about being eighty," Polly remarked on her milestone birthday, "is that I can't do splits in yoga anymore."

Pushing her multi-colored, hand-woven wool shawl, obtained during the same bargaining match in Nepal, securely onto her shoulders, she led her charges to the car, shielding them from a phalanx of reporters all boisterously and quite rudely, Polly pointed out, pushing their cameras and microphones toward the escaping party of four.

"How are you three holding up?" Polly asked as they drove toward Old Greenwich, a part of town with more than its fair share of mansions on the Long Island Sound. Stealing a furtive glance toward Lidia next to her and then through the rearview mirror toward the girls, she tried to determine the extent of their emotional trauma. A firm believer in the healing power of positive energy, a certainty she had picked up on Mount Fuji during the harmonic convergence of 1987, Polly believed she should go slowly, letting them talk when they were ready and in the meantime keeping it light.

"I must say, you look pretty good in your second-hand duds," she said, referring to the clothes she'd gathered together for them and brought to the hospital.

"Pretty cool, Polly," said Clarisse. "How did you know I like vintage jeans? These are so real—not like the ones they make to look old."

"Oh, I have my ways. I just consulted the Oracle of Apple Way," she said, nodding toward Lidia. As soon as the name of their street escaped her lips, Polly drew a sharp breath. "I'm sorry. I was trying to . . . I didn't mean to . . ."

"It's okay, Polly," said Lidia, gently petting Opal, who had precariously balanced herself between the back and front seats and who had put her head on the armrest separating Polly and Lidia. "You can speak the name of the street. We're going to have to go back to the house. We're going to have to talk about what happened."

Polly focused on keeping a cheerful demeanor as her heart went out to her homeless friends. "How do you like yours?" she asked, looking back at Carly through the mirror.

"I like my sweater," said Carly. "And the boots, too. So where did you get this stuff?"

"At Closet 2 Closet. You know, the Catholic Church thrift shop, on Putnam?"

"Honestly, Polly. It's all too much," said Lidia.

"Nonsense. Not another word." Polly turned to look at Lidia, her dark hair falling over the neckline of the lavender cashmere sweater Polly had picked for her. Lidia, at fifty-five, was older than most of the mothers with daughters the twins' age. Polly knew that Lidia and Owen had waited to have children, but now Lidia could pass for an older sister, the three of them tall and slim, with large, almond-shaped brown eyes and delicate features. It was hard to believe, thought Polly, that these three had been in her life for only a year, yet in that time they had come to be very important to her, filling a void that was deeper than she had realized.

Carly, standing five ten, weighing not an ounce over a hundred and twenty pounds, got the lion's share of attention, beauty being just one of her assets. She was smart and talented, an ace tennis player, and a trained soprano, and she would probably be named homecoming queen once the results of the recent election were announced. Given all the envy she could conceivably have mustered in her peers, she would likely have been universally hated were she not so down-to-earth and kind-hearted. Another of her assets: she was genuinely liked. Her interests at seventeen, though, surprisingly did not include boys. Unlike her peers, she'd rather be on the courts, or rehearsing an aria, or even reading, than going through the routine of dating, splitting up, and either causing or suffering the angst that generally ensued.

Clarisse, no less lovely, was just enough slighter and more subtle in her beauty to take a backseat to her ravishing sister. Had there been no Carly, Clarisse would be the standout girl at school. She was perfectly happy, though, to let her sister be at the forefront and under the scrutiny that came with first place. Clarisse too was a singer and a soloist in the school chorus, her musical talents extending to playing the guitar and writing songs, folk being her special interest. While Carly wore fashionable clothes and was a bit of a trendsetter, Clarisse tended to play down her looks, most days pulling her hair straight back into a ponytail and opting for large black-framed oval glasses instead of contact lenses. Still, she would no doubt be on the homecoming court.

Polly, trying to keep a conversation going, noticed the twins growing quiet. "I'm curious," she said. "Aren't phones on the top of everyone's replacement list? You must be wondering how you'll get by without them." And with that, the twins perked up.

After a quick trip to the mall for essentials and new phones, Polly and her houseguests made their way home for a light dinner of soup and salad, and they soon yawned their way to three separate bedrooms upstairs. Snuggled under down quilts smelling of lavender, Polly hoped they would sleep soundly, with thoughts of Apple Way and the tail of the plane sticking out of their house mercifully set aside for the time being.

"I don't know how to repay you, Polly," Lidia had said before falling into bed. It will take awhile for new credit cards, for new everything—"

"Don't say another word," Polly told her. "Everything will be fine. No need to worry. You'll see." Lidia smiled in return and the two said good night.

The Raven girls could stay with her as long as they needed, Polly thought, closing the door to Lidia's room. To be needed, that would be good, thought Polly. She had not felt that for some time.

The next day, after breakfast, Lidia found herself wrapped in a blanket in a rocker on the sun porch overlooking the Sound. Polly's home, the Niven Estate, as it was known in town, was a sprawling if somewhat rambling assortment of balusters, cupolas, porticos, and turrets, now all falling into disrepair. No longer able to afford the place, after what she'd only refer to as "the losses" earlier this year, Polly had given notice to her caretaker, gardener, and housekeeper. On the day of their departure, Polly had dipped into a generous portion of her remaining savings to be sure they would have enough to live on until other employment opportunities presented themselves.

Lidia knew that Polly had heavily invested in a recently revealed Ponzi scheme of mammoth proportions, and that she'd been struggling financially to hang on. The estate, one of the last old mansions directly on the Sound that hadn't been torn down to make way for new ones with the same sprawling features, was safe thanks in large part to Polly's deceased husband, John Paul Niven, the love of her exceedingly varied life. Had it not been for his other wiser investments, surely the house would have been gone by now. For the time being anyway, Polly had enough to keep going—if she lived frugally.

As the sun was making an effort to assert itself from behind the clouds, Lidia read an account in the *Greenwich Time* about the crash that had destroyed her house.

The pilot, Tina Calderara, 40, had a long history of stunt-flying and old-fashioned barn-storming, her publicist Anthony Holden announced at a hastily assembled press conference in her hometown of Dayton, Ohio. 'She was a skilled and careful pilot, having logged many hours in her single-engine Piper Cherokee. We cannot account for her running out of fuel on her way to a speaking engagement in Kitty Hawk, North Carolina, nor why she was flying over Greenwich, Connecticut, at 7:30 in the morning when she was due to land at Norfolk International at 8:00 a.m.' Speaking for the pilot's family, Holden added, 'The Walters send their sincerest best wishes to the family whose house was demolished in the crash, and while they are grieving for the loss of their beloved Tina, they are heartened to know that theirs is the only loss in this tragedy.' It was learned later that the Walters adopted Calderara at two years of age and that the stunt pilot legally changed her name as an adult.

"Poor woman, poor family," said Lidia to Opal, who'd joined her on the porch that morning while everyone else slept in. "Ran out of gas. That accounts for no explosion, but apparently no one knows why she was flying over Greenwich if she was on her way to Kitty Hawk." Lidia put the paper aside to stroke her dog. Opal, who had come out from under the chaise for a pat, was five now and had been a barely-weaned pup when the twins first brought her home. Both Lidia and Owen were reluctant to keep her, but the twins swore they would care for her themselves. And then they told their parents' Opal's sad story, the coup de grace to get them to keep her.

Opal, they said, had been abandoned, along with her five brothers and sisters, and was found in a cardboard box in a dumpster near school. Chloe, Carly's oldest friend, had heard the story on the news and had adopted one of Opal's brothers. She told the twins about the dogs, and the girls had stopped at animal control on the way home from school to see the pups for themselves. They took one look at Opal, the one climbing up the crate and wagging her tail, happy to see them, it appeared, and persuaded the clerk at the desk to let them take her home to show their parents, promising to bring her right back and to fill out the paperwork once their parents approved.

"All they have to do is see her," said Carly. "They won't be able to resist."

And so it was. Misgivings aside, Lidia and Owen relented and Opal took up residence on Apple Way. Lidia remembered how, when Owen left for good, Opal had sat looking out the living room window, waiting for him to return.

I guess we all waited, for a while, thought Lidia. She could still see the faces of her two sullen daughters in those days after Owen had left—Carly with her gently upturned nose and slightly downturned lips, staring into space, for hours, and Clarisse, her similar but somewhat finer features, dulled by her sadness.

Lidia thought back to her pregnancy; she'd been thirty-seven. After having devoted herself to her capital *C* Career for ten years and having made it to VP of mergers and acquisitions, Lidia had not known she was carrying twins until her third ultrasound, conducted at Lidia's insistence because, as she put it, "It feels like there's a party going on in there." Her doctor finally relented and was then embarrassed, having to explain Lidia's "hiding" twin daughter. "It happens sometimes, especially if one is larger than the other," Dr. Hanna Stevens had told her. Twins. It would be quite an adjustment, she and Owen had thought at the time.

"Owen called, just now," said Polly, interrupting Lidia's thoughts as she walked onto the porch and set down a tea tray. Lidia had been so lost in her memories that she hadn't even heard the phone ring. She wondered if the call had woken up the girls. "He'll call again later, he said. He just wanted to be sure you were all okay."

"Thanks, Polly, but you shouldn't be exerting yourself over us," Lidia said, reaching an appreciative hand toward her benefactor. It hadn't been that long ago when Lidia first started driving Polly to the Bendheim Cancer Center in Greenwich, Lidia recalled. She'd signed up some months earlier to be a driver in the Road to Recovery program because she had time on her hands since she had been let go, along with throngs of others, after the onset of the Great Recession. To lessen the pain of job loss, she had secured a pretty decent severance package, so she hadn't felt the crushing pressure of having to find another job, which was a good thing since so few existed.

Polly had needed to go for radiation treatments every day for six weeks. The only available appointments were at noon, a time that "ruined the day," as she had said the first time Lidia appeared at her door to drive her.

"I'm surprised they found a driver who could afford so much time and at such an inopportune hour to boot," she had said to Lidia.

Since that time their friendship had grown beyond anything Lidia could have imagined. From the first crack in the façade of polite conversation (Lidia had confided that her divorce had taken its toll on her and her twins), their bond had strengthened. Polly soon admitted to Lidia how lost she had felt ever since John Paul's death. It was as though they had found each other at a time of mutual vulnerability. Lidia had to admit that in the years she had devoted to career—before the birth of the twins and while they were growing up—she had been too frantic to cultivate good friends.

"I'm perfectly happy to have you and the girls here with me," said Polly, bringing Lidia back to the present. "What else would I be doing today? Besides, I'm just so grateful that you're all . . . When I think what could have . . ."

Lidia reached out for Polly's hand, gently patting it, at the same time looking away so her friend wouldn't see the tears forming.

"I think the same thing every time I look at them," Lidia said.

"Things have been tough, I know, Lidia—and now this . . ."

"In some weird way, I think I've been expecting, I don't know what, a cruel fate? I know that sounds horribly dramatic, but those first few years when Owen and I were, I thought, deliriously happy, I woke up every day and gave thanks for my charmed life: a handsome husband, money, a career—and then two beautiful and rare daughters—smart, talented, loving, and kind. And every day a little voice said, 'Be careful—such good fortune can't last.' It was like I was always scared. Every day I woke up happy, I also woke up scared. What is that all about? Vestiges of Catholic guilt? The belief that we are all sinners and don't deserve happiness?" She looked at her friend, as though hoping she might have an answer.

"Ah yes, religion. It does manage to keep us in line, doesn't it?"

"It was like there was a little comic book bomb, you know, the black ball with a lit fuse coming out of the top. I was always waiting for the bomb to explode. And then it did when Owen came home one day and put Robert right in the middle of us. The end of the perfect marriage—and I never saw it coming. Bomb goes off, right? But the funny thing is, that was small in comparison to whatever I thought my fears were. I mean, when I stop to consider. We are still alive. We are healthy. We still have our lives ahead of us."

Lidia looked over to Polly, who just nodded. She knew that Polly wanted her to talk, wanted her to process. This was Polly's gift to Lidia—her openness, no rigid "shoulds," no judgment, just a willingness to listen and to understand.

"I gave Owen so much grief over Robert and the 'disaster' he caused for us. But when the plane hit, I thought, so this is it—what I have known all along would happen. But no, it's not. It's not the end. We're homeless, but . . . Oh Polly, I'm rambling, I guess. I mean, divorce and this terrible accident—but we're still here. I am honestly grateful, in spite of it all. I've been so stuck in the breakup for the past three years, me, and the twins too, I think. Yet, there's so much to be thankful for."

Lidia turned to look at Polly.

"We have a wonderful friend who has taken us in until we get on our feet. We have insurance for all our losses. I guess I am still living a charmed life."

"Oh for heaven's sake," said Polly, leaning over to give Lidia a hug.

At that moment Carly and Clarisse burst onto the sun porch.

"Guess what?" asked Carly.

"At seven thirty yesterday morning," continued Clarisse, "when the plane crashed into our house, a bomb crashed into the moon—to find out if there was water."

"They're talking about on TV, CNN," said Carly.

"Some coincidence, huh?" added Clarisse, before they disappeared into the house again.

——————◗▬——————

By noon, the clouds had lifted, the temperature had risen, and Lidia had taken over answering the phone that had been ringing constantly since breakfast. All morning Polly had screened calls fiercely, reporters (there had been many) and other "snoops," as she called them, getting the "bum's rush."

Clarisse and Carly had begun setting up a light lunch of chicken salad and sliced Anjou pears on the sun porch. Polly and Lidia had just joined them when the phone rang again.

"Let it go," said Lidia, putting out a hand to stop Polly, who was on verge of stomping off to answer the offending ring. "If it's someone we need to talk to, they'll call back."

"It might be Dad," said Carly, placing a tray of dishes on the wicker glass-top table, not looking up

"We should talk to him, if it's him," said Clarrise, trying her best to sound nonchalant. "Shouldn't we?" She looked at Lidia imploringly—*As if for approval,* thought Lidia.

"Yes, I suppose you're right," Lidia said, moving toward the phone.

"Thank God," said Owen as soon as she picked up the receiver and said hello. "You're all right? I can't believe it. And you're sure, you, the girls, Opal, all okay?"

"It is him—your dad," Lidia called out from the living room, placing her hand over the receiver of Polly's heavy, square black telephone. "They don't make 'em like this anymore," she'd told the girls the first time they'd gawked over the old phone earlier that morning.

"I'm sorry, Owen. We were just sitting down to lunch, but the girls said I should answer in case it was you."

"My God, Lidia, I've been frantic. It's all over the news. What were you thinking, not getting in touch with me? And the girls—you—not answering your phones?

"I'm sorry, Owen. We're fine. It's been harrowing, but we're fine. Listen, I'm sorry about the phones, but it's been crazy. We finally turned them off."

There was silence on the other end. Lidia knew Owen was chewing on this—that the phones had been turned off, on purpose, without calling him first. She knew it wasn't admirable of her, but she was savoring (yes, that was the word, "savoring") Owen's feeling left out of the family—the family he had abandoned, after all.

Owen took a breath before continuing. "I know it's been hard on you, Lidia, but—you're my, you were my wife. Carly and Clarisse, they're still my daughters. I don't know what I would do if anything . . ."

After another few awkward seconds, Lidia jumped in.

"They're not ready yet, Owen."

"Not ready? It's been three years, and they hardly speak to me. Shouldn't they be adjusting by now? Who's not ready, Lidia—you or them?"

"Do you really want to get into this now, Owen? I thought you called to see how we were. We're fine, we'll be fine."

This time the pause was mutual. Lidia looked out at the girls in time to see them turn away. They had been listening through the open French doors.

"I've got to go, Owen."

"Whoa, whoa. Just a minute, Lidia. They're my daughters, and I will talk to them, so tell them to turn their phones back on, okay?"

Lidia felt the anger shoot up from the pit of her stomach. Readying herself to retaliate, she thought better of it. "Gotta go," she mustered and hung up the phone with just enough force to signal her muted fury.

No sooner had the phone struck the cradle than it rang again. "Mrs. Raven? It's Claudia Dobbs, from *Greenwich Time*. I was hoping you had a minute."

Claudia Dobbs had her own byline and wrote the "Out and About" column that Lidia read each week. Lidia was momentarily caught off guard by the idea that a columnist she actually liked would be calling her at Polly's house.

"This *is* Lidia Raven, isn't it? May I ask you a few questions?"

Lidia looked out the window at Polly and the girls, who now sat with full plates, while Lidia's own plate sat empty; she could see the girls weren't going to wait for her. Lidia debated whether she might just hang up on Claudia, regardless of how much she liked her column.

"So it appears there's a connection," she heard Claudia say.

What in the world was she talking about? Lidia wondered. "I'm sorry, I missed that. What connection are you referring to?"

"Between you and the pilot."

The Ravens of Ravenna

*L*idia, momentarily disoriented, took a few seconds to recapture the flow of the conversation.

"I'm sorry, a connection, you said. Between me and the pilot. Between me and Tina Calderara? I'm afraid I don't know what you're talking about." Lidia ran her fingers through her hair in exasperation. "How do you people even know I'm here?"

"You told a group of us when you left the hospital that Polly Niven had generously agreed to take you in. You said you were fine and that you and your family were very lucky under the circumstances."

Lidia, remembering her gratitude at the moment, now regretted her openness with the covey of reporters who had camped out near the entrance to the ER.

"Still feeling the effects of the drugs, no doubt."

"I'm sorry, Mrs. Raven. I don't want to alarm you, but I've been doing some research on the story, and it seems there's a connection, tenuous at this point, but who knows, there may be more to it." Then, taking a more personal tone, Claudia continued. "Look, I know you've just been through a very traumatic experience, the crash, loss of your home, your family endangered—that's why I was hoping, after you've taken a day or two to recover a bit, we could talk, person-to-person. I'll share with you what I've discovered. And maybe you could shed light on what I have so far."

Lidia felt her arms and hands go numb and then begin to tingle. This was followed by a deepening of her breath, and in a few rapid heartbeats, her feelings began to tumble in a confusing mass of fear, dread, and anxiety before finally settling on anger.

"I can't shed light on anything because I don't know what you could possibly be getting at. I'd never heard of Tina before yesterday. Are you suggesting that somehow the crash wasn't an accident?"

Lidia paused a moment to rake her fingers through her hair once again, pivoting haphazardly, but managing to continue before Claudia could respond. "And, by the way," she said, "if you're so sensitive to my recent trauma, as you so accurately put it, then I doubt you would call me the day after, making up some sort of melodramatic, weird, crazy story like this. Just, please, leave us alone."

With that she slammed the phone on the receiver, its after-ring continuing to reverberate as she plopped down on the sofa, arms folded tightly against her chest, as if to protect herself from what the future may hold. A reporter with a potentially juicy story. What was there to stop her? The idea that there was some point to all the madness, that she was somehow tied to that poor pilot, was more than Lidia could bear. Just as she felt herself giving in to despair, Polly and the girls came in. Lidia quickly tried to pull herself together; she unfolded her arms and brought them casually to her lap.

"I guess I'm more on edge than I thought I was," she said, looking up at the trio, who were obviously alarmed by the outburst since they'd hurried in from the porch. Lidia, with all her heart, did not want to worry her girls or her friend any further. They had all been through enough, but she didn't know how much longer she could keep burying her own mounting anxiety. Things were certainly piling on.

"What happened?" asked Clarisse tentatively.

"Are you okay?" asked Carly, the first to sit down next to Lidia and to lightly stroke her hair.

"Yes, yes, I'm fine," Lidia said, not too convincingly.

"Let me get you some tea," said Polly.

"No," said Lidia, reaching for Polly before she could take off for the sun porch. "All of you, just sit down. I'm fine, really." Realizing they had no idea what had caused her outburst, Lidia began to fill them in on what Claudia had told her.

"Reporters. They have no tact whatsoever. Never have had. Some things don't change," said Polly, alluding to something, though Lidia was not sure what.

"But aren't you at least curious?" asked Carly. "Don't you wonder what she may have?"

"No," said Lidia. "Not in the least." And with that she got up, looked toward the porch, and said, "I'm hungry."

———————◆———————

For several hours more the madness continued—phone call after phone call, more reporters hoping for an interview, some even going so far as to knock on the front door—but Polly had proved particularly adept at keeping the intruders at bay. Her last tactic had been to put a sign on the front gate: *No Trespassing. Premises Under Electronic Surveillance.* The discrepancy between the low-tech hand-written sign and the high-tech warning seemed to have worked, since no one came through the gate after that—and mercifully, the phone stopped ringing.

"Finally some peace and quiet, and the moon crash has taken us off the air," said Lidia, in the afternoon as she and the girls sank into the large overstuffed sofa in the living room to watch Polly's fifty-two-inch plasma TV. Since lunch, Carly and Clarisse had been on their phones talking to friends who were eager to learn all about the world of instant pseudo-celebrity the twins had fallen into. But now ready for a break from all the attention, they wanted nothing more than to be near their mother. Sitting next to Lidia, Carly pulled her feet up under her as Clarisse put her head on her mother's lap.

"Switch it to CNN, would you, Lidia, dear?" asked Polly, who was snuggled up in John Paul's old leather recliner next to them. "I'd like to see what they've been saying about the moon, poor old thing, rattled about like this."

"According to NASA," reported Wolf Blitzer, "the rocket and satellite strike was a success. It apparently kicked up enough dust for scientists to determine if there is water on the moon, and if so, how much. While there wasn't a dramatic splashdown, it looks like there's going to be plenty of data to sift through.

"I have here, commenting live from Cape Canaveral, Anthony Colaprete, principal investigator for the Lunar Crater Observation and Sensing Satellite mission, or the LCROSS mission, and Dan Andrews, the mission project manager . . ."

As the report went on, Lidia began thinking about the crash and of the loss of her family home. She began trembling, thinking of the girls, about their time under the stairs, waiting for rescue. And then about Tina.

"It's such an unbelievable coincidence that the moon and our house were struck at the same time," said Lidia, eliciting no response whatsoever as the assembled party continued listening to the news. Lidia, though, could not calm down and began to feel too on edge to stay put. At the same time, she was reluctant to disrupt the peaceful scene around her in the living room. She waited a few more minutes before giving into a growing need to find some information of her own to sift through.

"I need to check on some things. Polly, can I use your computer?" She turned to look at her friend, who was more relaxed than she had been all day. Needing to move but not wanting to disturb Polly's quietude, Lidia quickly added, "But don't get up. I can go myself." Lidia was increasingly worried about the toll all the commotion must be taking on Polly's recently returned stamina, although her friend seemed to have endless reserves of energy.

"Don't be silly. Let's both retreat to the musty old library. I'd like that."

One of the things Lidia admired most about her friend was her infinite variety. Old black telephone in one room, solidly perched on a maple phone stand, the likes of which was found now only in the remotest corner of antique shops, and a state-of-the-art Apple computer, dual screens, and printer in another. Polly was obsessed with the aftermath of the recent financial crisis and used whatever technology was available to keep a close eye on the remainder of her savings. The library, though, with its dark oak paneled walls, was a monument to the golden age of the printed word, holding shelf after shelf of first-edition volumes in serious jeopardy of moldering away, now that Polly rarely used air-conditioning in the summer or heat in the winter in this wing of the house.

"It's too chilly in here, Lidia. Let me heat this place up," said Polly when they closed the great oak doors to the library. "I could build a fire for you. That could make it cozy. I haven't had a fire yet this fall."

"Don't you dare do another thing, Polly. I'll be through in a minute anyway."

"What are you looking for?" asked Polly, plugging in a nearby space heater.

"I'm looking up whatever I can find about Tina." The screen, flashing from one search to another, lit up Lidia's face, until after several minutes, she concluded, "I'm not finding that much, but she did occasionally give speeches about the early days of flying, apparently. It says here she was a bit of an expert on the history of aviation. Oh, and here's one of her speeches. Is the printer on?"

"It should be, let me . . . now try it," said Polly, pressing the power button.

Lidia printed out a few pages and Polly retrieved them and handed them over to her. "Here, listen," said Lidia. "This is from a speech she gave in 2005, as keynote speaker for the Dallas Aviatrix Society's annual luncheon. Looks like the gist of it was firsts for women in flight—Bessie Coleman, first African American to earn a pilot's license in 1921; even Anne Morrow Lindbergh had a flight first, first woman to earn a glider pilot's license. The bulk of it, though, is about Amelia Earhart."

Lidia cleared her throat and read aloud:

"Man has always yearned to fly, but human flight was thought to be mere vanity. In Greek myth, Icarus flew too close to the sun, melting his wings of wax, causing him to fall into the sea—and to perish.

"Women aviators have always had to listen to warnings about the foolishness of their pursuit. The most famous, Amelia Earhart, didn't listen, though, and went on to accomplish great things 'Never interrupt someone doing what can't be done'—that's what she told the naysayers. And so she gathered about her many 'firsts,' but Amelia didn't fly to gain recognition, although she knew her accomplishments helped women everywhere to pursue their dreams. No, she flew for the love of it. I like to say that her name—the way it sounds, not the way it's spelled—suited her perfectly. Her 'heart' was in the 'air.' A-I-R-H-E-A-R-T. Her name could have been spelled that way.

"Then, as we all know, on July 2, 1937, she flew too close to the sun, in a manner of speaking, and fell into the sea never to be seen again. We grieve for her to this day. She is remembered mostly for that plunge from the sky—not for all she did, and not for her love of flight. Let us all be happy that she died doing what she loved."

"It gives me chills to read this," said Lidia. "Think of it; Tina died doing what she loved, too. It goes on to say that many women share Amelia's love, but here's something odd. She said that love of flying is sometimes an inherited trait—and that maybe she inherited it from her great grandfather, Mario Calderara. But that's funny because, well, that is the surname she went by, but she was adopted by the Walters of Dayton, so I don't see how she could know who her great grandfather was. Isn't that strange?"

"Indeed," answered Polly. "Who's this Calderara fellow?"

"I'm just Googling it now." Lidia took a few minutes to absorb what she was reading and then said, "Looks like he was an early aviator, Italian from Verona, but he did have an association with the Wright Brothers and had been to Dayton to visit them, and he was married to Emmy Gamba Ghiselli, whose family was from . . . Ravenna."

"Ravenna? Isn't that where your family is from, Lidia? Where your name comes from?"

"Well, yes. Our name was *DiRavenna*, before my grandfather

changed it to *Raven*. He thought it would be easier for people to remember and better for business. The logo for our orchards was a raven perched on an apple." She was trying to sound nonchalant, but Lidia's hands went cold on the keyboard. Claudia no doubt had pulled up this same information about Tina and Mario Calderara, and maybe something more about Lidia's own background.

Lidia's grandfather had settled in Connecticut after emigrating from Ravenna in the 1920s. He had started the same family business in this country that had been a success in Italy, cultivating apples. The DiRavenna's had a thousand acres of their own variety of Renette apples. The Renette, a tart, reddish, golden apple, was used primarily for baking, but Lidia's great grandfather was the first to distill it into a rich apple wine. At 14 percent alcohol, it delivered quite a kick for those expecting little more than juiced-up cider. *Il Nettare Delle Mele Renette*, as the wine was called, became a mainstay of households in the Emilia-Romagna region of Italy, and Lidia's grandfather believed he could transport the business to the United States.

It took until the 1940s for the orchards in Connecticut to mature. In the meantime, Rodolfo worked tirelessly as a superintendent of various Greenwich estates, all the while laying the groundwork for his own orchards to produce fruit and wine. When they did, his Renette apple wine became a best seller, and Rodolfo was able to devote himself full time to his business, bringing in his son, Rudy Jr.

When Lidia was growing up, her father used to tell her she, too, would one day join him in the orchards, but by the time she had completed her MBA, the business had faltered, the winery had shut down, and all but a few of the acres of apples had been sold off. The loss, Lidia and her mother were sure, was the cause of the heart attack that killed Rudy in 1986.

Lidia had always dreamed of running the business one day. Her pride and her memories led her to go from "Mrs. Owen Quentin Hardin" back to "Lidia Raven" when her marriage failed. The girls, in their anger, willingly followed her lead.

Now Lidia was brought back to her Ravenna roots—something she hadn't thought of in many years.

"Okay, so there's a coincidence here," said Lidia. "A city in Italy, but that doesn't translate to a connection. It doesn't mean anything. Unless maybe she found something else . . ." Lidia quickly Googled her grandfather's name and found several entries about the Raven apple orchards, but nothing that mentioned Ravenna or anything else to connect her to Tina or to Mario Calderara or to Emmy whatever her name was. Nevertheless, Lidia's heart was pounding.

"Maybe you should meet with her, Lidia. You know my low regard for reporters—but maybe, dear, you need to pursue this."

"I don't know, maybe. Something tells me to leave it alone. I'll give it some thought, though. But what are we doing in here?" said Lidia, turning off the computer, glad to get away from its harsh glare. "It's getting late, but it's still a beautiful afternoon. The sun is still out. How about a walk? We can take Opal and maybe the girls will join us."

Fall Colors

*V*ery early Monday morning, three days after the plane crash, a
nor'easter blew through southwest Connecticut, shaking loose
the red, gold, and orange leaves of the trees on the Niven estate. The
wind was still howling when Carly and Clarisse, dressed in clothes
hastily acquired in a shopping spree at the mall over the weekend,
were in the kitchen spreading jam on their English muffins. Lidia,
preparing one for herself, knew the twins were looking forward to
returning to school and to a routine away from all reminders of their
disrupted lives, but things were far from normal.

They were all living in a state of suspended animation—not able
to go home to retrieve whatever may have been salvageable. Their
home was the scene of an ongoing investigation, and no one could
tell Lidia when it would end. She was at a loss, like an astronaut float-
ing in space. Everything she did, everywhere she turned, she was
reminded of her precarious position. She and the twins got new cell
phones immediately, but all her contacts, her calendar, and her pictures were gone. Everything she had now was a result of the mall trip,
leaving her guilty since Polly had refused all offers to pay her back.
Overwhelmed and lost in her thoughts, Lidia didn't notice the twins
taking their empty and new backpacks from the table and heading
for the front door. Putting down the butter knife, she called to them
from the kitchen. "Girls, wait. I forgot to tell you. School is delayed
today. It was on TV this morning. They said ten o'clock. That's not
too bad, is it? Can I make you a real breakfast? Eggs? Pancakes?"

"I'd like eggs, over easy," said Polly from the mudroom, where she had just taken off her green rain boots and was now hanging her bright yellow slicker on a hook by the door. Opal, who had been with Polly on a morning walk, was vigorously shaking off the rain, causing Polly to shield herself with a towel she quickly grabbed off the next hook. "Watch it, Opal. Is that any way to repay me for our nice little outing?"

"I wondered where you two had gone off to in this weather," said Lidia as the pair walked into the kitchen.

"It's a perfect morning for a walk—makes you appreciate the warmth of a cozy kitchen when you get back. What's wrong, girls?"

"We can't go to school until later," said Carly. "But I don't get it. If you and Opal can go for a walk in the rain, why can't they open school?"

"Don't expect school to operate according to Polly's ways. She's invincible. But it is a little dangerous, isn't it, Polly, out in this weather, especially with those big old birches and oaks about to topple over?" Lidia took a container of flour off the shelf next to the kitchen window.

"I've been a storm-walker here for thirty years without incident—I suppose I'll just keep at it."

"Well, I said you were invincible. I just hope those trees are as sturdy as you are. I'm making pancakes and eggs. Who's in?"

———————◆———————

At quarter to ten, Lidia drove the girls to school in Polly's Subaru and dropped them off in the parking lot by the gym. "I'll be here right at two fifteen, okay?"

"Why can't we take the bus back?" asked Clarisse.

"Because I haven't told the office yet about our temporary address. Don't worry, I will, but listen," said Lidia, looking first at Carly in the front seat and then at Clarisse in the back. "I know you're happy to be going back to school, but don't get your hopes up about things being, you know, exactly normal. You're both going to be in the spotlight— a lot of questions thrown your way. The kids, teachers—they'll be curious."

"I know, Mom. We've already thought about it. We'll be able to handle it," said Carly.

"Right. We'll go all sad and depressed on them," Clarisse said with a grin. "So they'll feel sorry for us and leave us alone. Okay? Don't worry, Mom."

Lidia laughed. "Give me a hug, both of you. I should've known you'd be way ahead of me."

"See ya," they both said, all but flying out the door. "We'll be here at two fifteen," said Carly over her shoulder.

"Don't worry about me. I'll be fine," said Lidia out loud but to herself as her twins disappeared behind the glass doors. *They're handling this better than I am,* she thought as she pulled out of the parking lot. Thinking she should get back so Polly wouldn't worry, she was surprised to find d herself turning off Sound Beach Avenue, heading back to Greenwich. Her next turn was onto Apple Way.

She pulled into her own driveway as far as she could before the yellow police tape stopped her. Lidia got out of the car and began to walk along the cordoned-off area, her hand gliding along the tape, searching for some support, though it offered none, yielding under her touch. The fuselage of the plane was still surrealistically presiding over the ruins, reminding Lidia once again of the carnage that might have been had they not all been huddled under stairs at that awful moment. Whipped by the wind and with the misty rain still falling, the scene of wreckage looked even more ominous. Mental images she could not stop caused Lidia to tremble uncontrollably.

"I'm sorry, Ma'am, but you can't be here."

Stunned, Lidia quickly turned around.

"I didn't mean to scare you, but I had to let you know this site is under investigation."

"This *site* is my house," Lidia responded.

"You're Mrs. Raven?" The stranger extended his hand, which Lidia was reluctant to take. "Excuse me. I should introduce myself. I'm Special Agent Caligan. Harry Caligan."

"You're kidding. Harry Callahan—Dirty Harry. You're Dirty Harry?"

"Caligan, Ma'am. It's Caligan, with the Bureau. Of Investigation. Federal Bureau of Investigation. FBI."

"I got that, but I . . . You'll have to excuse me. I'm sorry for laughing, but this is too surreal. My house, there," Lidia said pointing. "And you, here. FBI. It's too much. And why are you here? Why is the FBI here? Can I see your badge?"

Lidia observed Harry Caligan and remembered having read somewhere that special agents had to be physically fit. Harry Caligan was that. He didn't exactly match the stereotype of a special agent from the movies, but he came close. At about six feet, Lidia estimated, he was lean and looked like he clocked more than a few hours in the gym each week. His brown hair, while not a buzz cut, was thick and close-cropped. But it was his blue eyes that got to her. Serious, very deep blue, and framed with crinkly lines, indicating lots of time in the sun. And he had a tan—a nice deep tan, she noted.

Lidia examined the leather folder with Special Agent Caligan's credentials. "Everything seems to be in order. I think that's what they say in the movies," she said, handing it back to him.

"I get that a lot, the jokes, but the job is real, and I have to let you know this is a crime scene, and as such, you can't be here. Not yet, anyway."

Lidia looked at Harry, and then at her home, fighting off two distinctly different emotions. She was drawn to this appealing man keeping her from going any farther on her own property, but then again, he was keeping her from what was rightfully hers, and this caused a bit of heat to rise up from under her lavender sweater. The heat was from anger, she told herself. *Anger, that's all,* she repeated, like a mantra. Pausing a moment to clear her throat, Lidia asked, "Why the FBI? And then she added, "I'm sorry for the jokes, but this is too much to absorb. The accident and now the investigation. Do they think it was a crime?"

"*Crime* is not the most accurate term, not at this point. The investigation is to be sure the crash that killed the pilot and destroyed your home was an accident and not something more."

"Like terrorism or something?"

"We have to investigate any crash like this to be sure. Like I said, I don't want to alarm you. I'm sorry, by the way, for your loss. It looks like it was a nice house."

"Yes, it was in our family for generations."

"I'll be getting in touch with you soon, Mrs. Raven. I'll have to ask you some questions—routine—but I want you to feel comfortable. Here's my card. If you have any questions in the meantime, you can call me."

"Thank you, Officer, or Agent Callahan."

"Caligan."

"Right, Caligan. But what do I call you?"

"Harry. Just call me Harry. Can I walk you back to your car?"

———◉———

Back at the Niven Estate, Lidia found Polly reading in the wicker chaise on the sun porch.

"You'll never guess who I met today, Dirty Harry. I loved Clint Eastwood in those movies—never forgot them."

After filling her friend in on her meeting, Lidia took Harry's card out from the pocket of the jacket she had borrowed from Polly and read it over several times, as though something embedded might appear if she examined it more closely.

"Are you a bit taken with him?" asked Polly.

Lidia looked up, quickly stuffing the card back into her pocket. "Taken? No, just curious. But he had nice eyes. He wasn't exactly the FBI type, you know, all hard-nosed, 'Just the facts, Ma'am'—that sort of thing. He seemed kind, like he understood what I was going through. But who knows." Lidia took note of the adrenaline surge she had experienced at Polly's words. *Was I taken with him?* she had to ask herself; and she had to admit the answer to herself: *I might have been.*

"But you saw something in him that you liked, or at least that interested you, seems to me." Polly flipped through a few pages of her leather-bound first-edition book and read aloud, "'There is no instinct like that of the heart.' Byron. I was just reading that line. It's from *Don Juan*, fourth canto. Sometimes we're drawn to people for reasons we don't know, but the heart knows, and it doesn't lie. I believe that."

Not ready yet (for reasons she did not quite understand) to admit her newfound feelings, Lidia responded, "He had nice eyes. That's all, Polly. Besides, I might have believed in all of that once, but where was my heart's instinct when I needed it most? I loved and trusted Owen, and we see where that got me."

"I'm sorry, Lidia. There are some things that just can't be fixed, no matter how it hurts." Polly got up from the wicker rocker and headed for the kitchen. "We have just enough time for a little lunch and a stroll out to Tod's Point. The walk will do you good."

By the time they had made their way to the bench on the farthest spit of land, the clouds had mostly lifted and the sun was intermittently making an appearance. Lidia and Polly huddled under a fleece blanket Polly had carried with her and stared out at the Sound, its waves crashing unthreateningly into the rocks a few yards in front of them.

Polly turned to Lidia, her brow creased with concern. "You know, Lidia, when I had my troubles, before my marriage to John Paul, I thought my life was over, but it wasn't. I'm sure, with all my heart instinct, that you will be happy again."

Lidia was grateful for this generous friend who had come to her later in life, when it seemed good friends were hard to find. She knew Polly had given up for adoption her only child when she was twenty-three. Polly's first love ended tragically; her first marriage didn't last. She had spent years in a spiritual commune in California before meeting and settling down with John Paul. But Lidia's understanding of the details of Polly's life was sketchy, and she had been reluctant to pry, but out on the point with the sun starting to warm them, Polly seemed ready to tell Lidia more of her story.

"I never thought I would speak of these things to anyone again, but it breaks my heart to see you struggling with the pain of the past few years of your life. Do you think that by sharing what has happened to me, it may help you in some way?"

Lidia took one of Polly's hands in hers and gave it a squeeze. "I want to hear whatever you want to tell me because I care about you, not for what good it may do me. I know you've led an interesting and at times difficult life and that you got through the hard parts—probably because of who you are, because of your strength."

Polly nodded. "Strength helps, but we don't always know our own strength until we're tested somehow. That's a profoundly interesting part of life—finding that out about ourselves." She took a deep breath. "Where to begin? We can skip the part about how I was born in a log cabin, but I will say I had a nice upbringing by very nice Midwestern parents, who didn't know what to do with me at times because I was different, to say the least, probably a little like the unfortunate Tina Calderara. By the time I was eighteen, I had taken off for Chicago, where I became a belly dancer to work my way through college."

"Belly dancer?"

"Yes," Polly laughed. "As you can imagine, there weren't too many belly dancing college girls at that time, but there you have it. I used to go to this Middle Eastern restaurant. I loved the music and the costumes and the sensual movements. It was all so enticing. So the owner, Ahmad Oman, as I recall, told me to come round on Saturday mornings when the girls practiced, and I could give it a go. I picked it up rather quickly. He gave me a costume, and for four years I danced at the Al Bustan. After I graduated with a degree in English, with no job prospect in sight, I danced some more."

"What did you want to do?"

"I wanted to write, of course, but I found I wasn't cut out for the writer's life, you know, locked in a garret, cold, and eating crumbs to get by. I was about to get my teaching license when I met my first love, Seth. He came into Al Bustan one night, intrigued by the blonde dancing girl. We managed to live on love until he was drafted.

You know, Lidia, it's an old but true story. Boy goes to war, leaves his
girlfriend who is pregnant, and doesn't come home. I was devastated,
so devastated that when I gave up our baby girl I was numb. It took
me years to recover. I went home and taught for a time, but the same
stifling landscape that had caused me to leave the first time began
to weigh on me again, and once again I fled. My poor parents—the
heartache I put them through. But I left for New York that time and
never looked back. I never saw them again."

Polly pulled out an embroidered handkerchief from her parka and
gently wiped her eyes.

Lidia felt her own tears beginning to form. She wanted to pull her
friend to her, to comfort her, but instead she put a hand over Polly's
and then withdrew it, knowing Polly needed to go on.

"In New York I decided to devote my life to the theater. Isn't that
what everyone does in New York, even still—work as a waitress and
audition? That's what I did. When I was twenty-five, I was getting
walk-on parts on Broadway—and I met Bradford Wilton the Third,
who was waiting for me outside the stage door one night. Brad came
from a well-to-do New York family, and they did not approve, but
we married anyway—a beautiful big wedding at St. Bart's on Park
Avenue. Brad was a beautiful man, with a very sweet nature, but he,
well, our marriage would be severely tested.

"I told Brad I wanted to find my daughter, and he backed me all the
way, but his parents were adamant that I give up all such thoughts.
It was the 1950s, and they were very conservative. Apparently there
was no way they would ever accept a daughter-in-law who had had
a child with another man. When Brad and I continued our search,
things got rather ugly. His parents turned on us with such vitriol.
They developed what can only be called a vicious hatred of me. Then
the unthinkable happened. They leaked a story about me to the *Daily
News*. Soon the history of Brad's belly-dancing unwed-mother wife
was read avidly by friend and foe alike. The Wiltons did not care.
They caused the scandal and then blamed me for it. It was irrational,
but they were out to crush me—no matter the cost. They couldn't

accept a daughter-in-law like me, and so their son would not be able to accept me as a wife—and their plan worked. Brad's weakness was that he could not take the notoriety, but mostly he could not take being alienated from his family. I loved him, and I think he loved me, but the harm had been done. We divorced.

"Once again I was devastated—but still standing. After the divorce, I went to California. What does one do in California? Movies, of course. So I waitressed and auditioned. I had small parts in some very bad films, all mercifully forgotten today. I drifted; I traveled. I went on spiritual quests. It was the 1960s, and I was in my thirties. I found my way to an ashram in Big Sur, where I stayed for a few years. By the time I was forty, I was ready for a more conventional life, so I came back to New York, got my master's, and began teaching at a private school on the Upper East Side. From there, some years later, I was recruited to teach in Greenwich, where I met John Paul, the true love of my life. We had a wonderful thirty years together.

"So there's a happy ending—except for the space in my heart that was always vacant, waiting to be filled one day by my daughter. John Paul hired an investigator, and we found her in Oregon. Kate turned out to be an independent outdoors girl, working as a forest ranger when we found her, but she didn't want anything to do with us, with me—wouldn't meet with me or even talk to me on the phone. She told the investigator, who actually approached her, she had one set of parents; she didn't need another."

"I'm so sorry, Polly. How painful for you—after all those years—finding her and then not being reunited. It's tragic, really." Lidia was undone by Polly's story. She knew Polly had suffered terrible losses—and yet she had endured. What must it take to go on after such pain? *I will never have her strength,* thought Lidia, humbled by the comparison.

"It was a blow, and I didn't know how to take what she had said. One interpretation was that she had had enough of parents, which could've meant her childhood was not happy. Or it might have meant she was loyal to her adoptive parents. I wanted that to be the case, so

I left it—her—alone. I take comfort in knowing she has, as far as I can tell, followed her bliss. I hope, I pray that is the case."

Polly looked at Lidia. "I think that's enough of the saga of Polly Cramer, Wilton, Niven. You know, Lidia, in the words of Edith Piaf, '*Je ne regrette rien*.' It's been a full, crazy, sad, happy life. What more can anyone ask?"

Lidia reached an arm around Polly and pulled her close. "Thank you, Polly. It does help. Really, it does."

"My stars, said Polly, looking at her watch. We have just enough time to get home for you to go and get the girls."

Polly, who had been quiet on the walk home thinking of those years before John Paul and then missing him terribly, decided it was time to put away her sad memories. She hoped, though, that by delving into her past, she might have helped Lidia cope with the present. The phone was ringing furiously when she and Lidia walked in the door, and Polly answered it immediately. The girls were getting a ride home with their friends, Jena and Chloe, and they had news. Polly relayed the information to Lidia, and within the hour, the four girls arrived, laughing and in high spirits. As soon as they had taken off their jackets and had put down their book bags, Polly motioned the girls to the sofa, where Clarisse began the introductions.

"Jena is my oldest friend," Clarisse told Polly, who saw behind Jena's red-framed glasses a pair of penetrating hazel eyes taking her measure.

"She's editor of our literary magazine and will probably be valedictorian. I don't know why she hangs out with us, do you, Carly?" At this, Jena tucked a stray strand of brown hair behind her ear and looked down at her boots. Polly had to look closely to see the corners of Jena's lips turning up slightly.

Carly frowned and shook her head no. "Way too good for us," she said. "And what about Chloe? She's our number-one gymnast and first-chair violist in our orchestra," Carly said of her sturdily built friend whose short blonde hair framed her open and friendly oval face. "Not too bad, huh?" Carly put an arm around Chloe, who was showing signs of a faint blush. "We've been hanging out since first grade."

"I'm so pleased to meet both of you, such accomplished young ladies," said Polly, gliding along on a current of fresh air listening to these young women. *How wonderful to have them here,* she thought, taking stock of her calm but sometimes gloomy days pre-Raven girls. "Now, come sit and have something to eat," she said, pointing to the plate of chocolate chip cookies she had baked while she and Lidia had waited for the girls to arrive "They're fresh from the oven. Wait just a minute. I want to get you girls some milk."

"I've got it," said Lidia, coming back to the living room and carefully placing on the coffee table a silver tray with four full glasses.

"Oh, cookies and milk," said Clarisse. "That's so sweet, Polly. Remember, Mom, when we were little, how you always said you wished you were a stay-at-home mom so you could give us cookies and milk when we came home?"

"Yes, I remember. So enjoy it—even though you're not so little anymore."

It was ironic, thought Lidia, that when the girls were young, she had been pulled in two directions. She had wanted, had needed to excel at work, to prove to herself that she could do it, could apply the business degree her father had wanted for her, but she had also, with all her heart, wanted to be at home with her twin daughters. She had been a little jealous, she had to admit, of anyone who had cared for them in her absence, starting with her mother and ending with Jennifer, the college student who ended up taking care of the twins until the girls graduated from middle school. There had been one more after-school helper before Lidia had decided the girls could be on their own for those hours until she got home from work. Then came the layoff. And now Lidia wished that the dark days of the recession would end soon so she could go back to the world where she had once felt so torn.

The girls, sitting snugly together on the sofa, reached for the cookies and politely began taking small bites.

"Well, you were right, Mom, about our being in the spotlight today, but not because of the accident," said Carly.

"Although some kids did say they were sorry about what happened to us, and some teachers, too," added Clarisse. "No, the real news— well, what's the big event at schools in the fall? Football and . . . what?"

Lidia and Polly looked at each other and shrugged their shoulders. "Let's see," said Polly.

"Oh my gosh, homecoming," said Lidia, immediately wondering which of her twins was on the court, causing her to worry about the hurt feelings of the other—and on top of all that had happened to them. In the recent chaos of their lives, she had forgotten about homecoming.

"Yes, homecoming," said the twins in unison.

"And, Mrs. Raven," said Chloe, turning to Carly. "Tell her."

Carly looked at her mother and said, "I'm on the court, Mom."

Lidia saw her daughter smile, but she also noticed she didn't look at all excited by the news. *Oh my God,* thought Lidia, *Carly is on the court, but Clarrise didn't make it.*

Isn't that fabulous news?" Chloe was beaming, but Lidia had a catch in her throat.

"There's more," Jena quickly added, prodding her friend to speak up.

"I am, too," said Clarisse, looking as unimpressed as her sister had a moment before.

Both Chloe and Jena seemed not to notice the nonchalance of their friends in divulging the news. They seemed genuinely ecstatic over their good fortune.

"Carly and Clarisse?" said Lidia, relieved that she would not be ministering to, most likely, a left-out Clarisse in the pre-homecoming frenzy about to ensue.

"We think it's pretty funny," said Carly. "I mean, this stuff was way more important to everyone than the fact that a plane just crashed into our house." She dusted a few stray crumbs from her jeans onto her linen cocktail napkin.

"And the other thing is, so many people said to both of us, 'Aren't you afraid your sister will win and you won't?' Like we would be jealous of each other or something. Anyway, it's so bizarre," added Clarisse, settling back into the cushions.

All four girls nibbled a bit more of their cookies and sipped a little milk before asking to go out onto the sun porch. "We just want to hang out a little before homework," said Carly.

As soon as they were lounging on the wicker rockers and chairs, Lidia closed the French doors and went back to Polly.

———●———

"I continue to underestimate those girls. I'm always so afraid one will be slighted or left behind with hurt feelings or be crushed—and I'm always wrong. They are so tough emotionally," said Lidia, sitting on the sofa across from Polly in the recliner.

Polly looked at her friend and considered her words before responding. "They have a good sense of themselves and of what's really important. You should be very proud, Lidia. You've raised two discerning, independent young women." Polly paused for a moment. She wanted to say more. She wasn't so sure about the girls and their emotional state, but she was afraid she might be taking too much for granted if she confronted Lidia on the subject. She was still learning when to proceed and when to back off with Lidia.

"I think they cut through what's trivial or insincere pretty nicely, but . . ."

Polly saw Lidia's back stiffen.

"But what?"

Polly decided against the direct approach. "Well, what you mean, you know, about their being emotionally tough."

Lidia answered immediately. "For one thing, you saw, all this homecoming business—and they're so unconcerned. And my God, they just lost their home, everything they own, and they're in there joking with their friends. And their parents are divorced, and they don't skip a beat. That's pretty tough to me."

Polly wondered if Lidia was aware of her defensive tone. Polly, on the other hand, was aware she had waded into some sensitive waters. She knew she had to tread carefully or risk offending her friend who was fairly fragile herself these days.

Polly leaned forward and said, "I'm sorry. You're absolutely right, but I don't know, I just think there must be more to it—they must have their moments, don't you think?"

"I'm not sure," Lidia coughed gently into her fist and then said again, "I'm not sure. I think they're doing okay."

Polly, hearing Lidia's voice soften, hoped for an opening to talk more.

"But then again, they have their very full lives to occupy them," Lidia said with finality. She turned toward the cookies and milk on the coffee table. "Homecoming court, both of them. Imagine that. Let me carry these things into the kitchen." She quickly loaded the glasses back onto the tray.

And that's that, thought Polly. Never one to admit defeat, she was determined to find another opening—even if the Raven girls didn't know they needed any assistance in getting on with their wonderful lives.

"I'm right behind you," said Polly.

———◉———

Later that evening, after Lidia had said good night to everyone and closed the door to her room, she pulled the reading chair over to the window and stared at the full harvest moon. Her thoughts were racing, what her house must look like tonight under the moon's glow—the tail of the plane shining like a neon sign, warning of what can happen when you least expect it. She thought of what Polly had said. She pulled her sweater around her. *The girls are fine, strong and resilient,* she told herself. *I'm the one who's always afraid, for them, and for myself. When did I get so protective of my feelings?* she wondered. *I used to put myself out there regularly to see what doors I could open just by taking chances. Has Owen done this to me, made me so fearful of being hurt I won't take chances anymore? Or have I done this to myself?*

The next morning, after the twins had left for school, Lidia asked Polly if she could borrow her car since nothing on Apple Way had been released yet, and for all she knew her car wasn't even in driving condition. She arrived at the *Greenwich Time* office at ten o'clock and asked the receptionist if she could speak to Claudia Dobbs. No, she did not have an appointment, Lidia said. It took some persuading, but as soon as the young woman behind the desk agreed to buzz Claudia's office, Claudia appeared in the lobby within minutes. "Let's go. Let me buy you a cup of coffee."

"I think I owe you an apology," Lidia said, moving to a table and chairs by the window. "I guess I was more than a little edgy with you on the phone."

"No apology necessary, Mrs. Raven," answered Claudia, stirring her double espresso with a wooden coffee stick. "Reporters can be pushy and obnoxious, I'm afraid. Tact and courtesy are not on the list of job requirements."

Claudia, a petite brunette of about forty, did not, today at least, seem pushy or obnoxious as far as Lidia could see. In a blue fleece pull-over, black corduroys, and suede ankle boots, she looked as though she might be more comfortable driving her kids to soccer practice than pursuing a hot lead.

"Call me Lidia. I've thought about what you said, about a possible link between me and the pilot, and I was wondering what more you could tell me."

"I was hoping you might have some information for me."

"What I told you when you called is true. I don't know anything, but if there's a connection, I think I should know."

Claudia put her cup down on the table and held it with both hands. "Well, I haven't been able to confirm any of this, but the pilot of the plane, Tina Calderara, claimed to have been the great granddaughter of an aviator, who was married to a countess from an old Ravenna family, the Gamba Ghisellis."

Lidia's first impulse was to tell Claudia she too had discovered this much about Tina, but of more interest to her was Claudia's claim about the connection.

"Yes, but what does any of this have to do with me?"

"How much do you know about your Ravenna family?" Claudia asked.

"Only that my great grandfather owned apple orchards there and that my grandfather came over to start the family business here. We never talked about the past. So how do you know about it?"

"Town records, property transfers, names of buyers. Your grandfather didn't change his name until after he bought the Greenwich property. With the right names it's pretty easy these days to track people down, to check old passenger lists of ships to find where people came from and when, for example. A lot of it is digitized." Claudia looked intently at Lidia and added, "Your grandfather, Rodolfo DiRavenna, came over on the SS *Leonardo Da Vinci*, leaving from Genoa and landing in New York in 1928. He bought the original parcel of land in Greenwich in 1931."

"That's very impressive, and as far as I can tell, accurate. Good researching skills, but that still doesn't add up to a connection, does it?"

"Maybe not, but here's the thing, Lidia. I went to the state library in Hartford and did some more research on your family's business here in Connecticut and discovered that your great grandfather's fermented cider had been famous in Italy. All very interesting, but not really amounting to much, until I found one line in an old newspaper story, an interview with your grandfather about how the Gamba Ghiselli family had lent your great grandfather the money that had given him his start. Turns out that one of their relatives was your great grandfather's biggest distributor in the region.

Lidia almost choked on her coffee and brought her hand to her mouth. "Excuse me," she said. "Okay, so that's a connection. It is." Lidia looked at the fingertips of her hands, spread out on the table in front of her. She drew her hands back and wrapped her arms around herself, looking out the window to see carefree shoppers striding confidently up and down Greenwich Avenue. Suddenly her own hometown seemed strange and distant, as though she would never be carefree on its streets again. *How will things ever return to normal if that poor pilot was actually linked in some way to me and to my family?* Lidia wondered. It was more than she could or would accept.

"So Tina's supposed great grandfather was married to someone from that Ravenna family who knew my family, and okay, she crashes into my house. Yes, that's quite a coincidence, but I can't figure . . . what could that mean? I mean, suppose she did do it on . . . purpose . . . I can't believe that, but suppose she did. Why on earth would she? All these years later, what could have happened that would make her do such a thing?" Hearing herself utter these words, Lidia was convinced. Of course the whole thing was impossible, and more. It was ludicrous.

Claudia was unmoved by Lidia's logic. She may have had no more information with which to make her case, but she did have a plan.

"In order to find out why, first I have to find out if Tina was in fact related to Mario Calderara, the aviator. I was hoping you might know something, but you don't. Privacy laws will make it nearly impossible to find out anything about her birth family, but I can talk to Mr. and Mrs. Walters of Dayton, Ohio."

On the drive back to the Niven estate, the wind picked up, sending leaves of red, yellow, and orange swirling across the road like small tornadoes. *That woman did not crash into my house on purpose,*

Lidia fumed, regretting her decision to seek out Claudia. She was sure she didn't want to know more, and yet of course she wanted to know more—all of it. Fear was again closing in, that sense that terrible things awaited her in the boundless, unknown world, things she could not control and, worse, could not stop from hurting her girls. Before they'd parted ways, Lidia had one request of Claudia. "Just, please, give me fair warning if you're going to publish anything that may be difficult for us, that could touch my girls, hurt them in some way. Can you promise me that?"

"This is what I do," Claudia had responded. "I'm a reporter." So that was it. Claudia would make no such promise. This was what she wanted to do—have a real story. "Not the soccer mom I took her for," Lidia said to herself out loud.

Salvaging What Remains

November storms and winds had blown the trees on the Niven estate all but bare. Polly watched as Lidia, standing at the kitchen sink, looked out the window. She was intently focused on the tallest birch on the property, bent almost in half by the wind. Without looking down, Lidia felt for the towel beside her and, drying her hands, continued to stare at the tree as it struggled not to snap. Polly could only imagine what her friend was thinking, but she assumed that Lidia, like the tree, must at times be on the verge of snapping. Polly returned to putting away the last of their lunch things. She struggled to stand as tall as possible, balancing on one arm as she stretched the other upward toward a high shelf, cup in hand.

"My reach is still pretty good, but I probably ought to bring all my dishes and glasses down a notch or two." She turned toward Lidia, who was still too engaged in her own thoughts to answer.

"My word," she said, as she joined Lidia to stare out at the near vanquished birch. "We've had a quite a fall so far, haven't we? More wind and rain than I've seen in quite some time. Microburst storms, that's what they're called. Things are definitely changing, climate-wise."

"Hmm," said Lidia.

"The good thing about them, though, is they're over pretty quickly. See, the wind is already dying down." Turning toward her friend, she added, "It would be nice if the storms in our lives passed as quickly."

"Huh? Oh, yes," said Lidia. Polly could see she was distracted. "I'm sorry, Polly. I was just thinking about the house."

They both gave a start as the teakettle rang out.

"It's for me," said Polly. "Will you have some?"

"Yes, thank you," Lidia said, as Polly poured hot water into two porcelain teacups.

"What's the matter, dear?" asked Polly, sensing a new level of distress. Lidia, who had been pacing as Polly prepared the tea, was now standing next to Polly, nervously tapping a finger on the counter. "Are you so anxious to have your tea?" she asked, smiling at her friend.

Lidia stopped tapping and laughed. "Sorry," she said. "I'm trying not to feel sorry for myself, even if it doesn't look that way sometimes, but damn it, why is it taking so long for me to get clearance to go back to my own house? Here it is November already. Three weeks—and nothing. At least they've thrown a giant tarp over some of the mess, but I know I've lost all the family albums by now, and who knows if I'll find my camera and the digital cards intact."

"Bureaucracy—it grinds along at its own pace," said Polly, handing Lidia a cup. "Green, nothing added, right?"

Lidia nodded, and the two settled in the living room, Lidia sinking into the couch and Polly into John Paul's leather club chair, her feet, warm in faux shearling slippers, up on the ottoman.

"It could snow before I'm allowed back," said Lidia, the tea and Polly's sympathy not having the hoped-for calming effect, Polly noticed.

"If things don't start moving soon, I'm going to get a black eye mask and black face paint, dress up like a cat-burglar, and, in the middle of the night, I'm going to Apple Way with as many garbage bags as I can carry. I'll take matters into my own hands. I'll tear that yellow police tape into shreds. I'll . . . well, that may be enough."

Polly laughed and saw Lidia begin to relax. "I'll go with you. It will be fun, but you know, Lidia, it hasn't been a month yet since the accident. I know it's hard, but I'm afraid your patience will be tried further before it's over."

"Yes—'the accident,'" said Lidia. "I'm glad you said that because you do think it was an accident, don't you, Polly?"

Before Polly could answer, Lidia moved up on the couch and put her cup down on the coffee table. "And I haven't heard a word yet from our intrepid crack reporter, Claudia Dobbs, or from our kind and understanding special agent, Dirty Harry. Both of whom, by the way, assured me they were 'on the case.'" At this Lidia made imaginary quotation marks in the air with the first two fingers of each hand.

She immediately drew them back. "Oh, tell me I didn't just do that. What's happening to me?" She slid back down into the downy comfort of the couch.

"Dear, it strikes me you need to do something, so you won't feel so helpless. I'm not advocating the cat burglar outing, but maybe you could start with something a bit more legal, some phone calls perhaps, to the police department, or, do you still have Agent Caligan's card?"

Lidia straightened and pushed her hair back. "It's around somewhere. Yes, I should get in touch. He told me to call. And Claudia, too. I need to call them both. You're right, Polly. I've lost my drive. I need to do something. And if the calls don't work, I swear, I'm cat woman."

——————●——————

Lidia knew exactly where Harry's card was, in the top drawer of her dresser. She had even added his name to the contact list on her phone, looking at it from time to time, careful not to touch his number for fear she would accidently begin the call she was not ready to make. Now, with a little assist from Polly, she decided to take action. *Someone needs to tell me why this is taking so long,* she told herself. Why not Harry?

In the afternoon, after telling Polly she had some insurance paperwork to attend to in her room, she closed the door. She didn't really need privacy, but she knew she might be nervous if Polly overheard her. Taking a deep breath, she took her phone from the dresser and pressed in Harry's number.

He answered on the first ring.

"This is a coincidence," he told her. "I was going to call you today. You can't see, but it's right here in my notebook, 'Call L. Raven, re: property, a.m.'"

Lidia sat down on her bed and took in Harry's voice, so different from Owen's tense tone, always expecting the worst from his conversations with her. And now, here was Harry, professional yet open, almost playful. Again she was reminded that he didn't fit her image of a special agent, but there was more. She was aware, for the first time, of how long it had been since she had wanted to hear a man's voice. This knowledge did not calm her, however, and she again started picturing those exploding cartoon bombs.

"That is a coincidence," she said, "because the reason I'm calling is . . . I wanted to ask, well, in addition to finding out what you could tell me about the investigation, maybe you know something there . . . I wanted to know . . ." Lidia could feel herself getting tangled in her words, not knowing where her sentences were going. *It's like being on some weird mental loop-the-loop,* she thought, and then she hunkered down for the rest of the wild ride. "If, or rather, when I could go by the house—it's been almost a month now—to pick through, to look through the rubble, to see if any of our things . . . I really want to salvage our personal things—pictures, albums—if there is anything I could take, recover, that might still be not ruined, or rather, that might still be salvageable." *Good grief,* thought Lidia. *Can't I say one intelligible thing?*

Harry was silent. Then he replied, "Right."

"I'm sorry. It's just that it's been a long time. And I'm getting nervous, about the property. I just want to see what's there." She sighed and realized she wanted to keep talking. "It's been very difficult. We had to leave so suddenly. We've got nothing from our real lives. Nothing feels normal anymore."

"I'm sure it's been very, very difficult," said Harry.

"It's not all bad. It's been easy to buy replacement things, insurance is paying for a lot, and we have a wonderful place to live, but I feel so cut off. Every time I want something of mine, I realize that it's not here. Then I think, it's at home—and I can picture right where it is—but of course it's not there anymore, either. Nothing is where it should be."

"We try to keep the victim, person, in mind, but we get wrapped up in things on our end, and we forget how it must be for people. I owe you an apology, Mrs. Raven. I should have been in touch sooner."

"Lidia."

"I'm sorry?"

"Lidia. Call me Lidia. Or Ms. Raven. It's my maiden name. I changed back after . . ." She stopped abruptly, embarrassed. She was saying more than she should.

"You told me to call you Harry. So you, too, call me Lidia."

"Lidia," he said.

She felt the heat in her cheeks begin to subside as Harry explained to her that the local police had concluded their search of the property. He told her the FBI was wrapping up its site work and had recovered what evidence was needed to continue the investigation from the field office.

"But just to let you know," Harry assured her, "the Greenwich police are still patrolling the property to be sure there's no trespassing. The area is still cordoned off."

"That's a relief, really. Thank you. But you said 'evidence.' Evidence of what?"

"There are some things I can talk to you about, and I have questions, too, of course. I know this has taken longer than expected, but you can go back to your property now, with PD assistance. That's what I wanted to tell you. I can set that up for you. I can be there, too, and we can talk then."

"Thank you, Harry. That would be good. I'll look forward to hearing from you."

Lidia hung up and sat for a while, staring at the phone. *All in all, not bad,* she thought, *aside from an awkward moment or two.*

On Friday afternoon she drove to Apple Way to meet Harry and police officer Dolan, who were there to guide her through the property. It was the first clear day all week. The sun warming her face, Lidia felt more hopeful than she had in some time, and there was no denying it, her heart rate picked up when she saw Harry walking toward her. He introduced her to Officer Dolan, a tall, broad-shouldered young man, new to the force, he explained, who appeared to be no older than her twins. But Lidia's light-heartedness diminished as they began walking through the rubble. Officer Dolan and Harry both pulled wheeled containers along the periphery as Lidia found things, a vase not shattered, her jewelry box, miraculously not damaged. She placed them carefully in the plastic bins. There wasn't much—the twins' trophies, not too scratched or dented, some clothes that could be cleaned and mended. Lidia was grateful that her filing cabinet was unscathed, and the files containing birth certificates and other documents, her divorce papers, were intact. The biggest disappointment of the day, though, was finding the family albums wet and crumbling; only some of the pictures of her parents and grandparents were salvageable. The girls would be equally disappointed to find their scrapbooks ruined.

"This must be what it's like after a bombing, she said. "I feel like I'm walking through a war zone."

Just then she spotted her digital camera, the edge barely visible, the rest hidden under a slab of plaster. She wiggled it out and pressed the power button. "It's a miracle," she said, waving the little silver box in the air. "The battery is still charged and the pictures are all still here. I have the girls' recitals, sports events, our last vacation to the Cape. I can't believe it." She turned the camera off and stepped over broken pieces of wood and plaster to find her way to the container Officer Dolan was pulling. After the rescue of the camera, there wasn't much else to be found, so much lay in ruins.

"My car, it's battered, but it may be all right," said Lidia, more hopeful than confident, looking at the caved in roof, the only part still visible in the debris that had been the garage.

Lidia noticed the young policeman and Harry exchange looks. "I wouldn't get my hopes up," said Harry. "I've seen cars in better shape that wind up totaled."

"Well, you've certainly made my day with that," said Lidia.

"Sorry, but it's probably better if it is. It may take some time, but a new car will be a safer bet."

"You're right. Look, I appreciate your help today, both of you," said Lidia, continuing to look in Harry's direction. It was comforting somehow . . . that Harry was offering a little guidance, even if it was only about her car.

Before leaving, Officer Dolan helped Harry load the containers into the back of Harry's van. Brushing off his hands, the young officer had some parting words about the clean-up work that would take place before construction could begin. "You'll want to watch that process carefully," he told her. "There's probably a lot that's hidden under beams and collapsed walls that's still in good shape. You'll want to oversee that as much as you can before good stuff gets hauled away or, worse, before it mysteriously disappears. There's only so much we can protect."

Lidia thanked him, said she would take his advice, and waved at the back of the PD cruiser as he drove away. She then spent a few minutes talking to neighbors who had stopped by to say hello and to express their sorrow at her misfortune. Out of the corner of her eye, Lidia could see Harry leaning against the van, patiently waiting for her. Mrs. Beltran was the last to say good-bye. She wrapped her ample arms around Lidia and then, releasing her, took Lidia's hands in hers and gave them a good squeeze.

"Give a hug just as big as that to those beautiful girls for me, Lidia. And don't forget a special scratch behind the ears for Opal—tell her it's from me. We miss you, all of you, so come home soon."

"We'll try," said Lidia.

Mrs. Beltran walked up the street, carefully guiding her impressive girth toward her house. Lidia glanced over at Harry, who gave her a sympathetic nod. She walked to him.

"I'll follow you back to the Niven place," he said, "and help you store these bins."

———•———

Lidia looked for Polly when they got back and then remembered her Friday afternoon yoga and meditation class. After Lidia and Harry had unloaded the bins in the garage, she asked him if he could stay for coffee.

Harry sat at the round white oak table in the bay window of the breakfast room as Lidia brought in two steaming mugs.

"Where are your daughters?" he asked. "I was hoping to meet them."

Sitting down opposite Harry, Lidia noticed the late afternoon sunlight still sparkling on the Sound.

"They're practicing for homecoming. They're both on the court— and the game is tomorrow night."

"I'm sorry I missed them." Then, changing the subject, he said, "I know you want to find out about the investigation so far, so here's what I know: Tina Calderara was apparently a very troubled woman, Lidia. We talked to her parents in Dayton, and they confirmed that for some time she had been delusional about her birth family. She had some sort of need to be connected with famous aviators, so she concocted a story that her grandfather was a well-known Italian flyer and that her grandmother was, and I hesitate to say this because you don't need to concern yourself with Tina's fantasies, but she thought her grandmother was Katharine Wright, Orville and Wilber's sister."

"Oh dear," said Lidia. "I knew about the Italian flyer, but not about…. I didn't even know the Wright Brothers had a sister."

"The Bureau is satisfied that the crash was an accident caused by bad planning and fatal error on the part of the pilot. How she got off course is a mystery, but she clearly knew she was running low on fuel. She was probably looking to land at the nearest airfield—Westchester would be my bet—and miscalculated."

"But she was so experienced."

"Pilots typically only get to make one big mistake, unfortunately. This one was hers."

Lidia looked down at her half-empty cup.

"So, our work is pretty much done. I'll finish up my investigation and report at the New Haven office."

Harry looked at her, saying nothing more. Lidia felt she was being pulled into the perfect blue of his eyes. She wanted to stay there longer.

"I better go," he said.

"No more coffee?"

"It's getting late. You can call me if you have any questions. After I've filed the report, I'll be in touch."

This last comment hung in the air between them. Lidia filed the moment away for later, knowing she would spend considerable time turning it over in her mind while reliving how deeply he had touched her with his gaze.

Harry pushed away from the table and stood to go. "So, Lidia, it's time to begin rebuilding your home. Have you given any thought to that yet?"

As they walked to the FBI van parked in the driveway, they talked about the decisions and the choices Lidia would be making in the next few weeks.

"I'm afraid I don't even know where to begin," she said.

At that moment, a car pulled in the driveway, dropping Polly off.

"Vivika, my yoga teacher, drove me home," Polly shouted to them as she eased herself out of the passenger seat. "I told you not to worry about taking the car for your meeting," she said as she approached them and extended a hand to Harry. "And you must be the special agent attached to this van."

"Yes, Harry Caligan. Nice to meet you."

"I'm sorry," said Lidia. "Harry, this is Polly Niven, my life-saver and good friend."

"Lidia and her girls are lucky to have you, Mrs. Niven," said Harry, extending a hand and clasping Polly's in his. "I've seen people in Bureau cases who've had no one they could turn to." Saying good-bye, he walked toward the van as Lidia and Polly stood, watching him leave.

As Harry was pulling away, he lowered the passenger-side window. "Lidia, a good friend of mine is an architect. I'm not supposed to make referrals, a matter of ethics. Just make sure you get a lot of recommendations from people you trust, but if you do call him, I'm sure he would be happy to talk to you. His name is Eric Porter."

"He's a handsome one, isn't he?" said Polly after Harry drove away. "And he does seem nice, Lidia. I think your instincts about him are correct."

———————◆———————

That night, after dinner, Carly and Clarisse were busy trying on the homecoming dresses they finally decided on after a last-minute trip to the mall. Both Lidia and Polly had tried to convince the girls that time was running short and found it hard to believe that the sisters were not more than a little casual about their impending big night but rather seemed genuinely opposed to the whole idea. At last the women prevailed and now looked on from the doorway of Carly's room as Carly looked at the back of her dress in the mirror.

"It's not too low, is it? I don't want it to be too low in the back. It's not too short?"

Lidia gazed at her daughter in her deep blue taffeta dress. It was strapless, and it dipped a bit lower in the back. Lidia thought Carly had never looked lovelier.

"Not at all, Carly. I think it's fine, and don't forget, you have a little wrap that goes with it. What do you think?" she asked, turning to Clarisse and Polly.

They both agreed the dress was perfect. Clarisse was just stepping out of hers, not waiting for opinions.

"But Clarisse, I haven't seen yours on you yet," said Lidia.

Clarisse continued putting the dress back on the hanger. "It's fine, really, Mom. It looks fine, but I don't want to put it on again, if that's okay."

Lidia looked at Polly, who smiled back. "Let me see it, Clarisse," she said as she took the bottom of the dress and then stepped back to look at it while Clarisse held the hanger. "Hmm. So this comes to the knee? And is it formfitting? It looks like it might be."

"The knee? No, it's shorter than that, and I don't want it to be too tight. You don't think it might be too tight, do you?"

"Well, I don't think so, but . . ."

"Okay, I'll try it on again," she said, stepping into the dress. As Clarisse brought the sleeves over her shoulders, she caught a glimpse of Polly and her mother looking satisfied. "You two are a pair of good witches, aren't you?" She turned to show them a pale champagne chiffon sheath with cap sleeves. "Too tight?"

"It fits you perfectly," said Polly.

"Yes, it does," said Lidia. "It's sweet and quite lovely."

"Thanks, but I just don't like all this fuss. It's embarrassing."

"Me either," said Carly. "I think this whole homecoming thing is a throwback to the 1950s, nothing personal."

Polly and Lidia laughed, nodding in agreement. "Yes, it is. Absolutely a throwback. How good of you to notice," said Polly. "I spent a good deal of the '60s trying to get people to notice how these 'dress-up events,' things like beauty contests, kept women from using their brains, but you know, honey, I'm not so worried anymore, not when I see girls like you and Clarisse who have their priorities straight. Right, Lidia?"

"Absolutely. Humor us; let us enjoy seeing you looking spectacular," answered Lidia. Then, remembering a message she had promised to deliver, her smile vanished. "But there's something else I want to talk to you both about."

Polly rose. "This might be a good time to leave mother and daughters alone," she said.

"No, please, Polly, stay."

Carly and Clarisse sat on one twin bed looking across at Lidia and Polly on the other.

"You know, girls, there's someone else who would enjoy seeing you tomorrow night," continued Lidia. "Your dad. He called right before dinner, when you were washing up. He'd like to come, with Robert."

Carly and Clarisse, known among friends and family for their dignity and composure, turned to each other, then stared at their mother and simultaneously said, "NFW."

"Well, if you're going to talk in code, I really don't see that you need me," said Polly. "'NFW?' What does that even mean?"

"I know what it means," said Lidia, "and really, girls, is that the most articulate thing you can say?"

"Mom," said Carly, collecting her thoughts. "Dad—we haven't talked to him or seen him in ages."

"We're estranged," added Clarisse.

"But it can't go on like this. You know that, don't you? It's been almost three years, and you've only seen him a handful of times since then." Lidia took a deep breath and said, "Maybe it's time to accept . . . for me to accept, too."

"Have you accepted?" asked Carly. "Accepted that with no warning he walked out on you, on us?"

Lidia saw that Carly was looking at her intently, as if trying to gauge her reaction, as if she, Carly, depended on Lidia's reaction before she could express her own. This realization was startling to Lidia—and yet hadn't she always known, hadn't she depended on her girls to be the firewall that kept her from having to accept? It was time for the firewall to come down, Lidia knew, but still . . .

"I'm trying, Carly. It's hard, but maybe it's something I, we have to do."

"But Robert?" said Clarisse. "He has to bring Robert? Isn't that a bit much?"

After half an hour more of a conversation that ended where it began, Lidia poked her head in at Polly in the library.

"Come in, dear," said Polly, looking up from her computer, taking off the glasses perched on the end of her nose. "How did it go?"

"It went nowhere." And then Lidia filled Polly in on the details.

"So they never relented? No Dad and no Robert?"

"Definitely no Robert, but there may be a chance I can convince them about Owen—if I tell them he'll come alone."

———————•———————

Some threshold had been crossed, Lidia knew. Her reluctance to move on was giving way to something new, even if the old anger and pain could still . . . would probably still . . . erupt. Lidia continued in her efforts to get the girls to relent. It took several more attempts on her part, at breakfast and in the car on the way to the hairdresser, but she finally prevailed—Owen alone, and no big reunion. After the game, the girls would go out with their friends—not with Owen.

"So essentially what they are saying is that I can go to the game, which is a public event, by the way, by myself. I can see my daughters from a distance, but they don't want to spend any time with me after," said Owen on the phone that afternoon.

"Essentially, yes," said Lidia, realizing how unbecoming is was for her to be taking pleasure from Owen's indignation, something that in the past she had accepted as her due. "Look, Owen, it's the best I can do. They'll see you after the game, just to say hello. They definitely don't want to go out with us, 'as a fake family,' is how they put it."

"Lidia, I know I've hurt you and the girls. I know how deep that hurt is and how hard this has been on you, but . . ."

Lidia said nothing, waiting for Owen to finish his thought.

". . . it's been hard on me, too."

Lidia felt her old anger flare up. She never let herself dwell on Owen's losses, nothing that would blunt her sense of abandonment. Nor would she allow herself to linger on what it would have cost

Owen—all of them—if he had continued to deny who he truly was. Now it was her anger that felt somehow blunted. She sensed it, but she wasn't quite ready to give up the fight.

"You made the decision to tear our family apart, Owen, not me," she said quietly.

"That's not fair, Lidia, and you know it. What should I have done?"

Lidia always knew that one day Owen would pay dearly for the loss of his daughters' love. He had been everything to them once, and he had loved being the object of their affection. She still had vivid memories of watching the three of them walking on the beach at the Cape when the twins were no more than three or four, Owen in the middle, the girls on either side, in their matching bikinis, reaching up at the same time to hold his hand as the waves came in. She had waited a long time for this moment—when the consequences of his actions hit him. But now, she wondered, had she been so focused on her own pain that she ignored what her anger was doing to those she loved the most? Had she somehow subtly seen to it that her daughters would not forgive their father? She always told herself she had been objective and had not turned them against Owen, but now she had doubts. Surely, she could have done more to help repair their severed relationship. She had always thought she would revel in this moment, the day when Owen's abandonment of his family would force him to see that he had lost his daughters' love. But listening to his breathing, his beginning to choke up, on the other end of the phone, Lidia did not feel satisfaction. He was right. She had not been fair.

"Owen? Are you all right?"

"No, Lidia. I'm not. You win. But let me ask you, would it have better for me to have stayed? Would that have been fair to any of us?

"Oh, Owen, don't. Please. Don't make me feel that all the years we had together were a sham. We were happy once, weren't we?" As soon as she realized she had posed that question, she retreated once again. "I can't. I can't get into this with you now, I can't."

"I know, Lidia. We can never get into it, but for all of us, not just me, we have to get into it. What I did that was wrong was to hurt you many years ago by not being honest with you or myself. I know I didn't handle things the way I should have with Robert, but at some point I had to admit that I was lying to myself and to you and the girls."

In the past, Owen's attempts to explain himself had only made matters worse, with Lidia charging ahead, releasing her fury on him, her rhetorical skills sharpened by anger. But for reasons she did not understand, the need to stand her ground was falling away. His words weren't landing like grenades she had to dodge, only to strike back with verbal assaults of her own. For the first time, in this war-torn field between them, a battered dove was trying to get through, carrying a message that had previously been denied passage

"I don't know, Owen," she said. "Maybe. Maybe somehow we have to find peace, all of us." Suddenly overcome with exhaustion, she added, "But I can't talk anymore right now." She hung up the phone.

———●———

Homecoming night was clear and cold. In the bleachers, people were huddled under blankets or bundled up in assorted layers of North Face and Patagonia outerwear. Lidia and Polly, wrapped in several of Polly's afghans, poured themselves mugs of hot tea from the thermos they had brought along, holding the mugs tightly, letting the steam warm their faces.

During halftime, when the homecoming court was presented, Lidia and Polly held hands while Lidia scanned the stands, looking for Owen. The girls on the court were all wearing strapless or near strapless dresses giving cover to their thighs at most. As a result, most of them walked in a teenage-girl hunch, indicating both the degree to which they were underdressed, given the weather, and the extent to which they were telegraphing their modesty at being singled out as special. Carly, however, stood tall, her wrap covering her bare shoulders. Clarisse walked so leisurely, it appeared she was out for a summer stroll. Their escorts, in dark suits, looked age-appropriately uncomfortable, not sure whether to hold hands, offer an arm, or walk singly beside their long-limbed, equally awkward partners.

"They must be freezing, poor things," said Lidia at the very moment she felt their bleacher row give a little bounce as Owen sat beside her.

"They look beautiful," he said, staring at his daughters.

There was just enough time for a few hurried hellos. As Owen reached across her to shake hands with Polly, Lidia took note of how well he looked. Always athletic, he had maintained his slender but muscular build. In his mid-fifties, he still had thick brown hair. Lidia remembered that she had once liked brushing away from his forehead a few errant strands as a last minute grooming gesture before they were to meet friends for dinner or a movie. Such little things; such a normal life. She always marveled at how quickly it had all unraveled.

In black wool slacks, a burgundy sweater, and a brown suede jacket, he looked every bit the successful man he was. He looked the perfect husband and father, roles he could yet play happily with Robert if he no longer had to fight Lidia for the love of his daughters.

The band stopped when the MC came forward to announce the winning couple. But first there were the obligatory jokes about the band, the coach, the team, a few teachers, and the cafeteria food. The laughs and the applause began to die down as it became apparent that the audience was anxiously awaiting the results of the vote for king and queen. And then came the announcement they had been waiting for.

The sound of the crowd and stomping feet became a muted roar overtaken by the pounding of Lidia's heart reverberating in her ears. She could see the people in the stands cheering. She saw Carly step forward to accept the crown, and then readjust her long flowing hair and step back beside her new partner, Jonathan Ketchum, the newly anointed king. She saw Clarisse, beaming and clapping vigorously, but Lidia couldn't see into her heart, to know what she was feeling at that moment, when her sister was singled out and she was not.

Owen leaned over and kissed Lidia just above the ear. "They're sensational, Lidia. You've done a great job," he whispered. "I'll meet you and the girls at the side entrance after the game, right?"

Lidia reached up and grabbed Owen's hand as he stood. "Stay, Owen," she said. "We'll go together."

After Owen sat back down, Polly gave Lidia's hand a little squeeze.

After the game and the big win for the home team, Lidia, Polly, and Owen began making their way to meet the girls, but it was slow going. Every few steps they were stopped by well-wishers who knew Lidia and her twins. "They're both so special, both deserved to win," she was told. Less welcome, though, were the numerous side-glances directed at Owen and then at Lidia, all but saying, "What's this?"

"I think you and Owen are stealing the show," Polly whispered to Lidia.

"For a family that doesn't like the limelight, we get our share of attention," replied Lidia. She was immediately brought back to the time just after Owen broke the news that he was leaving. She remembered the brief explanations she had tried to give to parents of the twins' friends and how the story of the breakup had taken on a life of its own—"Lidia Raven's Marriage in Ruins as Husband Runs Away with Another Man" was the headline she imagined everyone reading and talking about behind her back. Lidia began to feel the old nausea rising.

"I'd give them something to talk about if I were you," Polly whispered.

Lidia laughed and thought, *Why not?* She grabbed Owen's arm and held on. Owen leaned in and put a hand on Lidia's. *It might be 2009,* thought Lidia, *but we live in a stronghold of tradition where cultural change is slow. And I've been slow, too, to understand what Owen's been dealing with,* she said to herself.

When the trio arrived at the meeting place, the girls were already there, Chloe and Jena and several other friends waiting for them but at a distance. Lidia and Polly embraced the girls and congratulated Carly as Owen looked on.

"It's embarrassing," said Carly, "but thank you."

Lidia threw an arm around Clarisse and held her close. "And you," she said, "you're amazing."

"Thanks, Mom, but we're both just glad it's over."

Lidia stood away from her girls and looked at Owen, who took his cue to step forward, but in a few awkward moments the meeting was over. "Thanks, Dad," they had offered in return to Owen's compliments, but both quickly added that friends were waiting. There had been no embraces, no kisses. The girls waved good-bye and were gone. For the first time, Lidia felt sorry for Owen.

"That went well," he said.

"I'm sorry," said Lidia.

Polly was silent.

Owen walked both women back to their car. Polly retreated to the passenger side, saying she was chilly and eager to throw a blanket around her for the ride home.

Owen stood with Lidia before she too got into the car.

"I'm just trying to salvage my relationship with them if I can. I've missed so much."

"I know, Owen," she said, getting behind the wheel.

As she and Polly drove away, Lidia saw Owen through the rearview mirror, still standing there.

Thanksgiving

"This may sound New Agey, but in my experience, all healing, emotional or even physical, begins with letting go." Polly's words in the car on the way back to her place the night of homecoming were missing their target. Lidia was distraught, her feelings over what had happened with Owen so confusing that she was weeping. Crying, since her breakup, was something she rarely allowed herself, but tonight the tears were uncontrollable. Lidia was hardly aware of anything but her own turmoil as Polly continued.

"Let them come, dear," Polly said, easing her left hand over to steady the wheel as Lidia swerved slightly across the centerline.

At the house, Lidia's crying continued into the living room, where she ensconced herself on the couch and wiped her eyes with the embroidered handkerchief Polly had given her in the car. When Lidia reached what Polly had warned would be the staccato-sobbing phase of letting go (shallow breathing and short sobs), Polly came back from the library holding a copy of the *Bhagavad Gita*.

"It's the Isherwood translation," she said, looking through the first few pages. "Hmm . . . it's signed. Who knew? Anyway, you might want to give it a look. The reason I think so is because your new-found feelings for Owen seem to me to mean something momentous. And your kindness to him tonight is all part of letting go, as I've come to think of it." She patted Lidia's hand and said it was time for bed. "Will you be all right, dear?"

"Yes. Thank you. And I will—I will read the book."

"Good," Polly said, but as she turned to leave, Lidia called out to her.

"But my girls . . ." There were so many unresolved issues, and Lidia needed Polly to stay.

"Ah, yes. The girls." Polly sat back down, and the two of them talked for another hour, Lidia expressing her concerns and doubts. Could she truly forgive Owen? Would the girls ever forgive him? She was beginning to realize how much of a role she'd played in their lingering anger. How could she help them? Why was she suddenly feeling so sympathetic and weepy? At each turning point in the discussion, Lidia listened intently as Polly expressed her hope for the situation while emphasizing the virtue of patience.

"These things tend to work themselves out at their own pace, but the time will come when all this worry and angst will be resolved. Think of it this way. The heart is a muscle, so it's vulnerable to injury. Let's see, where can I go with this?" mused Polly, pushing herself back into John Paul's favorite chair. "Anger is an injury that tightens the heart, yes, that's it. Tightens the heart very much like a clenched fist." Polly made a fist and held it up in front of her for Lidia to see and, liking her example, continued. "A fist so tight, it hurts just to try to open it. The longer it remains clenched, the harder it becomes to open up. But sometimes for reasons unknown, something happens. No one knows where it comes from or why, but when it does, through some grace, some glimmer of hope, the heart begins to let go, to soften." At this Polly opened her palm before continuing. "In time," she said, "it returns to its pure pulpy red self, to its natural state of love and forgiveness." Polly was now looking at her opened hand pointing optimistically toward the heavens. She dropped her hand into her lap. "It needs a little work, but you get the idea."

"Yes, Polly, I do," said Lidia. "You're a joy, really. I think I can go to bed now. At least rest there until I hear the girls come in for the night."

"And one more thing about those lovely girls of yours: They do love Owen, very much. That's why they're angry, but they will forgive him one day—you'll help them do that. And when they do find their way, they'll be quite weepy, too. What you're experiencing now, these tears? That's the heart opening up. It's quite common to go on a cry-ing jag when that happens."

"But why now?"

"Hmm, I wonder. What's different lately? Has something or some-one gotten to you for the first time in a long, long time?"

"What could you be getting at?" Of course Lidia knew what Polly was getting at. She paused a moment, then asked, "Harry?"

Polly laughed and Lidia smiled, enjoying the mention of Harry's name, which for Lidia put a nice finishing touch on what had been a very emotional night.

"Something to think about, isn't it? Good night, Lidia."

"Night, Polly."

In her bedroom, Lidia sat at the writing table and wrote a note to each of her girls. In Carly's note, Lidia congratulated her daughter on her win, but more important—as Lidia saw it—praised her for her good nature and humor, which kept her from taking herself too seri-ously, even when she deserved to be a little proud of her accomplish-ments. In Clarisse's note, she mentioned her graceful acceptance and sincere joy over her sister's win. To both she wrote to ask their for-giveness for being angry with their father for so long. *"I'm afraid I've influenced you in some way, hardened your heart toward your father because you saw how broken my own was,"* she wrote to them both. *"I hope we can all learn how to forgive, for your father's sake and for our own."*

She read each note over and then tiptoed first into Carly's and then into Clarisse's room, checking to be certain she was placing the right note under the right pillow. Then she crept into her own bed, pulled the covers up over her shoulders, and reexamined her last conversa-tion with Harry while she waited to hear the girls come in.

When the twins returned, she listened as they tiptoed upstairs and, after a quick round of face washing, teeth brushing, and getting into their pajamas, crept into their rooms and into bed. First Carly and then Clarisse felt the carefully folded paper under their pillows.

———◆———

The next few weeks brought a degree of stress to the Niven household not seen since Polly's plans and preparations for John Paul's eightieth birthday party some years back. On that occasion, Polly had arranged for a jazz combo, a fancy caterer, a bartender, floral arrangements to bedeck every conceivable corner and crevice of the house and yard, a tent in case of rain, a dance floor, and an MC. These weeks, however, had brought a different sort of frenzied activity. For the girls, there were the college and scholarship applications to complete and send off. For Lidia, there was the excavation crew to be hired for Apple Way and architects to be interviewed. For Polly, there was much meditation to attend to, either in the studio she had fashioned in the front-facing turret on the third floor or at her favorite yoga center over in Glenville. This she did to maintain her sense of equanimity in the face of the high emotional pitch around her. "When you can't beat 'em, flee!" she had told Lidia and the girls, this being her mantra for such times.

The week before Thanksgiving, Lidia looked up from her to-do list and remembered with a tug at her heart that she had not yet heard from Harry. Putting that aside for a moment, she remembered also that she had not heard anything more from Claudia Dobbs, who had sort of promised to stay in touch. *I won't call Harry, not just yet, but I can call Claudia,* she thought. After several attempts to reach the *Greenwich Time,* all unsuccessful, Lidia called to Polly, who was in the library, to let her know that she was going out for a bit. Then, after taking the car keys off the hook in the mudroom, she proceeded to the garage and backed the Subaru out the long driveway onto the street.

At the newspaper office, she waited in the empty lobby for sometime before the receptionist returned, looking harried.

"No, I don't have an appointment," Lidia said before the young woman had a chance to ask.

After being told, "Ms. Dobbs is very busy," in several variations of the expression, Lidia asked the receptionist to at least buzz her office, which she finally did.

"Ms. Dobbs said for me to show you in, but you can't stay long."

Lidia was taken by surprise when she saw packing boxes, some full, some half-empty, scattered around Claudia's small office. Claudia herself appeared frazzled. Her frizzy brown hair was struggling against the fastener she wore to hold it back, strands breaking loose and threatening to cover her eyes, necessitating short bursts of breath from the side of her mouth to push the encroaching locks back.

"Oh, Lidia. Lidia Raven," she said, looking up from the stack of books she was about to lift and place in the box on her desk. "I've been meaning to call you, honestly. It's just that, well, things have taken a turn. In my life, that is."

Lidia waited for more, but Claudia returned to her task.

"It looks like you're moving. To a bigger office, I hope."

"Yes, it will be bigger, but it won't be here. I've been offered a job in Hartford, at the *Hartford Courant*."

"Well, that's good, a promotion, it sounds like."

Claudia nodded, and, after placing the books in the box, pushed back her hair and asked Lidia to sit down. Seeing the only other chair in the office was stacked with boxes, the two women moved them to the floor, and Lidia sat down while Claudia took a seat behind her desk.

"Yes, it is a bigger job, in their features department, and you know, there are no newspaper jobs today, so this—well—I couldn't turn it down."

"Of course," said Lidia.

"But, just so you know, I pitched the Calderara story, your story, about the crash, but they said there was a backlog as it was, and so it was dropped. I still think there's a potentially great story there, but I had to let it go, for the time being anyway. Who knows? Maybe someday."

"So, you never got in touch with the Walters, her family in Dayton?"

"No. I didn't. But tell me," said Claudia, beginning to pull items again for more packing. "How is the investigation coming? And are you rebuilding yet?"

Lidia began filling Claudia in on the details, but the more she talked, the more Claudia packed.

"Well, you're busy here," Lidia said, standing to go. "So unless I'm going to start packing too, I think I'll leave you to it."

Claudia looked up from her boxes. "I'm sorry, Lidia. I guess I am distracted. I have to be out of here this afternoon. I start my new job tomorrow. I'm lucky, you know—to have a job at all. This office will be closing soon—consolidating with the Stamford paper. That's the business today."

Lidia began moving toward the door.

"But I'll tell you, if I had my way, I'd be working on your story."

Lidia said her good-byes and left Claudia clearing the last of her shelves.

On the way home, Lidia wondered if there really was a story there. After all her efforts to deny it, she had to admit: Tina Calderara was often in her thoughts. Would she ever decide to see this through, to seek out the story on her own? Her newfound curiosity was soon buried, though, as Lidia threw herself into plans and preparations for Apple Way with the same zeal Claudia had displayed in vacating her old office. Tina and the story were relegated to the back of Lidia's mind.

————◉————

As the holiday drew nearer, one by one, the Ravens began to look up from their toil. The twins had sent out the last of their applications, and Lidia, with the help of Eric Porter, her new architect, had hired an excavator, Rocco Santini. Polly descended from self-imposed exile in her third-floor meditation studio. She stopped on the steps and asked, abruptly, "Who wants to help me plan the Thanksgiving menu—and who should we invite?"

The next few days went by in a blur. Before she knew what had hit her, Lidia was in the kitchen on Thanksgiving morning putting the finishing touches on the desserts, the part of the meal she had volunteered to take on. Polly had requested a variety of pies so she could have a wedge of each. The twins wanted anything with whipped cream—pumpkin would be great, they had offered. There were three others about to go into the oven. The apple, of course, was for Owen. That had always been his favorite. The peach was for Robert—not that Lidia thought she would ever be making him a pie. The last, pecan, was for Harry. As she was stirring the milk, vanilla, and nuts into the mixture, the absurdity of the situation hit her in the face like a, well, like a pie. How could she be baking for her ex-husband, his boyfriend, and the man who was beginning to occupy her nighttime dreams and daylight thoughts? More inexplicitly, how had everyone agreed to this arrangement? *My God,* Lidia thought, *how had the girls agreed to this most unlikely guest list?* Thinking back on it, she realized how unlikely it truly was that they had reached this point.

The day Polly finally ended her self-imposed meditation retreat to ask about Thanksgiving had been the start of it. When she had asked about the guest list, at first, Lidia and the twins had no suggestions. "Why not just us?" asked Lidia. Polly then explained how Thanksgiving was the holiday she and John Paul had loved most. "The house was alive with plans and preparations and guest lists that got longer by the day," she said with a mixture of joy and loss in her voice. "We always included those who either had no place to go or who needed to mend relationships that had been broken," she added.

It was here the twins began to groan. "We know where this is headed," said Carly.

They both looked at Polly, whose face had remained resolute.

"Well, not only Owen."

"Robert, too?"

Realizing what Polly was suggesting, Lidia felt things moving too quickly. How could she go from forgiveness—which she was earnestly trying to achieve—to entertaining her ex and his new mate on

Thanksgiving, of all days? No, it was definitely moving too quickly. She was about to intervene when Polly sighed and shrugged her shoulders.

"We don't have to decide right now," she said.

Lidia quickly looked toward her daughters, who shook their heads and seemed to take Polly's last comment as their cue to find somewhere else to be. Soon they were up the stairs and barricaded in their rooms.

Lidia was staring at Polly in disbelief.

"You're not serious."

"Wouldn't you like to invite Harry? I don't know why, but I have a feeling he doesn't have family."

"Don't change the subject, Polly, and yes, I would like to invite Harry, now that you mention it, but Owen and Robert?"

Polly ushered Lidia into the library.

"Not another leather-bound book and a pregnant-with-meaning quote," said Lidia.

After a brief search, Polly took a book from the shelf. "Here it is," she said, adjusting her reading glasses on her nose. "And, yes, another quote." She began reading:

> *From hope and fear set free,*
> *We thank with brief thanksgiving*
> *Whatever gods may be*
> *That no life lives forever;*
> *That dead men rise up never;*
> *That even the weariest river*
> *Winds somewhere safe to sea.*

"Well, that certainly is uplifting. You think I need to hear a poem about the joys of being dead?"

"It's Swinburne, 'The Garden of Proserpine.' No one reads Swinburne anymore, but John Paul did, and I found this verse underlined and starred."

Polly took off her reading glasses and, staring at Lidia, said, "I may be reading too much into this, but I think John Paul felt the weight of time near the end, and I think his great affection for Thanksgiving had to do with being thankful for life, even though, you're right, the poem is about death. But that's not my point, which is . . ." She paused, as though searching for the right words. "I think this poem meant something to John Paul because he knew how our grievances waste our precious time—and then it's too late. It's why he tried so hard to help me find Kate and why he was so sorry he couldn't give her back to me."

"I'm sorry, too, Polly. And I know how much you and John Paul put into these gatherings, but this guest list—Owen, Robert, and Harry— it's bound to create pain for all of us, especially the girls."

"Not necessarily. They may surprise you. And this lingering 'estrangement'—isn't that what Clarisse calls it? It will keep them from growing, from getting on with their lives, especially now when they're about to make a very big leap into the future, going away to school."

Lidia pressed her fingertips to her temples, shaking her head. "No, no—it's too big, too much to grasp."

"Why not leave it up to the men?" Polly suggested. "If they agree to come, then they obviously feel they can handle it. Maybe then you and the girls could too."

"I don't know . . . I can't think about it right now. And whatever happened to the idea that these things take time? Isn't that what you said? Why are you pushing so hard?"

"Am I? I'm sorry, Lidia, but sometimes opportunity presents itself, and you have to seize the moment."

"You know, you have a very nice way of adjusting your philosophy to suit the occasion."

Polly smiled. "I have a quote for that."

Lidia groaned.

"Let me talk to Carly and Clarisse," she persisted. "If they say, yes, would you be okay with it?"

"I don't know," Lidia said. Then she added, "I guess. But they won't agree, not in a million years." Lidia knew she was placing her faith in her girls' refusal so she wouldn't have to object too strenuously to Polly's ill-conceived plan. *It's cowardly of me, I know,* thought Lidia. But she stopped short of saying anything.

The next day, Lidia watched as Polly began to work on the girls. When they returned from school and had changed into tights and hoodies for their usual three-mile run, Polly quickly ran to the garage to unlock her bike. Lidia, looking out the mudroom window, saw Polly, helmet askew, catch up with the twins, gesturing for them to take out their ear buds. After dinner, Polly told Lidia to relax while she helped the twins clean up. "Go read a book or watch a show," she told her, taking the plate from her hand, steering her toward the living room. The next morning she volunteered to drive the girls to school. After Lidia picked them up that afternoon, Polly followed them upstairs, where she herded them into Carly's room and closed the door. Lidia, standing at the foot of the stairs, could hear muffled voices, but she couldn't make out what was being said. She tried to keep busy, but it was difficult to concentrate, and she found herself returning to the stairs, looking up, straining to hear. After what seemed like hours, Lidia wondered what else could possibly be said on the subject. She started up the stairs just as the door opened, and Polly emerged, arm in arm with the twins.

"You've been up there forever," said Lidia.

"But we've reached agreement," Polly announced. "It isn't the Sinai Peace Accords, but close."

"Carly, Clarisse? Is it true? You're both okay with this?"

They nodded, a little tentatively, Lidia thought.

"You don't have to do this, you know. You can change your mind. It isn't too late."

"It's okay, Mom. We're sure," said Carly.

"And we have to . . . you have to . . . call Dad. Thanksgiving is day after tomorrow," said Clarisse. "They probably already have plans, but we can ask anyway."

Lidia looked at Polly. "If this blows up in our faces, you know who will take the fall, don't you?"

Holding onto the banister and calmly walking down the stairs, Polly replied. "No one will take a fall, dear. We just check our grounding and put one foot in front of the other."

Later, after Polly had said good night, Lidia and Clarisse went into Carly's room and sat on the bed across from her. Lidia wanted to know how the agreement had been reached.

"She had us, Mom," began Clarisse, drawing her knees to her chest under her pink nightshirt. "Polly can be tough. Right away she totally pulled the old-age card. She said she wouldn't be around forever, and it was *so* important to her to see us put our 'anguish' over the divorce behind us. That's what she called it, 'anguish,' like it wasn't just anger."

"But that's what it is, Mom. Were mad, and why shouldn't we be? He didn't think about us, about you. He was just thinking about himself. It was so selfish. That's why we can't forgive him," said Carly. "I told her about the day Dad left, how I watched the car pull out of the driveway. That was pretty bad. I haven't forgotten that."

"What did she say, then?" asked Lidia.

"Nothing. She just hugged me."

"Then I told her that this would be nothing like real Thanksgiving, when we were all together on Apple Way," said Clarisse. "I started to cry and Polly gave me a tissue. Then she asked us if we didn't have happy memories."

"So then we started remembering all the good stuff," said Carly.

Apparently the girls had warmed to the idea of recounting the good times. Clarisse brought up the time Owen had patiently taught her to ride a bike, Carly about how he listened to her on long walks they took together.

"We kinda got lost in our memories," Carly said.

It was at that point, according to the twins, that Polly had asked them whether they thought he could still be that same father. "Don't you miss that?" she had asked them.

"I guess I've been so mad, I've forgotten about all the time he was there with us, when he was . . . our dad," said Carly, quickly sliding the back of her hands over her eyes before continuing. "Anyway, that's when we began to think, we should give this a chance."

Clarisse nodded.

"But you didn't agree it's okay to have your dad and Robert both here, did you?" Lidia knew she wanted them to say no, and she knew it was unfair of her.

"Oh no," they both said. "We agreed."

Lidia felt her stomach sink.

"Polly told us that if her plan didn't work out, this little dinner party, she would never bring the subject up again," explained Carly.

"It's worth it," said Clarisse. "She's killing us, Mom, and she promised she would leave us alone forever."

"Yes," said Lidia. "She can be very persuasive." *And I have to work on acceptance as well as forgiveness, it appears,* Lidia said to herself.

And that was how it had happened. The next morning, reluctantly, with heart pounding and palms sweating, Lidia called Owen, who answered the phone and said he and Robert were on their way to go shopping for the Thanksgiving meal they were going to make for themselves—alone. "What can we bring?" Owen had asked as soon as she posed the question.

"Nothing," said Lidia. "We've got the menu covered."

After a brief and awkward exchange, Owen said, "You don't know how much this means to me, to us. Thank you."

"Right," said Lidia, and she hung up. *I'm not there yet—on this whole acceptance thing,* she humbly acknowledged.

With heart pounding harder and palms a little sweatier, she called Harry. But there was something more than anxiety this time: hopeful anticipation.

"I'm glad you called. I was waiting until after the holidays to get in touch," he said.

"Until the new year? How did you know I'd still remember you?" Lidia replied.

"Not all the holidays, just Thanksgiving. I wanted to call, but I figured you'd be busy with family until then."

Lidia knew in this brief exchange, in the tone of his voice—and in hers—that something deeper was passing between them. Without words, their way with one another was changing, no longer requiring a pretext of formality.

Lidia took a deep breath and invited him. She smiled into the phone when, without hesitation, he accepted.

"I was planning on a quiet day with take-out turkey. My sister lives in Louisiana, and I didn't really have the time this year to make the trip."

"Is that where you're from?"

"That's where my sister and I grew up. We don't really know where home is." He paused, and then added, "We were adopted."

"Oh," was all Lidia managed.

"There's a lot we don't know about each other. Maybe now there will be time to fill in the gaps."

An intimate silence lingered between them before Lidia answered. "I'm looking forward to it, Harry. Oh, I almost forgot," she added. "My ex and his boyfriend will be here too."

After another pause, Harry said, "We better get started on that conversation pretty soon, to fill in the gaps."

Lidia let out a little laugh. "Yes, and I almost forgot, what's your favorite pie?"

"Pecan."

After she and Harry had said their good-byes, Lidia tracked down Polly, who was in the kitchen finishing the shopping list.

"Unfortunately, they all said yes," Lidia told her. "And how did you know Harry didn't have family? Well, he has a sister, but that's it, apparently. He's adopted. They're from Louisiana. He doesn't sound it, though. But how did you know about his family or lack of?"

"I didn't. There just seems to be a kind of sensitivity under the strong special agent veneer, a vulnerability that sometimes comes with childhood hardship. You know, like in Dickens, you either have an Oliver Twist orphan or an Artful Dodger orphan. Harry strikes me as an Oliver."

"Hmm. That's good, Polly. You're very insightful . . . but sometimes I wish you had majored in accounting."

"Let's go shopping."

"I'm right behind you."

———————●———————

As inconceivable as it seemed, in the end, Polly had prevailed, and now Lidia was pouring the pecan mixture into the remaining pie tin and placing all her pies on the middle rack in the oven. "Good luck," she said as she flipped up the door, closing it with a thud. "We're going to need it."

By 2:30 PM, everything in the kitchen was under control. The turkey with lemon and oregano stuffed with wild rice and pine nuts, Polly's main contribution, was almost done. Ready for a quick reheat were the maple syrup–infused butternut squash, Carly's handiwork, and Clarisse's roasted carrots and parsnips with shallots. In the refrigerator were a simple green salad and Lidia's favorite cranberry sauce with candied walnuts.

In the living room, the clock ticking away on the mantle was the only sound breaking the silence, except for the shuffle of Lidia's feet as she placed one black pump–clad foot in front of the other, keeping perfect time with the clock. Dressed in a grey flannel skirt and lavender cashmere sweater set, she was thinking she shouldn't have worn lavender. It had been Owen's favorite color on her. The girls, dressed in skinny jeans, ballet flats, and sweaters, one burgundy, the other dark blue, sat stiffly on the sofa. Polly, by contrast, seemed relaxed in the club chair, wearing a long black skirt, a flowing gold blouse, and a large turquoise pendant around her neck. Opal lay under the coffee table, head on paws, eyes shifting from sofa to club chair, in anticipation of something big, no doubt involving the food she had been sniffing all day.

"You three look like you're waiting for the executioner," said Polly, rising from her chair. "I think you need some refreshment. Lidia, I'd give you a stiff drink, if you'd take it."

"I'll have a scotch, neat," said Lidia.

"Oh, this is going to be interesting," said Polly.

"Girls, what would you like?"

"Hemlock," answered Carly.

"Cyanide," said Clarisse.

"Very funny," said Polly, heading over to the bar set up on the marble table next to the French doors.

"We can get it ourselves," said Carly.

"No, I keep the poisons under lock and key. You'll have apple cider and like it—the non-alcoholic kind."

Promptly at three, the doorbell rang.

"Oh my God, they're here," said Clarisse, putting down her glass.

"Mom, you get it," said Carly.

"I'm not getting it. Polly, you go. You're the one to . . . It's your house, and besides, you're the instigator," said Lidia.

"For heaven's sake. Of course I'll get it. But you three, pull your-selves together."

Carly and Clarisse nodded. Lidia swallowed the last of her scotch.

Polly walked to the foyer and opened the door. Lidia, looking over her shoulder, watched her open the door. "I'm so glad you could make it," Polly said, taking the flower arrangement from Owen. "They're beautiful. Eucalyptus and rose hips—how fabulous. Thank you."

"Polly, this is Robert," said Owen.

"How good of you to come, Robert," said Polly.

Handing her a covered pie plate, Robert said, "I wouldn't have missed it. And this is an apple pie for you, for all of us. It's Owen's favorite."

"Yes, I know. Come, join us."

Lidia rolled her eyes and faced forward.

She couldn't breathe when she saw Owen and Robert come into

the living room, Polly between them, walking arm in arm. She was sure Polly was smitten. Why wouldn't she be? Robert was as good-looking as ever, sandy blond hair, hazel eyes, and easy manner. They made a striking couple, both well dressed, elegant but casual; quite charming. She was sure her legs would not hold her when she tried to stand and that words of polite conversation would not come when she tried to speak. She was afraid she would instead blurt out the thoughts now screaming in her head. *Am I insane? How did I ever agree to this? I'll never forgive myself—or Polly.* Instead, what she said was, "Happy Thanksgiving. Would you like a drink?" And she dashed to the serving cart with the marble top , holding on for support, waiting for their reply.

Before they could answer, Opal jumped out from under the coffee table and began nuzzling Owen, tail wagging.

"Hi, old girl," said Owen, bending down to scratch behind her ears.

"Hi, Dad," said Carly and Clarisse in unison, not looking at Robert.

Rising, Owen stepped forward to give his daughters a hug, but they backed away. "Girls, you remember Robert," he said.

"Hello," they responded, continuing to look at Opal, now sitting on Owen's left foot, tail still wagging.

Robert looked at Owen, who shrugged his shoulders.

"Please, sit," said Polly, directing her guests to the side chairs by the sofa. "I'm going to take this delicious-looking pie to the kitchen and bring out the hors d'oeuvres, while Lidia gets you that drink."

Before she got the words out, she had three helpers on her heels, as Lidia, Carly, and Clarisse followed her.

"What are you doing?" she asked as the doors to the kitchen swung shut behind her. "Lidia, go back in there and give them a drink. And girls, what's going on? I thought you were okay with this."

"I know we agreed," said Carly. "But now that it's really happening, it's hard, Polly," she continued, her voice breaking. "Really hard. It used to be us celebrating with Dad, not Robert." Carly looked at Clarisse. Tears were now filling both sets of eyes.

"I guess we thought it would be a little easier," said Clarisse.

"I'm sorry," said Polly. "But they're here now. Can't we try to make it work?" When Lidia saw her daughters on the verge of tears, she began to tear up, too, waving her hands up in front of her face, as if to stop any sympathy that might be brewing. "It's the scotch," she said. "I never could handle it."

Carly and Clarisse stopped just short of tears. They always did when Lidia got emotional. Her pain trumped theirs, although they never said it, Lidia realized. And they were doing it now.

"We better get back," said Lidia. "We can do this, girls, right?"

Polly pulled a paper towel from the holder and handed it to Lidia.

As soon as everyone was settled in the living room once again, the doorbell rang for a second time.

"I'll get it," said Lidia, loudly and a little more enthusiastically than she had wanted to.

Polly explained to Owen and Robert that there would be a third guest. "Special Agent Caligan has been a big help to Lidia since the accident," Polly explained, "and Lidia's struck up a bit of a friendship with him, it seems."

As Lidia got up to let Harry in, she saw Owen and Robert smile weakly. She wasn't sure she or they or the rest of the assembled group was up to any additional pressure, but all seemed resigned to bearing it. *Poor Harry,* she thought. *What have I gotten him into?*

Lidia opened the door, and Harry immediately leaned in to kiss her on the cheek. Lidia's heart fluttered. He then handed her a tinfoil-covered casserole dish.

"It's oyster dressing, Bayou style. My mom made it for us every year."

"Thank you, Harry. I'm so glad you're here. Come in," said Lidia, practically pulling him over the threshold.

Harry walked into the room, Lidia pushing him along.

She knew that Harry was by nature and profession prone to keeping a low profile, not comfortable being the center of attention. He was, however, in spite of his best efforts, charismatic. Tall and attractive, he was hard to ignore, with understated self-confidence.

After introductions all around, Harry quite naturally paid special attention to Polly—thanking her for her kind invitation and complimenting her on her beautiful home, noting particularly the abundant photos in the room of John Paul, of travel photos of the two of them, and of other mementos, rather than commenting on the grandeur of the place. Lidia saw Polly taking it all in, her approval apparent in the warmth of her smile.

Harry complimented the twins—not on their loveliness—but on how proud of them their mother was. The twins, who never had to face a suitor for their mother before, were obviously okay with Harry, shooting glances of approval toward Lidia whenever they got the chance. Lidia, in turn, was encouraged. Was it possible? Could she let herself hope for a new beginning with Harry?

When he greeted Owen and Robert, he put out his hand to both men. This was accomplished in a manner so genuine, Lidia noted, that it had a calming effect on the entire gathering. The girls perched on the arms of the sofa so Harry could sit next to Lidia and allowed themselves a peek at Robert. Lidia, next to Harry, seeing his effect on everyone, began herself to feel more at ease. Opal returned to her spot under the coffee table, yawned, and soon fell asleep.

There was little conversation during the hors d'oeuvres, however, despite Polly's considerable skills at drawing people out.

"Owen, how is business going?"

"Not too many new clients these days for wealth management. I'm spending all my time trying to keep the clients I still have."

"Oh dear. Robert, Owen mentioned your photography. Is that what you do professionally?"

"I'd like to, but no, I'm not taking many pictures right now—just trying to keep the business afloat."

"Oh? And what is that?"

"I'm a corporate travel consultant. Not much of that happening."

"I see. Harry, working for the FBI, that must be fascinating."

"A lot of it is pretty routine, and what isn't, I can't talk about. Doesn't make me too interesting at parties."

"I see. Well, I think that turkey must be about ready," said Polly, rising to begin the holiday meal.

Lidia and the girls helped bring out the dishes, and soon the mood of the gathering picked up as the guests took their places at the table, thankful for the feast about to be consumed and for relief from the painful attempts at conversation.

Lidia made a toast to Polly and used the opportunity to thank her for all she had done—was still doing—for her and the twins. "She is a treasure I will be thankful for until the day I die," Lidia said before sitting down, fearing she would start to cry again.

Soon attention turned to the twins and their plans for college, the schools they applied to, the ones they wanted to attend, and their safety schools. This discussion was lively and managed to engage the girls, in spite of themselves. When they said their safety schools were U Mass for Carly and Penn State for Clarisse, there was a momentary silence and then a raising of glasses and a toast to these girls whose chances of getting into their first-choice schools, Amherst (Carly) and Brown (Clarisse), were probably pretty good.

Things went well, until dessert, when all the pies were spread out on the table.

Lidia's attention was on Robert's contribution to the meal. "So you made an apple pie, Robert."

"Yes," he responded. "It's Owen's favorite."

"I know," she said, realizing that of course Robert knew Owen's favorite pie. And Owen knew the meaning of apples in Lidia's life, in her history. His love of her various apple recipes, pies included, was part of their connection to each other. It was important to her to make an apple pie for this occasion—as a nod to the past—and now Robert had brought one to the table as well. She wasn't sure how she felt. She paused as though she were in a freeze-frame that only she could break.

"I made one, too," she said after a deep breath. "You can never have too many apple pies."

Owen smiled at her. It was in gratitude, she could see that. Her heart was opening, just as Polly had said. She thought she would get teary again, but instead she smiled back at Owen. There had been a passing of the guard in her comment and in his reaction, and it was good. Lidia looked at Polly, whose smile conveyed both understanding and encouragement.

"Well," said Polly. "I don't know about the rest of you, but I intend to have a taste of everything on this table."

After a bite or two of the pumpkin, Carly and Clarisse, sitting on each side of Lidia, asked if they could go to Chloe's.

"All our friends will be there. Chloe's mom's making dessert for all of us," whispered Carly.

"But the whipped cream," said Lidia, staring at the bowl filled with the frothy stuff, lovingly whipped by her own hand. "It hasn't even been touched."

Saying nothing, the girls waited for her response.

Lidia looked at Owen, who nodded slightly. She realized she had uncharacteristically looked to him for his opinion. It felt good not to be angry, taking every decision on. Maybe they could co-parent in harmony for a change. It was worth contemplating.

"Yes, it's okay," she said, "but say good-bye to us before you leave, okay?" she added as they left the room to get their jackets.

Everyone rose from the table when the twins came back. Carly wrapped a scarf around her neck and Clarisse pulled on her gloves. Once again, Owen stepped forward to embrace them, but they pulled back, said a quick good-bye, and in their parting words, did not include Robert, who then looked at Owen, who looked at Lidia, who felt a pang of sympathy she did not expect to feel.

"I thought we were making a little progress," he said to her.

"So did I," she answered.

"Things did go well," said Polly. "Look at how far we've come. The next time will be better, and the time after that. It will just take patience. Come, let's have some coffee."

Lidia let Polly's words sink in. *She's leading us through this—I hope she knows what she's doing,* she thought. But she had to admit: So far, Polly had been calling it pretty well.

In the living room, Polly engaged Robert in conversation about his collection of Civil War photographs. While Owen listened, Lidia and Harry slipped out of the room.

"This house is great," said Harry. "A lot of character—like its owner."

"Yes, exactly. Let me show you around a bit."

In the library, they admired Polly's first editions and walked over to the large Palladian windows, where they looked out on the Sound bathed in the last rays of sunlight.

From there they walked down the corridor to the conservatory.

"It's like a little bit of summer in the cold weather," said Lidia, of the glass enclosed structure with sunny wrought iron furniture and potted plants brought in for the cold months. "Polly's one extravagance when it comes to the fuel bill is keeping this space heated all winter. Isn't it great?"

Harry moved toward her, as though with a little encouragement he would embrace her. She did not back away but rather leaned into his side. In an instant she felt his arm encircle her waist, and they looked out over the expansive lawn in the fading light.

Lidia, not sure how she managed the nerve, but thinking of all the pies she had baked, all the anxiety she had endured over the last several days, thought she had earned this. She turned toward him, lifted her head, and closed her eyes. Harry pulled her to him and kissed her, a long gentle kiss.

Lidia fell into their first embrace, this first kiss, letting herself give into it completely. It was right and natural to be with Harry, to be in his arms as the late afternoon golden light was softening into dusk. When they finally drew back from one another, they lingered. Sitting together on the antique loveseat Polly and John Paul had had shipped back all the way from Venice one summer, they began to talk, to fill in the gaps, as Harry had said on the phone when Lidia, heart pounding, had extended her invitation to him. She had hoped for this very moment, not sure it would ever come. In the living room, Owen and Robert had just finished their second cup of coffee and were ready to go. As the two men stood, Lidia and Harry, returning, walked toward them.

"There you are. I think Owen and Robert are about to leave us," said Polly.

"I'm sorry. I hope we weren't too long," Lidia said, looking up at Harry. "We've been talking, and Harry has about convinced me that I need to find out about Tina, to see if we are in some way connected. I may be headed to Dayton soon, and—if he can manage it—Harry may come with me."

Rebuilding

*W*hy did Lidia agree to go to Dayton after weeks of avoidance? It was Harry who led her to the decision she knew sooner or later she would have to make. In the conservatory that late afternoon on Thanksgiving Day, he had asked her if fear was holding her back. "If it is," he said, "you have to deal with it—because, trust me, you'll regret later that you didn't dig into things when you had the chance. I don't think Tina did it on purpose, Lidia, but I know it's bothering you that there's some connection. Maybe that's what you have to find out."

Lidia knew she was afraid to find out if the plane crashing into her house hadn't been an accident. She didn't want to discover that Tina Calderara had intentionally come so close to the twins' bedroom. Such thoughts brought her to near panic, and so she was doing what she had begun to do since her life had been turned upside down. She turned away, denying the undeniable for as long as possible. She had done it at work before the bottom fell out. And again when evidence mounted that she was losing Owen. She had probably done it earlier, she had to admit to herself, when it was clear that Owen was gay and struggling with coming out. But when Harry confronted her with the truth about her habit of avoidance, it was as though she was discovering something about herself for the first time. It hit her with a force she could no longer ignore. To the world, she was competent, confident Lidia, but since that world had begun falling apart, on the inside she didn't feel so invulnerable. And now it was becoming clear: She would have to face her newest round of fears.

"I know you're right, Harry . . ."

"Chances are, there's nothing to it—the connection between you and Tina—but if you don't look into it, you'll never know. Wouldn't that gnaw at you?"

Before she could answer, he added, "There's a possibility I could get some time off to go with you to Dayton, unofficially, not on Bureau business."

This had been the clincher—the thought of Harry by her side.

"I would like that, Harry, for you to come with me," she had told him. "It would make the trip, the meeting, what I might find out—less daunting with you there."

And so the decision was made—Harry would put in for some vacation time, Lidia would get in touch with the Walters, and, if they agreed, the trip would take place.

As Harry and Lidia lingered on the loveseat that afternoon in the conservatory, with the sun going down, they continued to learn more about each other. Lidia told him of her fears and of how she was haunted by the image of Tina dying in the wreckage.

"I feel as though I know her, Harry, and no matter what I find out, we are connected. There's no escaping it. She must have felt so alone. How sad that she had to imagine a family she never had to fill her emptiness."

"I know a little something about that," Harry had responded that day. "My adoptive parents were good people. They told my sister and me we were adopted pretty early on, but I wanted more. I wanted to know where I came from, and since I couldn't, I made up a family—a whole heritage. My sister never really cared about who our real parents were, but I did."

"Who was in your imaginary family?" Lidia asked.

"Well, my thing wasn't aviators . . . You're not going to laugh at this, are you?"

"Never," Lidia promised.

"Okay." Then, leaning toward her, a little embarrassed, he said, "My mother and father were circus people. Animal trainers. That was how I imagined them."

"That's not funny, it's sweet. I can just picture little Harry out in the backyard, with a little chair and whip, maybe taming the family cat."

"Not far off, actually. But for my parents, it wasn't harmless housecats I made up. They trained much larger animals, very dangerous work."

Lidia felt a pang of sympathy as she guessed what Harry must have envisioned. "No, don't tell me . . . there wasn't a tragic accident with big cats, was there?"

"Well, yes, there was." Seeing the concern in Lidia's face, he put his arm around her. "But I didn't dwell on that, really—I needed some explanation about why my sister and I were adopted. I thought there must've been something awful that took them both from us. So, I made them the last of a famous dynasty of animal trainers, going back for generations. And I imagined animal training was something that was in my blood. I figured I would carry on the family name."

"I guess—with a dynasty and all . . ."

"The thing is, I did pursue it in a way—animals."

"What do you mean?" Lidia asked.

"Well, I wasn't always a Bureau guy. My degree is in marine biology. After graduating, I joined the service and trained as a Navy Seal."

A whole lifetime to catch up on, Lidia marveled. "A Navy Seal. That's pretty serious work, isn't it?"

"Yes," said Harry, laughing, "It's serious work. Don't you think I do serious work?"

"I mean dangerous."

"It can be. In the Gulf War, the first one, I was in the Marine Mammal Program."

"Isn't that where they used dolphins for something like mine detection?"

"Yes, that, and actually what I did was work with the dolphins on patrolling the waters for enemy intruders."

"Oh dear, I'm not sure I want to think about you and them out there, patrolling."

Harry pulled her closer. "I'm not telling you this to make you worry more," he said. "I just wanted you to know, adopted kids, well, they sometimes have vivid imaginations. It can help to make up for what's missing."

As a younger man, Harry had tried to find his birth parents—with no luck. The records were sealed, and he never got beyond that closed door. As far as he could tell, his adoptive parents either never knew and never asked about the mother and father of the two young children they had adopted, or they refused to tell what they knew. And that would probably mean something worse than a random car accident, he had told Lidia. "Maybe it was something they wanted to protect us from knowing," he said. "I was two and my sister was four, but neither of us have any memories of anything before we were adopted."

Lidia thought the conversation was over, but then he grew more serious and, looking into the distance as though he might've been talking to the parents who adopted him, he said, "In the end, though, secrets don't do anyone any favors. I'll wonder about them for the rest of my life." Then, turning back to Lidia, he added, "But it helps me to know I tried to find them." He seemed to be relieved, talking about it, Lidia surmised. And it made her happy that he had taken her into his confidence about something still painful to him.

"I know, Harry. I appreciate your telling me all this. Really."

———●———

Monday morning after Thanksgiving, Lidia steeled herself for the conversation with Mrs. Walters, who, as it turned out, was happy to talk to her and seemed almost eager for a visit.

"I'll be coming with Agent Caligan. I believe you spoke with him during the investigation. But his visit will be unofficial. He's agreed to keep me company," Lidia told her.

"That will be fine, dear," Mrs. Walters had responded. "He seemed like a nice man—very sympathetic. We weren't in such good shape, then, I imagine. Yes, that's fine, that he will be with you."

Harry and Lidia took a morning United flight out of White Plains to Dayton International later in the week. When they arrived at nearly one in the afternoon, they were relieved to see the sun shining on a cold but pleasant day. Their appointment with the Walters wasn't until three, so they grabbed lunch at the airport before getting their rental car and driving to Centerville, where the Walters lived.

At 2:45 PM, Lidia and Harry pulled up in front of an old two-story stone house. Soon the front door opened, and out stepped a woman who had to be Mrs. Walters.

"She's just as I imagined her," Lidia said out loud.

"Yes. She's waiting for us."

Mrs. Walters continued to stand on the front steps. She had pushed back her curly grey hair in order to rest one hand against her forehead, shielding her eyes from the sun. Her other hand rested patiently on her hip. She was a round woman of medium height in a blue shirtwaist dress topped with a crisp white apron that matched, in purity of color, her white sneakers. Here was a woman who probably bleached, starched, and ironed for a good part of most days.

As Lidia and Harry drew closer to the front steps, Mrs. Walters took her hand from her forehead and touched it to her heart. Her other hand dropped like a stone to her side. "Gracious, me," she said with a start. "You're Tina incarnate."

"I'm what?" asked Lidia, breathlessly, the old fear rising as an assault to her solar plexus.

"My goodness, dear, you look so much like my Tina," she said, lending a hand to help Lidia up the steps and into the house.

The three stood motionless in the foyer until Mr. Walters called to his wife.

"Emma, are you going to invite our guests in?"

This shook Mrs. Walters out of her stupor. "In a minute, Cal. We're hanging up coats." After she hung Harry and Lidia's jackets on the entrance coat rack, Mrs. Walters turned to them. "Let me walk into the parlor first and say a word or two to Cal. He hasn't been all that well lately. I want to prepare him." Mrs. Walters explained that her husband had been ill since the day he learned of the crash. Tina had been the sun in his universe, she said. His love for her was so central that after Tina's death, Mrs. Walters had to be the strong one, to keep Cal from total despair.

Although both had devoted their lives to Tina's happiness, their dedication had proved to be a trying task. "Her vision of a happy family didn't include us," Mrs. Walters told them. "Cal knew that. Tina lived in a world of fantasy, and she needed more than we could offer her. He came to see that, and it was very hard on him."

"I'm sorry," said Lidia, "about the resemblance. The pictures I saw in the news—I didn't see any . . ."

"Pictures? Yes, the ones I gave to the newspaper. They were from her air shows. She was in her aviator cap and gear, wasn't she? You wouldn't have seen . . ."

"Yes, of course. You're right," said Lidia. "Excuse me, Mrs. Walters. Why don't you go ahead and see about your husband."

In the few minutes it took for Mrs. Walters to return, Lidia, with Harry's help, had composed herself. When Mrs. Walters led them into the parlor to meet Mr. Walters, she held tightly onto Harry's hand, realizing once again how grateful she was that he was with her.

Cal Walters began to stand when he saw the threesome coming his way, straining in the soft light to see the woman he had been warned about.

Standing just under six feet tall and weighing two hundred pounds, even now, into his seventies, a little stooped and weary, Cal looked formidable.

When Cal saw Lidia come into view, he fell back into his over-stuffed chair. Emma rushed to his side and, assuring herself he was not in any immediate danger, fluffed the pillows behind him and stroked his forehead.

"Dear, this is Lidia Raven and her friend, Special Agent Caligan. You remember my telling you about him, don't you?"

"Mrs. Raven, Agent Caligan. Pleased to meet you," he managed.

What were they to make of the resemblance? This was the question the two couples kept coming back to, after Mrs. Walters brought out the albums and put them on display for all to see the uncanny likeness between the two women.

"I'm stunned," was all Lidia could summon after looking at pictures of Tina at age five, ten, fifteen, twenty, and on into her full adulthood. "She even looks like me as a baby. We could've been sisters, but of course that's impossible . . . crazy."

"This is some coincidence," said Harry, "but then again, you have two dark-haired, fine-featured, slim young women with brown eyes—they're bound to look alike."

Lidia nodded. They had come to get the bottom of things, but they couldn't rush to conclusions either. This reasonable approach was also comforting to Lidia, who still wanted to believe there was nothing between her and the tragic Tina. "Harry's right," she said. "It's probably just a coincidence."

Cal Walters continued to stare at Lidia, making her a little uncomfortable. He turned away briefly, but then looked her way again and began to speak.

"We adopted Tina when she was just two. We had tried for years for children of our own, but that wasn't to be. We didn't go looking for Tina, though. She found us, in a way," he said, turning to his wife, smiling, tears welling up. "Isn't that right, Emma? She found us."

"A neighbor lady and a member of our church came to us one day and said a baby girl, just two, needed a home. She told us we couldn't ask any questions, but that it was all legal, and through the church, and that we could have her if we went through some interviews and filled out some forms, which is what we did, and sure enough, quicker than we ever imagined, we had ourselves a baby girl."

"Right from the start, she was a handful," continued Cal. "Tearing around here, never still for a minute. She kept us real busy."

"And her love of flying, that started early, too," Emma interjected. "When she was ten, I found her one morning on the windowsill of her room, second floor—I'll show you. She had taken out the screen and was standing there in her pajamas, with a towel pinned to the shoulders of her PJ top. I screamed and ran to catch her, but before I could reach her, she threw herself out the window, arms out ahead of her, like she expected to fly. Well, she didn't. She fell is what she did. Luckily the forsythia were extra thick that year, and that's where she landed, right in the middle of a big thick patch of them. Come back in the spring and you'll see them, still there. They saved her life is what they did. She didn't break anything, but she was bruised and pretty scraped up. Remember, Cal?"

"Oh yes, I do all right. She told us that if Superman could do it, she could too. She wanted to fly, she said, and she didn't think it was fair that she couldn't. That was when we knew she was different, special and different, a real daredevil."

"Not long after that, she began telling us about her real family," Emma said, picking up the storyline. "She knew she was adopted; we didn't keep that from her. She said they all flew planes and that they were famous. I asked her how she knew, and she said she heard it in her head. She said they talked to her. At first we didn't think too much of it, but she kept at it, so we took her to see a specialist, a psychologist, who said she would grow out of it. And she did, sort of, but when she hit her late teens, she took up flying with a vengeance. And she was good at it, the barnstorming thing, the appearances in air shows. She became a family name around here. We didn't exactly approve, but we were proud of her, weren't we, Cal?"

"We were, in spite of ourselves. You couldn't help it; she was so determined to make a go of it. She worked hard at different jobs, babysitting and that, saved up her money, paid for her lessons, all her gear, and her flying time. When she graduated, she got a job as a dental assistant at Wright Patterson. That's the Air Force base here in Dayton—anything as long as it was near planes."

Harry and Lidia looked at each other and then at the Walters and smiled. The reminiscences had done them all good.

"For heaven's sake," said Mrs. Walters. "Where are my manners? I never even offered you a cold drink or coffee or . . . and I especially baked you a banana loaf."

"That would be lovely," answered Lidia. "But I was wondering, can we see the room? Tina's old room?"

"Yes, dear. Of course. But it's not her old room. She lived on her own for a long while, over near the base, but she came home, about a year ago, just said she wanted to come home. It made us happy, but then we knew . . ." Mrs. Walters took her husband's hand and looked into his eyes. "We knew something was wrong. It wasn't normal for a grown woman to want to come home, to be in her childhood room again." Mrs. Walters turned her attention to Lidia and Harry. "You see, I hadn't changed a thing. When Tina came back, the room was just as she had left it. And she didn't change a thing, either. It's still the same. Let me show you."

Lidia and Harry followed Mrs. Walters up the stairs, and they paused on the landing while she opened the door to Tina's small room, in which model airplanes, seemingly suspended in air, hung from every space, over her single twin bed, over the desk, in front of the windows and bookcases and over the white dresser, which was covered with stickers of vintage biplanes.

"Each one of these hanging planes is a replica that Tina glued together from model kits and then attached to fishing line," explained Mrs. Walters as they entered the room. "It makes walking around pretty hard if you're tall. Cal never could walk in here without stooping over." Mrs. Walters began to talk once again about her husband. She told Lidia and Harry that he had been a foreman and forklift operator at the GM plant in Moraine until the strike in '97, when he lost his health and finally his job. Fortunately, he retired with full benefits and his pension, she said, but those days took a lot out of him. The disappointment he saw in Tina's eyes when she looked at him took out the rest. "I don't know what she wants, Emma," he had told her. "A war hero, a flying ace? I don't know, but I'm not the father she wants."

Lidia noticed Harry walking around tentatively, ducking from time to time to avoid becoming entangled.

Mrs. Walters stood under each plane, pointing out special features and giving an impromptu tutorial about the ones Tina prized most: The Kitty Hawk Flyer ("Gave her the devil of a time putting it together . . ."), The Calderara Seaplane ("Rare, very proud she found it . . ."), the *Spirit of St. Louis* ("Authentic and expensive, put her back a pretty penny . . ."), Amelia Earhart's Lockheed Vega 5B ("Earhart broke two world records in this one . . ."), and the Lockheed Electra 10E ("Her last plane. The *E* stood for Earhart . . .").

Lidia stared at the crowded airspace, getting lost in the shimmer of light reflected off the tiny replicas. "There must be fifty planes here," she marveled.

"Fifty-two," said Mrs. Walters.

Lidia stood the longest at the model of Earhart's last plane, mesmerized by the silver fuselage with its meticulous details, the delicate lines of red paint on the wings and tail, the numbers painstakingly applied.

"You like this one, too?" asked Mrs. Walters, coming up behind Lidia, taking her out of her reverie. "It was Tina's favorite. She worked long and hard to get it right. I think it's near perfect." Then, walking to the window above the desk, Mrs. Walters gestured to Lidia and Harry, who came and stood by her.

"This is the window she flew out of in her Superman 'towel cape.' If you look right down there, you'll see where the forsythia grow in the spring."

Everywhere in the room was evidence of Tina's love—obsession. Bookcases lined the room, filled with volumes of flying, any kind, from *The Little Prince* to *Jonathan Livingston Seagull*. But most were about aviation history. Some of these, Mrs. Walters explained, Tina had read as a child. "She swore she learned to fly from an old book Cal found for her—this one," she said, pointing to a volume entitled *Stick and Rudder*. "When she grew up, she started collecting on her own. Some were rare and hard to come by, like these two, *Girl Aviators* and *The Light Bringers*," she said, lightly drawing her fingers across the two volumes laying side by side, their spines beginning to fray.

Lidia, standing next to Mrs. Walters, was drawn to another volume on the shelf. "What about this one?" she asked, taking down a brightly colored children's book entitled *My Brothers' Flying Machine*. "Oh, that," said Mrs. Walters, looking over at the volume Lidia was holding. "It's supposed to be written by Katharine Wright, Orville and Wilbur's sister, but of course, it's just make believe."

Lidia and Harry exchanged glances. "What is it?" Mrs. Walters asked.

"Well, it's just that, I guess you had told Harry earlier—when he first called to ask you a few questions—that Tina thought Katharine Wright was her grandmother . . ." Lidia explained.

"No, not grandmother, great grandmother. Gracious. Katharine died in 1929. She couldn't have been Tina's grandmother."

Harry looked at Lidia, chagrined. It had been his error, but it hardly mattered as far as he or the Bureau were concerned. It was all the fantasy of a confused and troubled woman. Lidia, though, who hadn't really thought of it until now, quickly did the math and thought how she and Tina could indeed share the same lineage, the same great grandparents, for example. Maybe not the Wright brothers' sister, but a family from Ravenna? It was not impossible.

"It's interesting, isn't it," said Mrs. Walters, "that Tina never seemed to wonder who her parents were. It was the earlier generations that interested her, the ones who started it all, like the Wright brothers and Mario Calderara."

"Why Mario Calderara?" Lidia wondered out loud.

"I never really knew," answered Mrs. Walters. It's just that Tina read so much growing up, a lot of history, and she learned about him that way. She used to say that Calderara saw the Wrights from time to time. I think the idea of a young Italian flyer having a fling with their sister was right up her alley. She must've loved the romance of it all. But that's where it stopped."

"Why do you think that is?" asked Lidia.

"My hunch is the bloodline stopped there. She ran out of famous flyers for the next two generations. She liked the ones who started it all."

Lidia's eyes fell on a picture of Tina on the desk. She was in full early aviator attire—cap, goggles, white flight suit—standing next to a full-size replica of an old biplane, the 1908 June Bug, the inscription said. It was a precarious-looking thing, with huge wings. Lidia couldn't quite see how it ever got off the ground, and yet there was romance to it. She could see that, being in that cockpit, defying gravity. She imagined Tina recreating man's early attempts at flight. It must have been like magic. Lidia could almost see Tina's eyes behind her goggles, full of wonder—and perhaps a trace of madness.

"Before we go, there's something I want you to have," Mrs. Walters said, opening the top drawer of Tina's desk. "It's Tina's last diary." Then, turning to Harry, she added, "You asked me if there were any letters or other things that may have shown Tina's state of mind before the accident, and I said no. I wasn't lying, Mr. Caligan. I found Tina's diaries after you called. She had been keeping them since she was ten, and I never knew. Can you imagine? Her mother, and I never knew. I found them after I began going through all her things. I wondered for a time if I should read them at all, but I decided, yes, and I'm glad I did." Mrs. Walters took a handkerchief from the pocket of the apron she was still wearing and wiped her eyes before putting it back. "I guess I should've called you when I found them," she said to Harry. "It hurts, some of what she wrote. I never told Cal about the diaries. I don't ever want him to know about them." She turned and looked out the window above the desk. "They just make it more clear, what we already knew. She was never really ours."

Then, turning to Lidia, she said, "Take it. It won't answer all your questions, but it may answer some."

Lidia's heart began pounding at the idea of reading Tina's thoughts, the idea of perhaps penetrating her mind, or perhaps of finding out that she had intentionally devised a flight plan culminating not at the airport but at Lidia's house. But of course this was impossible. If such a thing has been recorded in the diary, Mrs. Walters would have told them. Just the same, Lidia was reluctant. Mrs. Walters offered her the diary, but Lidia could not take it. Its childlike pink cover, clasp, lock, and key were all too symbolic of the troubled woman who wrote in it. Lidia didn't want to unlock her thoughts, at least not yet.

"I don't think I can take it. I don't think I can read it. It's too personal—and I'm not sure I'm ready to know what it may say."

Harry, who had purposely remained in the background as Lidia explored Tina's room, stepped forward.

"Thank you, Mrs. Walters. I can take it."

"No, Harry. I don't want it."

"Let me, Lidia. I may need to read it, officially. If I had known the diary existed, I would have included it in my report."

This satisfied Lidia, calmer now, as Harry took the book from Mrs. Walters. "Here, let me have it," Lidia said. "I'll put it in my purse, so Cal, Mr. Walters, won't see it." She took the diary and gently tucked it inside her bag.

"Come, dear," Mrs. Walters said to Lidia, patting her hand as she put the book away. "Let's go join Cal and have from tea. You, too, Mr. Caligan. I think you're going to like my banana loaf."

Harry and Lidia stayed with the Walters a while longer, listening intently as they reminisced about Tina's childhood. Each new story added to Lidia's growing suspicions about Tina. She was increasingly forming a picture of a troubled child who grew into a troubled adult.

After staying longer than they had intended to, Harry and Lidia said good-bye to Mr. Walters as Mrs. Walters followed them to the door, apologizing for having kept them so long. They assured her they had plenty of time to make their early evening flight back to White Plains. When they walked outside, however, they were unhappily surprised by the precipitous drop in temperature and by the freezing rain starting to come down heavily.

"Gracious, this weather. It's going to hold you up," said Mrs. Walters from the porch, as Lidia and Harry began making their way to the car. "It's typical, though," she called to them. "The day starts one way and ends another. Be careful, you two. The roads can be slick," she warned.

Harry and Lidia quickly ducked into the car and waved good-bye.

When they arrived at the airport, after proceeding at a slow pace, weather and traffic, as predicted, having taken their toll, Harry dropped Lidia at ticketing before going on to return the rental car.

"Our flight's been canceled," Lidia told him when he joined her fifteen minutes later.

"I know," he said. "I saw it on the monitor. The next flight out isn't until tomorrow morning."

They looked at each other, Lidia beginning to give in to the giddy anticipation that had been building since she first heard the cancelation announcement. Harry smiled at her and shrugged his shoulders. Lidia smiled back and took his hand.

"I'll call Polly and the girls and let them know we won't be home until tomorrow."

"I'll get us a place for the night."

———————◉———————

Is this me? wondered Lidia. *Am I holding Harry this close to me, cupping the back of his head in my hand, now moving my hands down his hips? Am I loosening his belt, so greedy, needing to hold him, all of him, in my two hands?*

Harry gently removed Lidia's sweater and unclasped her bra, stirring her deeply as he held her breasts. Lidia heard a little moan of desire as he steered her backward onto the bed, positioning himself above her, continuing to carefully take off her clothes—sliding her trousers down, then her panties. Lidia, matching his need to remove all remaining fabric between them, kicked off the clothes around her ankles, gently raising her knees.

Lidia was momentarily gratified when finally bare skin touched bare skin, but it was fleeting before a new and greater need shook her with great force. She fell into a world of profound sensation, one she had forgotten existed. She let herself go, yielding to deeper pleasure and yet more urgent desire. Harry was as ardent as she was, and like her, she could tell, was trying to hold back, making their first time together last a little longer, but when whatever restraint existed between them was no longer possible, they came at precisely the same time. With the aftershocks of pleasure still rumbling, she looked at Harry, who was staring at her, smiling. He lifted his hand to move a strand of hair away from her eyes.

After a moment or two of dazed calm, just lying there, Lidia enjoying looking back into Harry's deep blue eyes, he suddenly laughed a little and drew her under his arm, spontaneously humming, "Fly me to the Moon."

"Okay," said Lidia, who began laughing, too. "It was out of this world, Harry, for me, too."

"It that what you think, that it was out of this world?"

"Isn't that what your little song meant?" asked Lidia.

"Absolutely," said Harry. "Want to go there again?"

"Welcome aboard Flight 531 to White Plains. In preparation for our departure . . ."

As Harry and Lidia were complying with the flight attendant's instructions the next morning, securing their seatbelts and turning off their cell phones, Harry began softly humming again, "Fly Me to the Moon." Lidia poked him in the ribs, feigning embarrassment but glowing in the new level of intimacy between them.

About midway through the flight home, Lidia was able to turn her attention from the night before to the original purpose of the trip, the visit with the Walters. She began thinking about Tina's diary—and about her reluctance to read it. She remembered with some alarm the initial shock they all had over her perceived resemblance to Tina.

"I need to give this to you, Harry," she said, holding the diary out to him, after retrieving it from her bag. "I still don't think I'm up to reading it just yet."

Harry took it from her and put it in his jacket pocket. "It's okay. I'll read it and let you know if there's anything in it you should know. He turned in his seat to face her more directly. "Lidia, whatever harm Tina could have done to you—if she had ever intended any—has been done. She can't hurt you anymore. So what it is you're so worried about?"

"It isn't physical harm, it's . . . I don't know . . . It's the unknown. What if some of these supposed links between us amount to something? What if we look alike because we're related? What if there is something to the Ravenna link? Any one of these things, if true, would change what I think I know about myself, about my family. What if there is a link big enough to cause a woman to want to die—and possibly to harm me and the girls?"

Harry considered Lidia's words and then shook his head. "I guess I operate differently, Lidia. I don't think I would react until I knew more. Right now these possibilities—and I'm not trying to minimize them—seem pretty slim."

Harry sat upright in his seat with a jolt as the flight attendant's cart pushed into his armrest. "I'm sorry, sir," she said. "These things are hard to steer sometimes." Lidia and Harry nodded.

Dipping the wooden stirrer into his coffee, Harry said to Lidia, "Bottom line, I wouldn't get upset until I knew more, and if it was bugging me, I'd look into it."

"Well, that makes sense, but I guess I'm not that rational."

"Like I said, it's okay. I'll read it and let you know, but if there is anything, you'll need to check it out . . . and I'll be there to help you get through it."

This eased Lidia's anxiety. "You're becoming indispensable, Harry. I don't know how I would've made it through yesterday without you."

"I'm glad I was there. And like Mrs. Walters said, 'The day starts one way and ends another.'" Then, taking Lidia's hand, he added, "I wouldn't have missed yesterday—any of it—for the world."

They leaned into each other and joined hands, once again in the glow of their night together.

After a length of silence between them, Lidia raised the subject of Tina again.

"What do you make of Tina? After all the Walters said?"

"The trip confirmed what I suspected all along. She was very troubled. If anything, that's what I expect to see in her diary—more proof of her impaired mental state."

"You know, I don't think I realized until the trip just how disturbed she must've been."

"Makes you really feel for the Walters. All they wanted was to have a child and love her as their own."

Lidia held tightly onto Harry's hand as they began their descent, lost in thoughts of all he had revealed about his own childhood.

———◉———

It was late afternoon when Harry and Lidia finally pulled into Polly's driveway.

"Won't you come in, Harry?"

"No, I've got to get home. I have an early-morning meeting."

Harry walked Lidia to the door and pulled her to him, kissing her with an intensity that reminded her of how much had changed in the last twenty-four hours. She felt herself giving in to desire once again, and so, reluctantly, she pulled away. He looked at her longingly.

"Leaving you right now is the last thing I want to do," he said.

Lidia hugged him tightly, his words making their parting easier to bear. She was almost eager to be alone, so she could go over every detail of their time together, reliving each moment.

Inside the house, after their final light kiss good-bye, Lidia called out, "Anyone home?"

"We're in here," said the twins in unison.

"In the living room," answered Polly.

Lidia entered the room, and Clarisse sprang up to greet her with a hug and raised her hand for a high five.

Lidia giggled and gave in to the implication. "Okay, she said, high five back," as she slapped her hand.

"We want to hear all about it. Well, only as much as you want to reveal, dear. Gentle woman never kiss and tell," said Polly.

"It was . . . Harry is . . . I don't know what to say. Except that I think we're at the beginning of something here." Lidia knew she was blushing.

"It's great, Mom, really," said Clarisse, sitting down next to Lidia now on the sofa next to Carly. Lidia took Carly's hand.

Turning to Carly, she said, "You haven't said anything—is everything okay?"

At first Carly seemed reluctant to talk. She looked at her hand in Lidia's and then gently pulled it away and passed it over her forehead.

"No, it's nothing, really. It's just—I don't know, Mom. You've been through a lot, and . . ."

Lidia pulled Carly to her and gave her hug. "Oh dear. Honey," she said. "You don't have to worry about me. Look, I know this is a risk. Anytime you put yourself out there for someone, you take a risk. But that's okay. It's worth it, isn't it? When someone matters to you?"

"And he matters to you?"

"I think he's going to . . . I think, yes, Carly, he does," said Lidia, confirming for all and for herself, too, it seemed.

"Okay then," said Carly. "I guess I'm happy for you, too."

Lidia wasn't sure Carly was okay with everything, but she thought she would be in time. "Now, let me tell you about our visit to the Walters."

That night, after the girls had gone to bed, Lidia crept softly downstairs to Polly's bedroom across from the library. She had moved in there after John Paul died. "Too many wonderful memories in that room," Polly had said the day she opened the door to the master suite upstairs, showing Lidia the room. "I haven't changed a thing, but I keep it closed. It's like I can keep a part of us hermetically sealed in there—if I just leave it alone." She shut the door, and to Lidia's knowledge, it had not been opened since.

In front of Polly's new room, Lidia knocked softly. "Can I come in?" she asked, opening the door a crack to reveal a sliver of light, indicating Polly was still up.

"Of course, dear. Come in."

Lidia pulled her lavender chenille bathrobe around her and sat next to Polly on the bed.

"Do you want to join me under the covers?" asked Polly, pulling back the pale pink silk duvet. I keep it pretty cold in here."

Lidia slid in next to Polly, propped herself up on the pillows, and pulled the covers up over her shoulders.

"Anything you want to talk about?"

"You and John Paul, you were always very happy, weren't you, even though it took you a while to find each other." Lidia said. "Even after you were so hurt by your first marriage . . ."

"Wondering about your Harry, are you?"

"Yes," said Lidia. "I am. We shared a wonderful time together last night, not just physically—that was pretty great, though—but the sense of being so close to one another. It was so natural, and it felt so comfortable. I've been without that for so long. In fact," Lidia paused, "I'm not sure Owen and I ever had that. We were happy together, but so much of our happiness was about being young and going through exciting times together: marriage, children, careers. We were good partners, but maybe never such good lovers or soul mates. I guess we were never soul mates."

"And do you think you have that—all those things—now with Harry?"

"It's too soon, Polly, but maybe."

"You think you might, that the potential is there?" Polly amended.

"Yes, that's it exactly. I think it may be possible. I feel that way, and I think Harry does, too. And that's exciting to me and also scary."

"Now, why scary, Lidia?"

"I know I sounded confident with Carly—and I meant it—but still you have to wonder, can it really be this good? If it is, will it last?"

"Well, I liked what you said to Carly. And I hope you won't put up obstacles to what might be your own happiness."

"I'm trying, I really am. I want this to work."

"I just don't want to see you limit yourself. Too much self-protection pushes away the good and the bad. You've been hurt and have suffered, but you have to be open in order to find the good that may be waiting for you."

Lidia uncrossed her arms as the covers dropped from her shoulders. She drew a forefinger over the embroidered silk cherry blossoms on the duvet. "I know you must want to shake me sometimes, Polly, but I'm just not fearless like you. I'm trying, honestly. I know Harry's a good thing. I'm trying not to blow it."

Polly settled back and put an arm around Lidia, giving her a little hug. "That's good, Lidia. Self-awareness is a wonderful thing. Let me tell you something about John Paul," she began, fluffing up her pillows. "I had lovers in my day, and I had been married before, but our intimate lives, behind that closed door upstairs, gave me more earthly pleasure than I could have imagined. And it wasn't just the sex. We loved each other, deeply, that was the important thing. I used to put my head on his chest just to hear his heart beat. I wanted to blot out all other sounds in the world. I thought if that heart could just keep beating into my ear like that, I would be happy forever." Polly reached for a tissue on the nightstand. "I didn't want to start crying, but sometimes it just comes over me, even now, even though I've adjusted to living a life of missing him every day."

"I'm so sorry, Polly."

"You're a dear, Lidia. But listen to me. As much as I miss him, I wouldn't trade a moment we had together. You see, it's worth the pain. Even if it ends in loss, it's worth it. Don't miss out on that, if that's what you have with Harry, and I think you might."

The next day after breakfast, when Lidia had just sat down with the newspaper, the phone rang. Lidia's heart jumped. It was Harry, she was sure.

"Hello," she said, a little flirtatiously.

There was silence on the line. Then, "Hello? Mrs. Raven? This is Rocco, Rocco Santini. I'm calling about rebuilding—your house on Apple Way?

The Best and Worst of Times

*O*n the drive over to Apple Way, Lidia turned on the windshield wipers of her new dark blue Forester, acquired after a relatively mild battle with her insurance company when she insisted her battered car be totaled. (*Insistence, thanks to Harry,* she thought, smiling as she reflected on the first time he had said anything personal to her... that day on Apple Way among the wreckage of not only her home but of her old life, as it turned out.)

The light flurries of the morning had given way to a light snow. *December already...* It was hard to believe it had been almost two months since Tina's plane had turned her life upside down. In some ways, it had been the worst year of her life—losing her family home, seeing her girls endangered, being homeless—but in others, it was the best—her growing friendship with Polly, the good fortune of her daughters, and finding Harry. *It's crazy,* thought Lidia, *without the worst thing that could've happened in my life, I never would've met Harry, one of the best things to have happened in a long, long time.*

As she turned into the driveway, her heart sank, in spite of having just counted her blessings. The rubble was as she had left it, but now it lay under a light cover of snow, like a shroud.

Coming into view was a man, probably in his mid to late sixties, with broad shoulders and a full head of wavy white hair. With his red jacket and black pants, he looked like Santa, a more vigorous version. *And without the big belly,* Lidia thought as she got out of the car.

"Hello, Mrs. Raven, I'm Rocco," he said, extending his hand.

"Thanks for coming out. I wasn't expecting this snow, though—a little early, huh?"

"Yes, but I'll tell you, after the year I've had, nothing surprises me anymore," said Lidia, shaking his hand.

"Yeah—I'm sorry," said Rocco, looking toward the ruin in front of them. "It looks like it was a real nice house. Old, historic, I mean. Too bad. Now they tear down these old houses, but yours—it got torn down for you."

"Thanks, Mr. Santini—Rocco," she said responding to Rocco's raised hand, which went up as soon as she had used his last name. "And you, too, please call me Lidia. Yes—the house, it was in my family for four generations. My grandfather built it when he came to this country from Italy."

Rocco's eyes brightened. "Oh yeah? Where from?"

"Ravenna," Lidia responded.

A little less enthusiastically, Rocco said, "Calabria. My family is from Calabria."

"Um. Not neighbors, are we?"

"Might as well be two different worlds, huh? It's always like that for Italians, isn't it? If you're not from the same place, you might as well be from a different country."

"I suppose, the whole North, South thing, like in this country."

"Only worse," said Rocco with a little laugh. Then, turning his attention back to the house, he said, "Let's walk. I want to tell you what's next."

As they slowly made their way around the property, Rocco explained how he and his crew would complete the demolition and clean the site, readying it for rebuilding.

"We'll be excavating below grade, where the basement is, preparing it for new construction. I won't know how extensive that work will be until we get the site cleared and can get down there."

Lidia frowned, concentrating on what she had just heard. "You know, I haven't been in the basement for years, since before my mother died, but it is a maze down there. It branches off into different sections, almost like separate rooms. My grandmother told me that Grandpa met down there with his cronies—for rounds of hard cider and cards. There's a room toward the back, with a table and chairs and with a long wooden rack on the wall for hanging coats. There's a summer oven down there that he apparently used in the winter to heat the place up when his friends came over."

"Hum. You don't hear stuff like that anymore. Real old world, huh?"

Lidia hadn't thought about her grandparents, Nonna and Nonno, much over the years. When she was a child, she thought of them as weary old time-travelers, coming from an alien time and place. Everything about them was different—their clothes, dark and heavy; the way they spoke, uttering many words she could not understand at all and others so buried under strained pronunciation that she hardly recognized them. Her own parents were distant enough to her as a child, but at least they were from her world, speaking to her only in English, not wanting her saddled with a language that would set her apart from other children. She was surprised as an adult, after her grandparents were gone, looking at old pictures of them and thinking how young they had looked, vital even, with a hard strength in their eyes. How difficult it must have been, leaving everything behind to start over in a new and strange world. It hardly registered in her younger days—the courage it must have taken.

After bringing Lidia up to date on permits and other details, Rocco told her he expected his work to be complete soon after Christmas. "We want to get the basement cleared and prepped before there's a hard freeze, so pray for good weather." Then, looking at his watch, he said, "I guess that's about it. I've got another meeting in Stamford. If you have any questions, let me know. And you can come out and see what we're doing anytime, Mrs. . . . Lidia, but you'll have to wear a hard hat starting Monday."

Rocco walked Lidia back to her car. "Porter says you're following the old footprint for rebuilding?"

"Yes," answered Lidia. "I'm putting up the same house, just as

Grandpa built it, with the improvements we made over the years, of course, but basically the same house."

"Good for you. You don't see much of that anymore. Now it's all tear down the old and put up something too big for the property. I don't know how some of this stuff gets past the review board. Well, yeah, I do, but that's a different story."

———————◆———————

Quite a satisfactory meeting, thought Lidia, on the drive home. She liked Rocco and was glad the rubble would soon be cleared. She looked forward to seeing the new house going up. Porter had told her if the weather was good, the house could be ready by late spring.

In the new year, we'll be back at home, she thought. Then she remembered that the twins would be going off to school in the fall. How many other changes would she see in the coming months, she wondered. Just then she felt a rush of excitement rising up. It was hope. She would look forward to the new year with hope, even without knowing what awaited her. One thing she knew for sure, though. She was glad that soon she would be putting this one behind her. *The year 2009—it will be gone but not forgotten,* she thought.

That night, Harry called.

"I was beginning to worry," said Lidia, teasing him a little for not calling sooner. But Harry either ignored her implication or was too intent on what he had to tell her to respond.

"For a lot of reasons, I couldn't sleep . . . all good, about you . . . just to keep that straight. But then I remembered the diary, so I pulled it out and started reading." Before he began to fill Lidia in on what he had learned, images of his sleepless night flashed by.

———————◆———————

After spending an hour tossing and getting tangled in the covers, Harry got up and thought about getting something to eat or maybe watching a little TV. Then he remembered Tina's diary. The diary had started, likely enough, on New Year's Day, 2009.

January 1. Back at the Walterses'. Life near the base not all I had hoped. I hear the planes taking off and landing, but what good is that, really? I spend my life preparing Novocain shots, helping people feel no pain, as if we don't all go through life looking for our next shot. No, it's flight I want, perpetual flight. Without that I might as well be anywhere, like here with the Walters. (If you ever read this, "Mom and Dad," I only refer to you as "The Walters" when I talk to myself in my diary, but don't feel bad about it. You've been very good to me, and I appreciate it. I must be a disappointment to you, almost forty, and I've come home to live here, with my planes and my books.)

The next ten to twenty pages were more of the same. Not able to fulfill her dreams, she was becoming increasingly despondent. She seemed delusional at times and then also aware of how she was not normal—no friends, a job she considered menial, no interest in love, a family, the things other people strive for. "*These are not goals, they are impediments!*" she had written.

Harry saw a pattern emerging that was in keeping with his impressions of Tina as troubled. Now he saw her as self-absorbed and, despite her claims of appreciating the Walters, with a bitterness bordering on cruelty—especially when she wasn't flying. Her dental assistant job, which she saw as servile, kept her in Dayton during the winter and unable to travel to air shows in the South or on the West Coast. By March, she was desperate to fly.

March 10. I'm not sure how much longer I can go on living this earth-bound life. Once Amelia started flying, she was never grounded the way I have been. Cal, with his nose to the grindstone—where has it gotten him? He's given his life to his "job," and where has it gotten him? And Emma? Never met an apron that couldn't use bleach and a little more starch.

As Harry continued to read, he remembered the pictures of Tina—an attractive woman, eerily like Lidia, although he had downplayed their resemblance. But how unlike Lidia, who had embraced life—in spite of her anxieties. When she married, she threw herself into her life with Owen. When she divorced, she kept going, making a home for the girls, and when that home crumbled around her, she gathered her family up and moved on. Thinking about Lidia caused an emotional rush he hadn't felt in years. In fact, he wasn't sure he had ever felt as strongly about anyone.

The contrast between Lidia and Tina was stark. The more he thought about it, the more he pitied the dead woman—and felt sympathy for the Walters. The hapless Walters. Tina had broken their hearts, and they defaulted on hers, not knowing how to help this child, this woman who was a mystery to them.

Then Harry came to this entry:

July 25. Yesterday was Amelia's birthday. I took off work and flew the Piper Cherokee to her airport, but first I flew over the house where she was born in Atchison. It did me good to pay tribute that way, we have so much in common, our love of flying, knowing nothing else matters, willing to give it everything. I spent the night near the airport and flew back today. The most alive I've felt in a long time. Holden thinks he can get me a few shows this summer. I think I can save up some money and ask Cal for a loan and buy the Cherokee. If I'm not flying, I'm not living.

Aside from her more upbeat tone, almost manic, Harry noted that she had purposely flown over the house where she said Earhart had been born. He thought about what Lidia's reaction would be, reading that, if she ever agreed to read the diary at all.

Buying the plane and traveling to air shows had boosted Tina's mood through the remainder of the summer, but by September, she had fallen back to earth.

September 3. The Walters insist I find another job. I told them I couldn't hold one down and fly—and flying is what I want. If I could fly year round I'd leave here and never come back. Since I'm not working and not flying, I'm reading—the only escape I have from earth. Went to the library—am researching my great-grandparents.

The next entry caused Harry to bolt up in his bed.

September 6. For years I believed that Mario and Katharine were my great-grandparents and that I was a part of that grand time, but it may be that I am not related to Katharine at all and that I am related to Mario only through his marriage. How odd to contemplate that there is no Calderara-Wright blood running through my veins. What a fool I am, abandoned again by father and mother. I am no doubt just an ordinary earthbound foolish, foolish girl, related most likely to the Ravenna clan of horseback-riding, villa-living aristocrats.

Harry scoured the rest of the diary to see if there was any evidence to back up Tina's suspicions of her true heritage. He found no clue that would have led her to these conclusions, no references to research or other credible sources. He did find evidence of a deteriorating state of mind, however, from that day forward. The October entry was her last.

October 1. To make them feel better I have seen the psychiatrist again, but I am not taking my medication, although they don't know that. I feel sorry for the Walters. I haven't found another job. It would hurt them irreparably to know I've been flying on the days they think I'm looking for work. So far there are no buyers for Air-Heart. *I may have to give her up. At least she's insured.*

Much of the content in the diary was disturbing. Tina, troubled as she was, may have been capable of doing harm to herself and maybe to others. But thinking like the Bureau agent he was, Harry saw nothing more than a horrible coincidence . . . if there was some sort of connection between Tina and Lidia. The woman, on her way somewhere else, ran out of gas and was dead. No, the problem would be with Lidia. How would she cope with more evidence of a possible connection?

The very last pages of the journal were a collection of quotes from books and poems about flight. Harry closed the diary and turned out the light but was still unable to sleep.

———————●▶———————

The next morning, he had wanted to call Lidia right away, but her reaction to the diary stopped him. She had treated it like a land mine, to be avoided at all costs. Throughout the day he argued with himself.

Why tell her anything? The harm's been done, whether intentional or not.

But it's dishonest. It treats her like a child you have to protect.

So? Why not protect her? She's vulnerable on this.

Is this the way you want to start out, shielding her from what won't go away just because she's afraid right now?

By the time Harry called Lidia, he had made his decision.

"You've read it?" Lidia asked.

Harry heard the phone brush against her earring. He pictured her moving it from one ear to the other, probably to hear better, to drown out the noises around her, the girls talking on their cell phones, Polly listening to her records. He could hear Opal barking faintly in the background.

"Yes," Harry answered.

"Was there, was there anything . . . bad?"

There was time to change his mind. Harry took a deep breath and forged ahead.

"Remember when you didn't want to go to the Walters, and I said I'd be there with you? That helped, I think, having me with you, right? Well, I'm still here—and I will be . . ."

"It's too big, Harry—all of this," Lidia interrupted. "What am I going to do—if there's a connection, if she did it on purpose? If it's true, won't it just lead to more anxiety? I don't see how knowing will make things better."

Harry didn't say anything. He was thinking about his own attempts to find his parents, about how overpowering his need to know was, like Tina's in a way. Maybe he was putting all this on Lidia because of his own past. Maybe he should back off.

"I know my past gets in the way sometimes, and I'm afraid I'm pushing this on you because I know what I would do, I'd jump on this so fast—I'd want to get to the bottom of it," said Harry.

"My fears, Harry. You've said it, and Polly, too—I let them stop me. I should do this just to get control over whatever it is I'm so afraid of. Whatever is out there, waiting for me to find out, I don't have to be afraid of it."

Lidia paused. Harry waited for her to continue, and when she didn't, he asked, "Does this mean you'll read it?"

"Yes."

"Lidia, that's great. You won't regret it—I know it. And like I said, you're not in this alone, even if it gets to you at times, I'll be there."

"I can tell by what you're saying there's something there, Harry, in the diary I mean, but it's okay, and yes, knowing you're there—it is a comfort."

"It's going to be all right—you'll see." Harry wanted to put Tina and the diary aside for the time being. "When can I see you, Lidia?"

"Now," she answered.

"I'll come get you."

———◉———

After they hung up, Lidia went upstairs and pulled open the closet. Looking for something to wear, she was struck by how life had changed. It was as though she had been in some time travel machine and now she was standing in front of a closet that wasn't hers getting ready to be with a man she didn't even know just a short time ago. She buttoned up a silky blouse, stepped into her jeans, and slid into a soft dusty rose pullover. She looked in the full-length mirror hanging behind her bedroom door and adjusted the jeans low on her hips. She ran her hand through her hair and realized she had been fussing with clothes that would soon be hanging over a chair in Harry's bedroom. She smiled at her reflection in the mirror. Life was different all right, and because of Harry, in spite of everything, it was better.

Polly nodded at her, and Carly and Clarisse walked her to the door when Harry's car pulled into the driveway.

"So where are you going, exactly?" asked Carly.

"Well," started Lidia, wondering just how direct she should be. "I think we're going back to Harry's."

"Oh," said Carly. "Okay, have a good time."

Lidia saw that Carly seemed a bit uncertain.

"Thanks, Carl," she said, realizing she was using a nickname she hadn't used in some time, since Carly was a tomboy of ten. Looking at her daughter standing there, nearly grown, she felt a surge of motherly protection—the way she did on so many milestones in the past. And now, so much more lay ahead, so much change.

"Okay, Mom," said Clarisse, opening the door for her mother. "Remember, it's a school night, so curfew's at, what, say midnight?"

Lidia laughed and hugged her daughters before leaving.

"Don't wait up," she said, leaving.

———◉———

As soon as Lidia closed the car door, she turned to Harry, who pulled her to him. Their kiss was long and deep, searching for satisfaction but stoking their desire instead.

Harry pulled himself away from her and put the car in reverse. "Let's get out of here," he said.

Lidia thought she saw Carly, or maybe it was Clarisse, draw back from the window when she saw Lidia look up toward the house. *Owen's the only man they've ever seen me with. This must be a little strange,* thought Lidia, and then, putting the house and Polly and the girls out of her mind for the time being, she leaned toward Harry, and put her hand on his thigh.

———◉———

Harry lived in a three-bedroom Cape not far from the Sound in Rowayton. He had moved there five years ago when he joined the Bureau, wanting to be near the water. Rowayton's quiet, small-town feel had appealed to him right away, he told Lidia on the drive over. A sailor, he liked that the boat launch and dock were within reach and within his means, without having the yacht club atmosphere of other Connecticut towns so near the water. His habit on Saturday mornings was to grab a cup of coffee and sit around with the old timers at the weathered clubhouse before taking off for a few hours, sailing up to New Haven and back before lunch.

Harry had left the front porch light on. Lidia saw in the grey shingles and stonework of the exterior an understated house with character and warmth, much like its owner, she thought. By the time they got inside, she formed no impressions of the interior. She was far too absorbed in Harry. Her passion, which had abated on the way to Harry's, now intensely came upon her. In minutes they were in Harry's bed. By the time they arrived there, they had already shed their clothes.

When they finally made it back to Polly's house and Harry kissed Lidia good night at the door, all the lights inside were out.

"I hope I didn't keep you too long," he said, brushing away a strand of hair that had fallen over her eye. "I know we have to take this more, more, what? I don't know what to say, I want to be with you, but I know you have the girls to think about. I can't just drive up and steal you away whenever I want."

Lidia put a finger to his lips. "I know, Harry, but we're in it now, all of us. We'll figure it out. This is all new to them, to me." Then, looking up at him, she cupped the back of his head with her hands and said, "Besides, we won't always be in this crazed, super-sexed mode."

"Oh yes we will," he said, pulling her closer. "I don't ever want to lose what we have here."

In her room, Lidia was too tired to do anything but go to bed. As she was hanging up her coat, she felt something heavy in one of the pockets. The diary, she remembered. Harry had given it to her on the way back. She took it out and looked at it, a child's book, thought Lidia. A grown woman, writing to "Dear Diary." Picturing Tina sitting at her desk and picking up a pen to begin writing, Lidia felt a sudden shift in her emotions. Instead of fear closing in on her, she felt calm, as though a window had opened and was letting in light and air.

We're all like children, really, looking for whatever it is we think will make us happy—a person, place, or thing to love, to love us back. Isn't that what drove Tina, her love of flying, her need for a family that suited her passion? Isn't it what is driving me, causing me to act like a teenager, like my own daughters? We're all the same, fragile, vulnerable children in a fathomless universe where we hardly register. Lidia wasn't sure why the notion of being a speck in a vastness beyond comprehension would be comforting, but somehow it was. *We're all in this together,* she thought as she pulled the covers up over her shoulder.

She settled into bed, deciding to save the diary for the next day. Then, thinking of the past few hours, she felt Harry's arms around her, one hand on her breast, his breath in her ear. She felt the stirring of desire, but then sleep overtook her.

————◉————

In reality, it took Lidia a few days to open the pink book that now lay on the desk in her room. She wanted to be sure her newfound courage was not fleeting. It had come unbidden, like grace, she thought, and she wanted to be sure it was real. In her phone calls with Harry over the last few days, he never asked her about the diary, unless she brought it up first. She knew he was giving her time to come to it on her own terms. She appreciated that.

When, by the third day, she knew she could face down her fears, Tina, and her diary, she took the book to the conservatory, sat on the loveseat she had shared with Harry not so long ago, and opened to the first entry, January 1.

By mid-afternoon she had read all the entries, including the one about Tina's developing certainty of blood ties with the family in Ravenna. Those words had shot lightning through Lidia's veins, rising up and out the top of her head, but still she read until she finished the last entry in October. *At least she's insured* . . . What an odd sentence, out of the blue, really, but Lidia couldn't escape its implication. This seemed to suggest, as she had suspected all along, that the crash was no accident.

Determined not to give up until she had touched every page, Lidia read through the remaining pages of quotes from books and poems that Tina had copied into her diary. Near the end, Lidia found a folded sheet. She opened it and read:

> *What if I knew the limits I impose*
> *Would amount to nothing if I chose*
> *To see my life another way?*
> *What if I opened doors now closed*
> *And from my chair I rose*
> *To chart a brand new day?*
> *Could I without regret . . .*
> *tip my wings to one I never met*
> *before I ventured to be free?*

This was no copied poem. This was Tina's own. And Lidia took in the fullness of its meaning. *She tipped her wings above my house, and then she set herself free.* "The crash was no accident—and neither was diving into my house," Lidia said out loud, pushing the book away from her, watching it hit the floor, its pages splaying out from under its pink cover. But still she was not afraid.

———————◆———————

In the kitchen the next morning, Lidia told Polly about all she had discovered in Tina's diary.

"You've wanted this, Lidia, to overcome whatever was holding you back, and now you've had a breakthrough. Now you can face, without fear, whatever else you may uncover," said Polly.

Lidia was determined, she said, to get to the bottom of the

remaining mystery: why Tina had wanted to crash into Lidia's house and what the Ravanna connection between them was.

"There was nothing in the diary to explain what she had discovered—only that she was devastated to learn she was not related to any famous flyers. She had been to the library. She must've found something there," said Lidia, circling the rim of her coffee cup with her finger.

"Maybe that's where you start, too," said Polly, putting away the rest of the breakfast things.

"Maybe."

Just then the twins came into the kitchen after their morning run, shedding their fleece jackets, caps, and gloves and tossing them onto the old wicker desk chair in the alcove where Polly kept her cookbooks.

"It's freezing out there," Carly said.

"And I think it's getting ready to snow," said Clarisse.

"By the way, when are we going to get our shopping done? It's almost Christmas," said Carly, grabbing the package of oatmeal on the counter. "Want some?" she asked, turning toward her sister, who nodded yes.

"I can't even think about Christmas," said Lidia. "We should be excused this year. Carly, pour me some more, would you?" she said, holding out her coffee mug to Carly, who was standing next to the coffeemaker, pouring milk on her oatmeal.

"Well, this seems the appropriate time to bring the subject up, since we're already talking about it. I've been meaning to ask," began Polly. "Shall we have another holiday gathering here at the house, for Christmas, and then maybe do something special for New Years?"

It took a matter of seconds for Carly to shoot a "code red" in Clarisse's direction and then for Clarisse to stare down Lidia, who then looked over at Polly sympathetically and said, "I think the Ravens may want to take a pass this time, Polly, if you don't mind."

Polly walked over to the kitchen table where the three of them now sat—Lidia stirring milk into her mug and the twins sprinkling brown sugar over their oatmeal. "Well, that's fine," she said, sitting down among them, "but what are your plans, then?"

Carly wiped her mouth with her napkin. "I don't know about the whole time, you know Christmas Eve and Christmas morning, but Chloe's mom and dad have invited Clarisse and me to their ski house in Vermont for Christmas week through New Year's. A bunch of us kids are going."

Polly looked at Lidia. "Oh, I didn't know."

"Yes," said Lidia. "They've talked to me about it, and I said fine. After the last few months, I think they could use some time away with their friends, and besides, depending on your plans, I think Harry and I may be up for a little getaway ourselves, but we both agreed, we're not leaving you."

"Leaving me? I didn't want to firm up my own plans until I knew yours. I've been invited to a yoga and meditation retreat in Bali with my friends from the center, so it looks like I can say yes."

After sighs of relief all around, it was agreed that the Ravens and Polly would share an intimate candlelit Christmas Eve dinner together. Christmas morning the twins would go to Owen, now that the freeze between him and his girls was showing signs of some thawing. After the memorable Thanksgiving dinner, with Lidia's encouragement, Owen had become more persistent with the twins. He called more frequently, cajoled them into going ice-skating on the pond in Old Greenwich—something they loved to do when they were little. He had invited them over for dinner—with Robert—and they had gone. Things were definitely improving. The girls were beginning to forgive Owen, and to accept Robert. These breakthroughs, Lidia knew, were largely because the girls now saw that she was happy with Harry, but she also knew that much of the credit for the new state of affairs belonged to Polly. After all, it was her determination that had started the whole thing.

"I have a request," said Lidia, full of gratitude for her friend. "I want us to raise a glass, or our coffee mugs, to Polly." She paused and turned toward her friend. "Without you, these last two months would have been unbearable. You've taken us in and made us a part of your family. And more—while our house is being rebuilt, you've been busy helping us to rebuild our lives. Thank you Polly—and I'll stop here because I'm about to cry."

"Hear, hear," said the twins together.

Polly put down her mug and smiled. "Dear ones," she said. "That is all well and good, and thank you for the tribute, but you obviously don't realize the repairing you've brought to this old house—and to me." Pulling a handkerchief out of her sweater pocket, she said, "Okay now, let's dry our tears and get on with our day."

It was agreed then that on Christmas day the occupants of the Niven Estate—Polly and her three guests—would happily go their separate ways, for a little while at least, taking up residence together again on New Year's Day.

Ringing in the New

*T*wenty ten. *It's finally here,* thought Lidia as she put down her suitcase back home at Polly's after having said a lingering good-bye to Harry. She was the first one to return from their various destinations. The twins had sent a text saying they would be home in time for dinner. Polly had called Lidia on her cell phone earlier to say that her plane would be arriving on time and to ask Lidia to defrost the leftovers from their Christmas Eve dinner. Owen had left a message saying he could drop off Opal anytime, just call. Things were returning to normal, not that anything was really normal, but the holidays were over, and the daily round of activities was about to begin again—school, rebuilding, researching into Tina's discoveries. And then there was Harry, who, it appeared, was in it for the long haul. Though things weren't necessarily normal, they were definitely good.

That evening, Polly, the twins, and Lidia settled into the living room after a dinner of leftovers (Cornish game hens, roasted potatoes, and Polly's special recipe for haricots verts—it's all in the herbs, Polly declared) to share pictures and stories of their time apart.

"Here's one of Carly and Chloe on the chairlift before the accident," said Clarisse, adding a note of alarm to an otherwise pleasant evening in front of the fire.

"Accident?" said Lidia, sitting up in her chair.

"Yeah, they skied the moguls right after this was taken, and Carly nearly killed herself."

"It wasn't that bad," said Carly, "but I did twist my knee in a funny way and took the rest of the day off."

"Yeah, reading. She and Chloe read the rest of the day up in their room, and we had perfect powder that day, too," said Clarisse, shaking her head.

Lidia was up in a heartbeat, moving Carly's leg back and forth, satisfying herself that there had been no harm done, and causing Carly and Clarisse convulsive glee at Lidia's expense.

"Mom," they said. "Mom, what are you doing? What do you think you can tell? Dr. Mom, secret M.D. You've been holding out on us," said Clarisse.

"Are you sure you didn't hurt yourself? Maybe we should take you to see Dr. George in the morning," said Lidia, undisturbed by the mirth.

Even Polly joined in before deciding it best to change the subject.

"If you can pull yourselves together for a moment, I have something for each of you," she said, lifting a canvas satchel she had stowed by her feet. She reached in and pulled out brightly colored little bags, tied at the top with shimmering gold string.

Lidia took her seat between the girls. *So like Polly,* Lidia thought as all three of them began untying their packages. *Generous even when she was juggling her accounts to make ends meet.*

"You shouldn't have done this, Polly. We already exchanged Christmas presents," said Lidia.

"But it's always nice to get more," said Clarisse. "Just kidding, Polly. What I meant was, thank you."

Then each pulled out little gold charms hanging from gold chains. "They're likenesses of Hindu gods and goddesses," Polly explained.

"Yours is Ganesha, Lidia."

"He's an elephant," said Lidia, clasping the necklace behind her neck. "And he's adorable. Thank you, Polly. How very sweet of you."

"He's the remover of obstacles. May he remove any that you encounter." Lidia and Polly exchanged glances, reminding Lidia that she had vowed to begin her research into Tina's Ravenna connection in earnest when she came back from her trip with Harry.

"I'll wear him every day," said Lidia, pressing the gold figure against her chest.

"I know this one," said Carly, dangling the four-armed god in front of her face. "It's Shiva, Lord of the Dance."

"You know then that he represents endings and beginnings, just as we sometimes end certain things to begin again, to recreate ourselves."

Carly looked at Polly, puzzled, Lidia thought, but she said nothing.

"Now that you and Clarisse will be going away to school, you'll both be starting fresh, in a sense," Polly quickly added.

I love him, Polly. Thank you."

"And yours, Clarisse . . ."

"Yes, and mine—she's got four arms, too."

"That's Saraswati. She's the goddess of knowledge. And she plays an instrument. See it there? It's not a guitar, but she's a musician, like you."

"You didn't have to do this. You're too good to us."

"Don't be silly, and besides, you'll make me feel bad if you scold me for getting you something. It makes me happy to do it."

Clarisse was the first to get up to hug Polly, followed by Carly and Lidia.

"Okay, enough. Now you'll make me feel bad for all the attention. My trip to Bali, by the way, was sensational."

"We've hardly had time to ask, what with Carly's fall—and then these wonderful gifts. Tell us all about it, Polly," Lidia said.

"It's as wonderful as ever—full of energy and passion—enough to invigorate even an old broad like me. Speaking of passion, how was your trip, Lidia?"

Momentarily caught off guard, Lidia began to feel the blood rising from her neck to her temples, a full-on blush, but she quickly recovered.

"Okay, Polly, just like you—get the attention away from you. Well, it may surprise you to know that Harry and I are not always locked in torrid embraces."

"Mom, please," said the twins.

"Spare us—TMI," said Carly.

"Believe me, I'm not going into any details, I just wanted you to know that we have a lot in common and really enjoy each other's company."

"I'm sorry, Lidia. I'm afraid I started it all," intervened Polly. "So what did you do?"

"As it turns out, we didn't drive to Newport to walk the beach in winter, although that would've been nice, too. Harry surprised me with two tickets to New Orleans."

Polly and the twins were struck silent, until Lidia filled the vacuum.

"Harry's from there, remember my telling you? He volunteers there when he can—since Katrina. His parents are dead, but he still has a sister there, outside of New Orleans. We went to see her. He hasn't seen her for a while. So we went." She was rambling, she knew, but they just kept staring at her. It was Carly who broke the silence.

"So is there something you need to tell us? Should we be looking for a ring on your finger or something?"

Lidia held up her left hand, to show them it was bare. "It's nothing like that. But, well, Harry is in my life now, that's all."

————◉————

"I'm going to need a remover of obstacles," Lidia said to Polly later as she clutched her new necklace. "I think my relationship with Harry is going to be an adjustment for the girls. After all, Harry—more and more—will be seen as taking Owen's place." Lidia's brow narrowed. "It's confusing, I mean, first they were so angry with Owen, they would hardly see him, and now that they are accepting him, loving him again, I think, won't they come to resent Harry? I want them to accept Harry, too—to be happy I'm with him."

"I think they are happy for you, Lidia, and for you with Harry," said Polly as she settled back into John Paul's club chair in the living room. "They just need some time to be sure it will be okay—for you more than for them, I suspect. I think they're concerned about you more than anything. They don't want to see you get hurt again. They're just recovering from Owen. Ironically, I think they've just been able to forgive him because they see you happy now."

"You see things so clearly, Polly, more than I do. It's your gift, and I'm sure you're right about them being worried. Join the club. I'm worried, too. I don't think I could take another heartbreak, and I'm in pretty deep here."

The trip to New Orleans had been more than physically satisfying. Lidia and Harry were as compatible during daylight hours as they were during their nights together. He'd shown Lidia where he grew up. He took her to see some of the houses he had worked on after Katrina, and then he took her to meet his sister, Jo.

Jo, a social worker, mother of two teenage boys, had been a widow for five years. She lived in St. Tammany Parish on the North Shore of Lake Pontchartrain but worked in St. Bernard Parish. "I love my work," she'd told Lidia over breakfast, "but it gets to me sometimes. It was bad before Katrina, but now—I'll tell you, the cases I deal with can be hard. Sometimes I don't know." Sparing Lidia any further details, Jo just looked down at her coffee and shook her head. Watching this no-nonsense, unadorned woman, whose greatest indulgence was hanging around in her bathrobe until noon on Saturdays, handle with grace and good spirits her house, boys, and brother with this perfect stranger, Lidia couldn't imagine her backing away from much.

On the last afternoon there, Jo asked Lidia to join her out back to sit on her new porch swing. "I like coming out here in the evenings when the sun goes down. It fills me with peace," she said. "Then I go back in, tackle dinner, and try to get the boys off their computers."

Lidia laughed, but she expected that something more was on Jo's mind.

After a few minutes, she said, "My brother has never brought a woman here to meet me. I always knew his girlfriends when he was younger. They were from here, but when push came to shove, mostly them pushing for something more, Harry always backed away. He's had some serious relationships over the years, I suppose, but you know, Lidia, he's never been married. Almost fifty now, my baby brother, and never loved a woman enough to get married."

Feeling a little uncomfortable, Lidia finally said, "I'm not sure why you're telling me this, Jo."

"Just a heads up, I guess. You may be the one, if that's what you want."

"I don't know that yet, and I don't think Harry does, either. This is all pretty new for both of us."

"Well, I'm just saying—he's never brought anyone to meet me. I'm the only family he's got, and I know he always wanted a family of his own, but he wanted to get it right."

When they left that day, she hugged Jo and whispered in her ear. "Don't worry. I want it to be right, too."

And Jo whispered back, "I hope it works out."

Lidia realized, sitting next to Harry on the plane back home, watching his eyes gently flutter after he had dozed off, that her fascination with him, her crush, her infatuation—call it what you would—had become something more.

Now, sitting back home with Polly, she pondered what all of this might mean for her future. "You know, Polly, I'm pretty sure I'm in love with him," she said, smiling.

That Old Gang of Mine

*L*idia sat in a hard, straight-back chair on the first floor of the Greenwich Library, stretching her back, trying to find a comfortable position. Pressing the forward button on an old microfilm reader, she looked away from time to time to stave off the waves of nausea threatening to send her scurrying to the restroom. She hadn't expected this, feeling nauseous when the advertisements and words sped by in a blur as she looked for feature articles, hoping to catch a glimpse of her grandfather, his picture or his name.

The unsettling dizziness reminded her of childhood bouts of car sickness, sitting in the backseat of the family Chevy between her mother and Nonna while in the front seat her father and Nonno talked about baseball, usually about the good old days of Joltin' Joe and the Yankees. Her mother invariably would notice Lidia's discomfort and pull her onto her lap so Lidia could look out the window and get some air. This warm memory of those now gone cleared away the queasiness as though a summer breeze had just blown through.

Lidia turned away from the screen and gazed out the window, reflecting on those long-ago days when she and her family had piled into the car for the long ride to Jones Beach to meet up with other transplants from Emilia-Romagna, especially those from Ravenna. She hadn't paid much attention to the old people who hugged and kissed her grandparents as they plopped their blankets and picnic baskets down on the warm sand. Lidia, in those days, was too busy looking for kids her own age, Americans preferably, so she wouldn't be miserable listening to a language she didn't want to hear and to music she didn't like, tinny voices and strange instruments coming from the transistor radio her father had brought along.

Taking a deep breath, Lidia returned to the microfilm and pushed on.

She had learned from the reference librarian that Old Greenwich had had its own weekly newspaper, the *Town Ledger,* for years in the fifties and sixties and that old copies had been filmed. "We don't have much demand for this one; we're lucky to have it at all," the librarian explained. "We won't be digitizing this title anytime soon, but the years you're interested in are here." And with that she handed Lidia the box containing the rolls. When she was halfway through the late fifties, she saw an advertisement with the logo of an apple with a raven perched on top. Unless she had missed something, this was the first time an ad for the family business had shown up in the weekly. Then in the features section of the same issue, she saw her grandfather in a grainy black-and-white photo. The headline read, "Renette Apple Cider from the Raven Orchards Turns Liquid to Gold." And under the photo was a caption: "Pictured here is Rodolfo Raven with one of his apples."

The article's glowing assessment of the Raven Orchards' success caused a flutter of pride in Lidia's chest. In the photograph, her grandfather stood next to one of his trees with his hand cupping a plump ripe apple. He was wearing a flannel shirt tucked into a pair of canvas work pants, each leg in turn tucked into a high-cut leather boot. His thick silver hair was pushed back from his tan face. He had a strong straight nose and an appealing smile that revealed a set of handsome white teeth. *Who knew,* thought Lidia, *that Nonno was so dashing.* She shook her head, remembering her young self and her impression of her grandparents as relics of a strange past she could not understand and about which she had no interest.

The article was written with a "rags-to-riches" slant, focusing on Rodolfo's drive and determination to buy his own orchards, although it didn't quite fit the narrative Rodolfo was relating to the inter-viewer—that he, Rodolfo, was merely duplicating his father's success in Italy. The article closed by saying, "Anyone who is willing to work hard can enjoy the American dream, right here in Old Greenwich, Connecticut." Lidia plunked in her quarter and made a copy of the article.

After a break for lunch in the café downstairs, Lidia returned to the dizzying task at hand. Then, later in the afternoon, she read a headline from June 11, 1960. "Local Businessman Honored by Chamber of Commerce," which was accompanied by another picture of her grandfather, this time receiving a plaque for Businessman of the Year. He was wearing a white dinner jacket and shaking hands with the president of the Chamber. Lidia could just make out Nonna in the background, photographed applauding and looking up at her husband admiringly. *They really did make it in America,* Lidia thought to herself, as she began scanning the accompanying article.

A lot of it was a rehash of the content that had appeared in the previous article a year or two earlier, but in this one, there was a quote by Rodolfo that touched off a memory, something Claudia had told her the day they had met for coffee in Greenwich. *I owe all my success to my father, who made it possible for me to plant his dream in the new country. And my family owes thanks to the Gamba Ghiselli family of Ravenna for all they did to make my father's dream a reality.* The hairs on the back of Lidia's neck prickled. Her grandfather went on to mention the name of one man in particular, Ruggero Gamba Ghiselli, who apparently gave him a loan and his backing to start his orchard business in Ravenna. She wondered if this was the same benefactor Claudia had mentioned. Lidia also wondered how deep the relationship with the Gamba Ghiselli family had been.

She printed the page, stuffed her papers into her bag, and made her way to the rows of computers behind the information desk. There she wandered up and down, looking for exiting behavior—someone packing up. But every spot was taken by, from the looks of the computer screens she glanced at, jobseekers working on résumés and applications, or by students no doubt making avid use of Wikipedia for research projects. Finally, she observed a young man with a mop of unruly hair beginning to yawn. Then came the stretch with a deep back arch, arms spreading in two directions and into his neighbors' spaces on either side. This looked promising. Sure enough, he quickly brought his arms down and reached for his backpack. After tucking away a few stray sheets of blank paper, he rose, and Lidia deftly scooted in behind him. "S'cuse me, sorry" she said, acknowledging her swift move to take his place.

She began Googling, starting with Roger Gamba Ghiselli. One of the first entries to appear linked the name with Lord Byron, the nineteenth-century poet. The more she looked, the more the reference was confirmed, the name soon morphing to the Italian, *Il conte Ruggero Gamba* (1770-1846) of the illustrious Ravenna Gamba Ghiselli family.

Well, what does this have to do with my family, or with Tina? The dates were too long ago to be of relevance, but the more she read, the more intrigued she became. The allure of the Byron-Gamba family connection could not be denied. She was hooked by the time she read these lines, ascribed to Bryon and written in a letter in 1819, five years before his death:

But all this is too late. I love you, and you love me, at least, you say so, and act as if you did so, which last is a great consolation in all events. But I more than love you, and cannot cease to love you. Think of me, sometimes, when the Alps and ocean divide us, but they never will, unless you wish it.

Lidia wondered who had inspired these lines. She didn't know much about Lord Byron, but in her college Brit lit class she had studied enough to have learned the basics: the good-looking, reckless lover who debauched many a fair maiden in the course of his travels; the tragic adventurer who died of fever in Greece during his attempt to join the fight for freedom against the tyranny of Turkey. But the history of this love, more than likely his last, had eluded her.

The letter was written to eighteen-year-old Teresa Gamba-Guiccioli, the daughter of Count Ruggero Gamba. And in spite of all Byron's past romances, his late love for Teresa was no mere dalliance. Was it possible he had finally found true love? The more Lidia read, the more tragic the love affair appeared to have been.

Further research brought her to a website on the Gamba Ghiselli family, in Italian. She pushed the translation icon, and, several pages in, a portrait of Teresa Gamba Ghiselli appeared, supposedly painted on the occasion of the young woman's eighteenth birthday, around the time she first met Byron. Lidia drew a deep, sharp breath—the long neck, the slender body, the abundant hair, the almond-shaped eyes. "She could be Tina," Lidia muttered. "A younger version of Tina . . . or, of me?"

She read on. When Teresa was seventeen and recently returned from convent, she was married off to a rich sixty-year-old count, Allesandro Guiccioli, making her then Countess Gamba-Guiccioli. The meeting between the pair was recorded thus:

The girl waited obediently while the Count lit a candle and examined the young woman before him, circling her several times. Without haste, he took up his pen and signed the document previously presented by her father, sealing the matrimonial agreement. Count Ruggero then addressed his daughter, letting her know, without question, the elderly gentleman was soon to be her husband. There would be no discussion. A daughter's obligation, after all, was to comply with her father's wishes.

Beginning to feel sorry for this unfortunate girl, soon to be married to someone old enough to be her grandfather, Lidia almost missed the significance of the next entry. Teresa had two brothers, one who died young, and another, Ippolito, who was the father of Amelia—who married Mario Calderara. Teresa was Amelia's aunt. Lidia could not help but wonder how much of this Tina might have known.

Returning to the screen, Lidia quickly scanned the remaining information. The last line of the entry mentioned a memoir Teresa Gamba-Guiccioli had written later in life, after she had married a

French marquis and had become Madame la Marquise de Boissy. The book, written in French, championed her lost lover against those who continued their attack on his reputation, even after his death, Lidia read.

So, figured Lidia, Teresa met Byron not long after her marriage to the Count Guiccioli, entered into a liaison with him, lost him to death several years later, and stayed in love enough to write about him years later after yet another marriage. Fascinated, Lidia wanted to read more, but, looking at her watch, realized it was getting late. It was the end of the first week back at school, and the twins had agreed to a family dinner. Polly had a new recipe for shrimp in clear noodles she wanted to try out. "I got the recipe from a friend in Bali," she had announced that morning. "It's more complicated than it sounds, so be here," she had called out as they'd all piled into the car.

Lidia hurriedly searched the library holdings to see if there was an English version of the book available. There was. She quickly gathered up her things and went to search the stacks. It was there. Lidia pulled the weighty volume from the shelf, holding it to her chest, knowing that soon she would be telling Polly about all she had discovered and that after the dinner things had been put away, she would be in her room reading *My Recollections of Lord Byron and Those of Eye-Witnesses of his Life.*

Although Lidia knew Byron had led a bohemian life, she was surprised to learn the rest of it—not only his casual entanglements with so many men and women, but also the relationship with his half-sister, his ill-fated marriage, and then, his reputation in ruins, his departure from England—a permanent break from his homeland in 1816, leaving behind a daughter, Augusta.

That night, Lidia sat up in bed reading, absorbed in Byron's life as told by Teresa. Later, after turning out her nightlight, she tossed restlessly, not able to get the images left by her reading out of her mind, Byron alone, sailing up the Rhine into Switzerland, maligned and bereft, then settling in Geneva near his fellow poet and friend, the famous Percy Bysshe Shelley, and Shelley's soon-to-be wife, Mary Godwin—and Claire Clairmont, Byron's lover. The following year, Claire gives birth to Byron's daughter, Allegra, born in England after the Shelleys and Claire leave Geneva. Bryon does not go with them, instead traveling through Italy and writing.

Lidia's head began to reel trying to follow the complicated relationships, even though Polly had warned her. "They led wild lives, those two," she had said, " with many entanglements."

Lidia continued her reading to discover that in 1818, when Shelley saw his friend again in Venice, gone were Byron's vigor and youth, no longer the slim dashing figure of but a few years ago, his thick, curly locks replaced with unkempt hair, turning grey. Was it possible that he was but thirty?

Lidia, half-asleep, let the book fall on her chest. In a dreamlike state, she envisioned the pair from her reading—imagining Byron's chance meeting with the young and charming Countess Teresa Gamba-Guiccioli, his infatuation with her from the start. She is married to the old Count by this time, it is true, but only she, it seems, can bring the sad poet back to life. They spend hours together. He is surprised by the depth of her intellect. She is a devotee of the Italian poets. She and Byron lie under the trees, reading to one another. He knows one day she will be reading his poetry to another, but that does not matter now. Now she is the breath of life to him. He follows her to Ravenna. In time he is a friend of her brother, Pietro. He will be accepted by her father, Ruggero, as well. The Gamba family is moved by his revolutionary spirit, by his desire to fight for a world where all are free from tyranny, they themselves freedom fighters, members of a clandestine group against Austrian rule. And Byron is writing. The sweet words pour from him like scented water from some miraculous spring. She, the beautiful Teresa, is his muse.

Late in the night, Lidia awoke from her dreamlike state, turned her light back on, and continued reading.

The couple openly see one another in spite of Teresa's marriage to another. Finally, she leaves her husband's house. Late in 1821, Byron travels to Pisa to be with the Gamba family, where Teresa is, after her father and brother are forced to leave Ravenna for having supported an uprising destined to fail.

Byron is nourished by his love, but there is no escaping the sorrows of life. His daughter Allegra dies of fever in April the following year. Little does he know then in his grief that by mid-summer, he will lose Shelley, who will drown sailing in the storm-tossed Bay of La Spezia.

In September, Byron follows Teresa once more, this time to Genoa, where the family has settled, seeking protection from retribution for their political beliefs and actions. By the following year, Byron heeds the call himself to fight for freedom. In December, he says his good-byes and sails for Missolonghi to help the Greeks fight the Turks.

Lidia then read of the fever that would finally kill Byron a few months later. She wondered if he was already weakened when he left Teresa. Was he touched by her tears and his recent losses, his sorrow beginning to fuel the fever that would take him? Whatever he may have felt in those months after leaving Teresa, by April, Byron was dead. *Teresa would never forget him,* Lidia thought, closing the book. She would love him always, writing about him years later, after she had taken up a whole new life and identity, yet never forgetting, reading his poetry to the young admirers who sought her out, almost unaware of their presence, sitting at her knee, so absorbed in her lost lover's words.

Lidia threw off the covers and walked to the window, where she saw the full moon's light still bright.

Why do I care about these people? she asked. Was it because there was some assumed relationship—some connection to her? She only knew their story had touched her deeply. *Who are they to me?* she continued to ask herself as she crept back to bed and soon fell, finally, into a deep sleep.

————◆————

Lidia was awakened the next morning by the sound of someone knocking on her closed bedroom door. She opened her eyes, surprised by the amount of sunlight streaming in the window, and then glanced at the small clock on the nightstand by her bed.

"Oh my God—it's nearly ten," she said, jumping up, remembering the twins' plans to go skiing today.

Quickly opening the door, she saw Polly standing there, holding out a cup of coffee.

"It's cappuccino," said Polly, and handed Lidia the steamy brew.

"Thank you, Polly. I can't believe I slept so late. The girls . . . did they leave already?"

"Chloe's mother picked them up an hour ago. They were fine—excited and had everything prepared. You know how they are."

Lidia held the cup with both hands, feeling the warmth rising to her face as she lifted the coffee to her lips, then taking a sip. "I can't believe I overslept like this. I was up most of the night reading."

"Ah, yes, Byron and Teresa." Polly answered. "It didn't end well, did it?"

"No," said Lidia, thinking of the anguish of the star-crossed pair, hearts and promises broken, children and lovers lost. Gloom was overtaking Lidia, even now in the light of day.

Lidia, standing there at the top of the stairs, coffee in hand, began to tell Polly about her late-night reading and troubled sleep.

"Yes, I know the story," said Polly. "I'm sorry for your bad night. Their affair, it's terribly sad, isn't it? I knew of the young woman, Teresa, who was presumably his last love, but I must admit, I never read her entire memoir, only translated excerpts."

Lidia looked at Polly in amazement.

"Don't be so surprised, dear. Lord Byron has long been one of my favorite poets, so naturally I've spent some time on his biography—and on his many conquests. I'm chagrined, actually, not to have read the book you pored over last night."

Lidia smiled and shook her head. Holding up her cup, she said, "Thanks again for this, Polly. I'll be right down."

"I would've let you sleep longer, but you had a phone call earlier, well two, actually. One from Harry. Says he'll pick you up tonight for dinner at eight-ish, and the other from Rocco. It sounded like it might have been important."

In the bathroom, Lidia washed and rinsed her face, feeling more cheerful as she anticipated a night out with Harry, but at the same time, she couldn't help feeling that the call from Rocco might be an omen of some kind related to her dreams and reading.

She looked into the mirror as she wiped away lingering drops of water, staring at her reflection as though the face she saw there belonged to a stranger. She paused to observe the long neck, abundant hair, straight nose, and the almond-shaped eyes, like her daughters', like Tina's, and now—like Teresa's. The face staring back at her, familiar but also strange, hid some secret knowledge.

In the bedroom, she opened the closet and looked for something to wear. It was promising to be a lovely day, cold but with bright sun, not a cloud to mar the brilliance of the January sky. Under the influence of her nighttime reading and half-asleep imaginings, Lidia chose a long black wool dress, black tights, and leather boots. She walked down the stairs to call Rocco, throwing a purple velvet shawl over her shoulders, her long dark hair getting caught under its weight.

After she hung up the phone, she went looking for Polly. Not in the living room, not on the sun porch—too cold—not in the kitchen or the library. Finally Lidia found her friend in the conservatory, deadheading her begonias.

Lidia stood in the doorway.

"My God. You look like you've seen a ghost," said Polly, putting down her basket and scissors.

"I sort of did. Rocco found an old iron lockbox behind a wall in one of the rooms of the basement. It must have belonged to my grand-father, but I don't think it was his—originally, anyway. Rocco said the box was engraved with R. *DiRavenna I*. My great grandfather was Rodolfo the first. Grandpa was Rodolfo number two. Grandpa must've hidden it in the wall."

Why? she had wondered. *Why hide it? What could have been in there, needing to be hidden in a wall? Jewels, maybe? A gun? Secrets?* Lidia's money was on the latter, even if she was betting with no one but herself.

"Anyway, Rocco says it's locked and wants to know if I want him to open it for me. Says he'll meet me over at the house, show me where he found it, and open it, if I want him to . . ."

"So I guess you told him yes, and that you'd meet him, to see . . ."

"I didn't tell him to do anything. I thanked him and said I'd be in touch."

"And now you're standing there looking like . . ."

"Like I've seen a ghost, I know," said Lidia as she reached for the loveseat and sat down.

Polly sat beside her. "Not just that—you look, well, dressed to go out. Had you thought you'd go see Rocco? Did you know he'd have something for you to see, before you even called him?"

"I don't really know, Polly—maybe. It would be reasonable to think he wanted to tell me about some new idea for the house, but never this. Some sequestered box."

"Well, I think it's pretty exciting. Aren't you eager to find out what's in it? If it's your great grandfather's, it's like walking back in time, opening a door to history. Fascinating," she said. "Who knows how long it's been since that box has been opened."

They both sat quietly for a moment, contemplating the contents waiting to be discovered.

Lidia spoke first. "It is exciting, Polly. Everything you say. But I have this very real feeling that there's something in there, something related to this whole mystery linking me to Tina, so I'm a little . . ."

Polly waited, but Lidia was at a loss for words.

"A little anxious, maybe? Needing some time to catch your breath before rushing over there?"

"Yes. Exactly," Lidia answered, relieved to have words put to her feelings.

"Perfectly natural," said Polly. And with that she stood, gathered up her basket and scissors, and turned her attention to her plants.

"If you want, Lidia, I'd be happy to go with you, when you decide to go."

Lidia smiled, looking a little less anxious. "I'd like that, Polly."

———◆———

By noon, having shed her shawl and boots, Lidia had washed the breakfast things and had tidied up the girls' rooms, remaking their hastily put-together beds, and dusting, careful not to move any jewelry or scarves strewn about, mindful not to be too intrusive. She had also helped Polly water the plants in the conservatory. Running out of things to do, she announced she would like to polish the silver on the sideboard in the dining room. "It's something I've wanted to do for a long time," she told Polly, who responded by saying, "Of course. Polishing silver—everyone's favorite activity on a beautiful day." Lidia noted the sarcasm, but said nothing. She opened the sideboard's bottom doors and pulled out a container of polish and several soft cloths. Lidia managed to clean two large serving pieces and a carving knife before she turned toward Polly, who'd just come into the room with a stack of recently ironed linen napkins.

"How long before you can be ready to ride over to Apple Way?"

"I just have to grab my coat."

"I'll call Rocco."

The Iron Box

*B*y the time Lidia and Polly pulled into the driveway, Rocco, leaning against his truck, was just finishing the last of his lunch. He motioned them over while quickly wiping his mouth and then stuffing the napkin and foil wrapping into a paper bag. "I was already here when you called," he said to Lidia. "C'mon—how long could you stay away? I knew you'd change your mind. Hi, Mrs. Niven. You come to see what's in the box, too?"

Lidia saw Polly smile, put her head down, and then begin to blush a little. She'd never seen Polly blush. Lidia looked over at Rocco, who was focused on Polly and smiling.

"Call me Polly, please. And, yes, I'm here for the opening. Wouldn't miss it, Rocco. Could be quite fascinating, you know."

Rocco placed his hand on her back, guiding her in the direction of the large hole in the ground where the basement was still intact.

"I'm glad you came. It's right over there, at the top of the steps," he said, motioning in the direction of the old house. "I want to show you both where I found it."

Lidia, who had been amused by the exchange between Polly and Rocco, soon became absorbed by what she saw before her. *My, house, it's completely gone,* she thought, looking at the property, razed to its foundation. Just the stairs and the old basement remained.

"I guess it's a shock, huh, Lidia? You haven't been out here in a while. The last time I think part of the house was still standing."

"Yes," said Lidia, trying not to sound as shocked as she felt. "It looks so strange, this empty space." She imagined the house as it once was. On the top floor, she saw Nonno and Nonna standing at an open window, waving to her. At the front door, she saw her mother and father holding each other, smiling.

"Ghosts," she said.

Rocco and Polly, who had gone ahead of her, turned at once.

"What?" asked Rocco.

"Dear?" said Polly.

"Nothing," said Lidia. "It's nothing. Where's the box, Rocco?"

After a few more steps, she saw it resting on the bricks by the stairs leading to the basement.

"My God, what is it, some sort of medieval shrine box?" she said, bending down to look more closely at the mottled iron case, no bigger than a shoebox, with its delicate lace-like decorations, a greenish metal, different from the rest and still intact, in spite of its fragility. Lidia sat on the top step, picked up the box, and turned it around in her hands, pausing to take in her great grandfather's name, the engraving still crisply visible. Lidia began to tremble. A family relic in her basement—it was exciting, to be sure, but there was something more. There could be something rare inside, or possibly nothing at all. The pounding of her heart reminded Lidia of her excitement— and also of her reluctance to know. But she was determined to see it through.

"I don't know," said Polly. "It looks later, sixteenth- or seventeenth-century maybe. It's too decorative to be religious, I think." She bent down next to Lidia. "May I?" she asked before picking it up.

"Of course," said Lidia. On second thought, it looked to her like a rather substantial antique jewelry box—or gilded cash box, maybe.

"I bet this will clean up nicely," said Polly "I think the overlay, the filigree, is copper. See how it's kind of green? The way copper weathers? It's verdigris." Holding it up in the sun, she continued. "Look at the top and the sides, it has little rosettes, and in the middle on the top, a face—see, with the mouth open? Oh, and here, on the side, in the front, that little flower with the opening, that's the keyhole."

Lidia knew Polly was an ardent lover of literature and fine old books. Now it appeared she also knew something about antique iron and copper boxes. There seemed to be no end to the variety of her interests.

"Right, and it's locked, but there's no key," said Rocco.

"It's quite charming, whimsical and elegant, all at the same time," continued Polly. "Could be quite valuable in its own right, regardless of its contents."

"But without a key, how can we open it? It would be a shame to break it open," Lidia said.

"Oh no, we mustn't break it," said Polly.

"I don't think we'll have to, ladies," said Rocco. "I'm not a lock picker, but I have some tools that may work—if you want me to try."

Lidia looked at Polly for some encouragement.

"I think that would be fine," said Polly. Then turning to Rocco, she added, "But do be careful with the decorative copper. It might break."

When Rocco walked back to the truck for his toolbox, Lidia drew her coat collar around her ears and crossed her arms around her chest. The day was warming up, but Lidia was shivering. Polly put an arm around her.

"This should do it," said Rocco, walking back, holding up a slim implement that looked as though it would fit in the opening. Polly handed him the box. After a few minutes of maneuvering the pick-like tool, the lid of the box popped up a fraction of an inch.

"I think I got it," said Rocco, still holding the box and slipping the implement into his tool belt. "Do you want me to raise the lid the rest of the way?"

"Let me," said Lidia. "I'd like to open it, if I may." Rocco gently passed the box to her.

Holding it in her hands, Lidia was reluctant to lift the lid. She was afraid her world would forever be divided between before she opened the box and after. She was dramatizing, she knew, but the other possibility, equally distressing, was that nothing would change, that this ancient overwrought box contained nothing but old worthless receipts, recording business dealings long passed, with no current value or meaning.

"Before I open it, can you show me where you found it? I want to see where it was. Maybe I've walked by a hundred times, never knowing it was there."

Rocco nodded, and Lidia handed the box to Polly, who stayed above.

"I promise I won't look, Lidia," said Polly. "You'll be the first to see what's inside." Rocco and Lidia walked down the stairs.

"It's funny," said Lidia. "I haven't been down here in ages, even though the hot water heater is here, the fuses, the stuff that makes the house go, actually. Owen used to do all that stuff."

"Well, you don't have to worry about that. We're putting in a whole new electrical system—and I'll be sure you know how everything works before I leave."

Rocco led the way to the last room in the basement. In spite of the sun, at this depth, the room was blocked from light, and Rocco had to shine his searchlight on the wall in front of them.

"It's here," he said, lighting up the space. "Hold this." Rocco handed Lidia the flashlight. "I want to show you how I found it." Lidia took the light as Rocco began moving his hand over the wall.

"I was checking for stability, with the bricks, when I came to this one. See how it's not even with the others? When I felt this, I used a probe in the space, and it moved, very easily, so I rocked it a little, and it practically fell out. The space behind the brick was deep. Look inside."

Lidia drew near and bent down slightly to look into the space where the brick had been. Rocco pointed the searchlight into the opening, and Lidia saw a smooth recessed area, deep into the wall.

"Whoever dug this out went into the foundation and cemented the space—top, bottom, and sides—to keep it protected. Whoever it was, he must've thought this was a way to keep the box safe, but, mostly, I guess, private."

"My grandfather," said Lidia. "It would've been my grandfather who hid it here, for some reason, but originally the box must've belonged to my great grandfather. That's his name engraved—the one you told me about on the phone."

After Rocco replaced the brick, Lidia ran her hands along the wall, feeling the rough, cool surface, imagining her grandfather at work, making a safe place to secure his secrets.

"Well, let's go see what's in it, then," she said.

When they got back to where Polly was standing, she held out the box to Lidia.

"You know," she said. "You don't have to do this in front of us. You can take it home and read the contents in private."

"We've had enough secrets in this family, I think. Besides, I'm not sure I want to be alone. Who knows what's in here, so . . . let's find out."

With that, Lidia opened the box.

Inside was a brown worn velvet pouch, its sides tucked around what appeared to be envelopes or folded papers. Lidia pulled out the pouch and handed the empty box to Polly. She began trying to untie the knotted and frayed leather cord that was drawn tightly closed at the opening.

"I think I'd better sit down to do this," Lidia said, walking over to the top step of the basement stairs.

She placed the bottom of the pouch in her lap and began again trying to untie the cord. She picked at the knot with a fingernail, and finally it began to loosen. She reached in and began pulling out the contents.

"It's letters," she said, looking at a stack of papers, folded, with broken wax seals. "Mostly letters. Some look very old—with sealing wax; others are newer in envelopes and stamped." Then she pulled out another velvet pouch—red with a similar leather cord—this one opening easily. She reached inside and extracted its contents. In her palm rested a gold locket and chain. Lidia looped the chain on her finger and let the locket drop, dangling it in the sun.

"Look at that," said Rocco.

"It's lovely," said Polly.

Lidia, heart pounding, said, "I think the locket will open. There's a clasp, but I don't want to break it."

"Pry it gently, Lidia. If there's resistance, leave it. We can always take it to Terry. He has the jewelry store on Greenwich Avenue. He'll know what to do."

Lidia pried it gently with the tip of a fingernail. The clasp released, and the locket opened.

"Look. It's a picture—of a young woman. Goodness, who could she be?" Polly leaned in to get a better look. "From all you've told me, Lidia, I'm wondering—about the connection with that other Ravenna family—and the way you described her. Do you think it could be Teresa? Byron's Teresa?" asked Polly.

"I don't know," said Lidia, wonderstruck. She passed the locket to Polly so she could examine it more closely.

"It's history, right here in front of us," Polly marveled as she held the piece up, turning it from side to side. Then Polly carefully passed it to Rocco.

"She must be in your family. She looks like your girls, if you ask me," he said, quickly passing it back to Lidia, who looked closely at the face in the locket, wondering if indeed the portrait could have been a young Teresa.

Lidia had to admit, the lovely woman looked a lot like the image she had seen on the screen in the library. Lidia placed the locket back in its pouch—away for now—but she was eager to learn more, the misgivings she had felt earlier, now vanished.

"It seems a lot of people resemble members of my family these days," said Lidia. Then, turning to Polly, she asked, "Your friend, the jeweler, could he tell us more about this piece—its age, maybe?"

"I'm sure he could."

"Good. That's one thing about this widening mystery I can do at least, find out more about this lovely little gem."

Lidia put the pouch in her coat pocket and then turned to opening the letters, starting with an older one, careful not to tear it at the fragile folds, but she stopped when she heard Polly unsuccessfully try to hide a gasp. Seeing Polly's reaction, Lidia concluded that the letters were too fragile to be opened while sitting on the foundation of her recently razed house, and she announced it was time to go. She placed the contents as she had found them into the brown pouch and into the metal box.

Turning to Rocco, she said, "I know it's a lot to ask, but could you come with us? You speak Italian, right? And can you read it, too? From what I've seen so far, everything's in Italian."

Rocco looked unsure, but then he turned to Polly, who said, "We'd understand if you have other work to attend to."

"Well, no, I don't, actually. I could go over for a little while. Sure, why not?" And so Rocco was enlisted as translator.

Back at Polly's, the trio took to the library, where Lidia and Polly threw back the heavy drapes and turned on all the lights, making sure Rocco would be able to see in the dark, wood-paneled room. Polly cleared off John Paul's large desk, pushing the computer keyboard back so there would be room to spread out the letters. Then she went to make tea.

"Don't get too far along without me," she said as she was leaving the room. "And if you'll excuse all my dos and don'ts—I must sound like a fusty old librarian—we should wash our hands before touching the paper. At least, that's what I've been told over the years—about caring for old paper—because of all these old first editions, you see," she said, waving at the bookcases surrounding them. "We should probably be using archivist gloves, but anyway, just touch the pages as little as possible. And then there's all this light. Oh well," she said. "After all, it's not the Dead Sea Scrolls, now, is it?"

Lidia and Rocco dutifully excused themselves to wash their hands in the guest bathroom down the hall. When they returned, Lidia was first to pick up a letter, one of the older ones, its sealing wax having been broken almost two centuries ago. The paper was nearly transparent with age, like old skin, the deep creases at the folds in danger of tearing. Seeing the date, 1825, Lidia cautiously touched only the edges, as though she were ministering to a frail relative.

"Rocco, can you read this?" she said, carefully handing the sheet to him.

"*Carissima amore*, Dearest love," he began as Polly came in and put the silver tray with the teapot and cups on the table in front of the leather couch. He paused then, giving her time to pour the tea and get settled.

"Please, continue, Rocco," she said, passing him a cup.

"It's hard to make out," he said, holding the paper up to the light, "but I'll try."

The script, rendered in black ink, was neat and straight, written by someone given to great precision. Although taking up only one sheet, the tight lettering enabled the writer to say a great deal, to pour out his heart, in fact. By the end, it was clear to the listeners, the letter was not by an ardent lover, but by a father intent on comforting a distraught daughter.

The little group was silent for a moment, taking it in—the content, the years separating the writer from them. It was as though a curtain had been pulled back, allowing a rare glimpse into the past, a past that somehow did not seem so distant.

Lidia spoke first. How does he sign it, Rocco?

"*Tuo padre amorevole*—your loving father."

"Of course. He doesn't name her or say anything about their relationship in the letter, but of course it's his daughter, with all the references to her childhood and then to her adulthood and to her terrible loss of the love of her life," said Lidia.

"There may not be any names, but by the date and the circumstances described, it's possible that this letter is from the Count to his daughter, Teresa," said Polly, walking over to take a look at the letter Rocco had placed on the desk. "Written after the death of Byron. Somehow your great-grandfather came into possession of some of the Count's correspondence—and the locket with the picture of his daughter."

"But why? Why would it come to be in my great-grandfather's stack of letters? That my grandfather then hid in the basement?" asked Lidia. "Very strange, if you ask me."

Polly turned, her back against the desk. "I don't know. I guess we just keep reading."

"I may need something stronger than tea," said Rocco.

———————◆————————

The threesome settled in for what proved to be a long afternoon, Lidia and Polly replenishing their cups with tea and Rocco drinking several bottles of beer.

With only a few letters remaining unread, the little party paused and, seeing it was nearly dark, decided it was time to take stock of what had been revealed so far. Polly started the summation.

"Well, let's see. We haven't been completely systematic. That is—we've sort of jumped about a bit, but from the signatures on the older letters, it's clear to me the ones from the 1800s are from the Count, as I had suspected from the beginning," said Polly, still holding the last letter read. "From what you've told me about the family connection with the Gamba Ghisellis—and that part about your family owing them a debt of gratitude. We may not know everything, but we know about the connection—and the timing—it's a good bet, I'd say." She smiled over the top of her reading glasses first at Lidia and then at Rocco.

"You may be right—the one from the father to the grieving daughter could be from the Count to Teresa. Poor girl, she was so in love with him, Bryon, that . . ." Lidia's voice trailed off as she thought of Teresa in those first days after learning of Byron's death: a young woman, privileged, her whole life still waiting for her, yet inconsolable. Lidia hoped the love of her father had helped her to get through those dark days. Then, realizing Polly and Rocco were waiting for her to finish her thought, she continued.

"Teresa would have needed the support of her family, of a loving father, to get through her grief," Lidia said. "But we still don't know why letters from the early nineteenth century—from the Gamba family—are mixed in with my family's."

"We know there's a family connection, from what you've found in your research, but I think there's another hint," said Polly, looking at Lidia—as if to gauge her readiness to hear Polly's theory.

"Okay," said Lidia, tentatively, knowing a rather large shoe was about to drop.

"We have a lot of letters here written years later from a Pietro to your great grandfather, many thanking him for support with Pietro's workers, for whatever went on there, labor disputes, I guess, that your great grandfather was apparently able to help with." Polly looked over at Rocco and continued. "Thanks to Rocco's translation, we've actually learned quite a bit." Rocco smiled at Polly. She continued. "And then, remember, the one about Pietro's oath to help Rodolfo in some way, as a way to express gratitude, it seems. This would be when the debt comes into play, after the Count and Teresa, so there is a family connection that goes beyond the debt—or your family wouldn't have come to own the box and its contents. You see? Somehow these two families, yours and the Gamba Ghisellis, became linked. The 'debt,' I suspect, is a *quid pro quo*, of sorts. That's the mystery still to be solved."

By this point, Polly was pacing back and forth, pointing her finger in the air with each new thought.

"I know you're on a roll, Polly, but in the newspaper article I found, my grandfather thanked a Ruggero Gamba, not anyone named Pietro," interrupted Lidia.

Polly let her arm drop to her side and stopped a minute. "Well, I can't answer that," she admitted. "Maybe we can't answer all the questions that remain on the basis of these letters. Now, where was I?" She began pacing again.

"These letters, the 'Pietro letters,' let's call them, are all dated in the late 1800s, so, as we've already said, we're beyond Teresa now, and into the generation that gave birth to the early flyers, like Mario Calderara." Polly stopped to look at Lidia.

"You remember from your reading that Mario's wife was called 'Emmy,'" but in Pietro's letters, he references a daughter named Amalia. My hunch is that she is the Emmy married to Mario. These are the people of your great-grandfather's generation. And your grandfather for some reason had these letters passed down to him from his father."

Lidia sat, brow furrowed, thinking this over. Rocco, at this point surely feeling tired, announced, "I'm not really following, ladies. It's great stuff, don't get me wrong, but I have to get going. I'm supposed to meet my daughter and her husband for dinner at their house tonight. She always worries when I'm even a little late." He looked around the chair where he was sitting. "My hat," he said, holding it up. "Anyway, when you get it all figured out—you're a pretty good detective, there, Polly—let me know what you find, okay?"

Lidia and Polly jumped up.

"Thank you so much," said Lidia, taking his hand. "I don't know what we would've done without you."

"Don't mention it," he said, putting his hat on. Then, looking in Polly's direction, he took it off again. "Thanks for the tea—and the beer—Polly."

"Rocco, you've been a dear. You're welcome here any time. Let me walk you out."

While Lidia waited for Polly to come back, she began turning the pages of the letters Rocco had read. She was looking for one from Pietro, one about a deeply troubling family episode. It had been addressed to Amalia, and it was about her sister who had died. She looked for the words *sorrella* and *morta*.

"Yes," said Polly, when she returned and Lidia showed her the letter she was reexamining. "I wanted to talk about that one next. The sentence that stuck with me when Rocco was reading, '*Tua sorella è morta per me.*'"

"'Your sister is dead to me,'" said Lidia. "Not the same as saying, 'Your sister is dead,' is it?"

"Not quite. The letter didn't go into great detail, but there had been a scandal involving the sister that had caused a terrible breach with the father."

"Right," said Lidia. "And there weren't any references to it in any of the other letters, were there?"

"Not that I recall," said Polly. "We've learned a lot today, Lidia, but your work here is just beginning."

"I think you're right. And you know, Polly, I'm ready to have at it."
As soon as the words were out, Lidia knew they were true. She was
eager to dive into the widening mystery.

"That's the spirit."

———————●———————

Later that evening, after hot chocolate with the twins and hearing
all about their skiing adventure, Lidia quickly dressed for her night
out with Harry, their first since the holidays. Harry had made res-
ervations for them at Pierangelo, a pricey choice, but he had been
putting in long hours on an escalating case and told Lidia when they
sat down that he had been looking forward to seeing her all day.

While Harry didn't go into details about the case that was keeping
him so busy, Lidia was happy to fill in the gap by telling him about
her day.

"It's pretty exciting, all right," said Harry. "And look at you—not
about to pull the covers up over your head anymore and wish it
would all go away."

That Harry approved of her new found curiosity, her desire to get
to the bottom of things, was gratifying to Lidia. She knew she had
turned a corner. "You know, there may be a very real connection
between me and Tina, Harry. In the end, I may find out we're related
in some way, but it's still hard to think that the connection caused
her to . . . end her life that way. I hope where I'm going with all this
doesn't end in that scenario—that she did it on purpose."

Harry gently pushed the plate of amoretti cookies aside and
reached for Lidia's hand. "Whatever is out there, Lidia, you'll handle
it. I know you will. I knew you'd get to this point," he said. "And you
know why? Look at all you've come through. You've been strong and
up to the challenge all along. The whole thing with the house threw
you, but it would've thrown anyone. It's not a small thing to have a
plane crash into your house."

Harry let his hand linger on hers. The light from the candle cast a soft glow on the table, on Harry, on everything. Lidia felt her face beginning to warm.

Rather than going back to Polly's, they found themselves at Harry's, and after a night of enjoying one another physically as much as they had enjoyed each other's dinner company, their morning lovemaking threatened to make Harry late for work. He told her then that he had received a call shortly after he and Lidia had fallen asleep. A special investigative unit was being formed, and the work would get underway at nine o'clock in the morning. Harry took a few last sips of coffee.

"Are you sure you don't mind a cab home?" he asked. "I don't like leaving you like this so soon on Sunday."

"Of course I'll take a cab," she said. "I'm not some fair damsel in distress, for heaven's sake."

Harry turned to her. "I'm sorry to be so tied up, Lidia. It looks like this case of mine is about to blow open. As soon as we have a breather, we have to talk, seriously talk, okay?"

Lidia felt a quick flutter in her chest. "What? Harry? You can't possibly leave on that note. I don't know whether that's a good thing, or—" Seeing the look on Harry's face, she knew the time was not right to press him. "Oh my God" she said, Are—you breaking up with me?"

Lidia, standing close to Harry, wearing one of his shirts loosely draped around her, looked at him and smiled playfully, taking the coffee cup from his hand. After their night and morning together, breaking up was not a likely option, she knew, and yet Lidia was a little unsettled by the news of the investigation that was leading to his sudden departure. Harry never talked much about his work—he couldn't really—and Lidia knew there was always the risk of a dangerous assignment.

Harry laughed. "Breaking up? Not quite," he said, "not quite." He took the cup from her and placed it on the counter before taking her hand and gently pressing it to his mouth.

And then he was gone. Lidia drew his shirt tight, hugging her arms around her waist.

Friends and Lovers

*R*occo is an interesting man, don't you think, Lidia?" asked Polly, turning onto the Post Road on their way to Greenwich Avenue. "I mean, he's a bit rough-hewn in a sense, but also rather courtly." Polly stared at the road ahead, a smile beginning to tilt her lips upward.

Lidia knew an opinion was not really called for. Polly had already made up her mind about Rocco. She liked him and did not need confirmation about him from her friend. The question was rhetorical, indicating only that Polly was open to talking about the man she found interesting. This resoluteness was a hallmark of Polly's character, thought Lidia, this and her everlasting affirmation of life. Here she was in her ninth decade and considering a relationship with a younger man.

"Wasn't it good of him to stay with us all afternoon Saturday translating my letters?" Lidia decided a question of her own would be the best way to start the conversation.

"I've decided to give him a little encouragement. I think he wants to ask me out, but he's not sure how I'll take it."

"Why do you think that?"

"He said so—when I walked him to the door." They were stopped at a red light. Polly looked in the rearview mirror and tapped her fingers on her forehead, gently putting her bangs in place. "His exact words were, 'This was nice, Polly. Maybe I could take you out for tea sometime, or beer.' Dear man, he seemed a little uncomfortable, as though he were being too forward."

Lidia had thought to tell Polly about Harry and their future "serious talk," as Harry had put it, but Polly's budding romance seemed to take precedence at the moment.

"So," continued Lidia, "how will you encourage him?"

"I'm going to call and ask him where one goes for a good cold beer and a hot cup of tea. The rest will be up to him." Glancing in Lidia's direction, Polly grinned, her blue eyes gleaming. "Dear me. Does this make me a—what do they call it—a cougar?"

"Yes," answered Lidia, laughing. "Yes, I think it does." *Good for you,* thought Lidia, admiring her friend's pluck, as they turned onto Greenwich Avenue.

"Look at that," said Polly. "A parking space right in front of the store. That's a good sign. Not easy, finding parking on the Avenue."

A few minutes later, Polly's friend Terry, wearing white jewelers' gloves, was carefully extracting the gold necklace and locket from the envelope Lidia had put them in. Terry had abundant chestnut brown hair and a boyish vitality, making his age difficult to determine. He wore wire-rimmed glasses that he had temporarily placed on the display case next to him in order to bring the jeweler's loupe to his right eye, beginning his examination. He was wearing brown corduroys and a dark blue sweater pulled over a light blue oxford cloth shirt. He looked like a college professor, a genial professor, Lidia thought, but she was too preoccupied to linger on such observations.

She caught herself lightly tapping her fingers on the glass and quickly drew her hand away. Nervously awaiting his verdict on the piece, she began walking up and down the long narrow aisle, casually looking at the sparkling rings, bracelets, and necklaces laid out before her in the glass cases on either side. Polly, in the meantime, was talking to one of the saleswomen, who obviously knew her.

Lidia, unmoved by the trove of jewels beckoning, was thinking about the gold necklace now in Terry's hand and mostly about the face in the locket. Who was it? Who had painted it—and when? The hair and clothing seemed timeless. Every detail could conceivably give Lidia another piece of the puzzle, but nothing was adding up to anything yet.

"Lidia," she heard Polly call, motioning for her to come. Terry had completed his examination.

"Well," he began, fitting his glasses over his ears. "The necklace itself is a twenty-two karat sautoir, or rope chain. Sautoirs are long, like this one. It's about twenty-eight inches, I'd say. They're called 'opera length' when they're this long—sometimes they're even longer and then looped into double strands."

When Terry paused, Lidia asked, "And the locket?"

"Yes, the locket. It's also twenty-two karat. Nothing unusual about it. It's in good shape, though, not scratched or anything, considering its age."

"Its age? How old is it?" asked Polly.

"I'd say it's early twentieth century, not so old, but still, for a locket that's probably about a hundred or so, it's in fine shape." Then, turning it on its side, Terry looked more closely at the locket's hinge. "Do you mind if I open it? I'll be careful."

"Oh, of course. I mean, we have. There's a portrait inside," said Lidia.

"Splendid." Terry opened it, and after further examination, he pronounced the locket in fine working order. He looked at the portrait and then at Lidia. "A relative?" he asked.

"We don't know who it is—yet," answered Lidia, feeling resolve straightening her spine. She was certain now she would find out who the young woman was even if she didn't know where to begin.

"A few things are a little hard to explain," he continued. "On the one hand, these necklaces with pendants or lockets were quite popular during the Edwardian era. On the other, miniature paintings in lockets were from an earlier time—before photography. Then again, the portrait could've been painted from a photo, I guess." Shaking his head, he said, "I'm not clearing things up much, am I?" He put the necklace back in the envelope, holding it with both hands. "Odd," he began. "You'd expect a miniature of a lover—or a lock of hair. Hair was quite common, too. But instead, there's a picture of a young woman—could very well have been a friend or relative, I suppose." Handing the envelope to Lidia, he said, "Anyway, I think we can conclude the necklace and locket are solid gold, early 1900s. That can be said with some certainty."

Lidia extended her hand to Terry. "Thank you so much," she said. "You've been a big help. How much do I owe you?"

"Don't think of it. Nothing, you owe me nothing. It was a pleasure. Lovely, really, but I'm afraid I haven't helped you very much."

"On the contrary. You've made me more certain than ever that I have to find out who this young woman was."

———————◆———————

On the way home, Lidia slumped down in her seat and closed her eyes, her mind filled with images of antique metal boxes, faded letters on crumbling paper, foreign words, velvet pouches with leather cords, and old jewelry—none providing clarity to the questions dogging her. She did not know where to turn next in unraveling the mystery of Tina, the connection with the Gamba Ghiselli family, and the identity of the girl in the paining.

"Is there anyone still alive whom you could call or write? Anyone who knew your parents, who might know more of your family history than you do at the moment?" Polly asked.

Immediately Lidia thought of her mother's address book, one of the few intact items she was able to recover from the ruins of her house on Apple Way. It had been inside the filing cabinet she had salvaged the day she walked the property—the day she met Harry.

"Polly, you're brilliant," said Lidia, opening her eyes and sitting up. For the rest of the drive home, she told Polly about the Sundays when her family went to Jones Beach to meet up with other *paesani* from Emilia-Romagna, most of whom were from Ravenna. "I, of course, don't remember any of them. I was too busy being disdainful of the foreigners my grandparents loved seeing. But maybe, just maybe, my mother kept the names and addresses or phone numbers of the people they used to meet. Wouldn't it be a miracle if some of them were still alive and in the same place?" Lidia wanted a miracle. She felt she was due something to break the current logjam of unknowing.

"All things are possible," said Polly. "You just have to put it out there, to the universe."

Before Lidia could run upstairs to rifle through the filing cabinet she kept in her room, she and Polly were met at the door by the twins, who were accompanied by Jena and Chloe.

"Guess who's got a boyfriend?" asked Carly.

Lidia looked at the foursome, smiles all around, though only Clarisse was sporting a blush.

"Well, I'm going to guess it's not you," answered Lidia.

"Right you are. One more try?"

"Not necessary. I can see by the downcast eyes and the red cheeks—hmm, just like a Victorian heroine—that it must be . . . Clarisse."

Jena said, "Yes!" at a decibel level, causing Polly to cover her ears. Soon Chloe and Carly joined in the merriment.

"Oh my word," said Polly. "Whatever happened to the feminists of yore? In my day, men were taken in stride. Have a boyfriend, if you want, but screaming? There was no screaming."

Lidia, listening to the scene unfold, thought about Polly's own attraction to Rocco. She had to admit, Polly was taking it in stride and going after what she wanted. She wasn't blasé about it, just in control, it seemed.

Lidia watched as Polly went to hang up her coat.

The foursome then settled into the comfort of the living room to fill Lidia in on the details.

Derek Duncan was not who you would expect for Clarisse, as it turned out. He was a total jock, as described by Jena, "but in a good way." While he was not one of the school's literati, as both Jena and Clarisse conceded, and while he was captain of the football team, he was, thankfully, also a first-rate poet. "We're publishing two of his poems in the *Sangraal* this spring. "They're really deep—dark, but very deep."

"Well, deep, that's good, but I'm not so sure about the dark part. Not too dark, I hope," said Lidia, on hearing the news. "And his grades, how are those, and his manners, and his attitude toward women? You know, those things that a mother would like to know about?" inquired Lidia.

He got the seal of approval on all counts, according to all four girls, and—not to be discounted—he was dreamy.

"Wavy black hair and blue eyes to die for," said Jena, looking happily at Clarisse.

"Well, that's all well and good. So how did all this come about?" Turning to Clarisse, Lidia asked, "What happened that makes it official, that he's your boyfriend? Do kids still go steady? Did he give you a ring?"

"No, Mom. We've been going out for a while now. I guess I haven't wanted to talk about it just yet. But to answer your question, we both just decided we wouldn't go out with anyone else—just each other. So that's what's different now. We're at another level now."

"So it's more serious now," Lidia said.

"I guess so," replied Clarisse. "You could say that."

Lidia looked hard at Clarisse as she took this in. *How did I not notice?* Lidia wondered. This caused her to think that maybe she had been too involved in her own world—with Harry—and too absorbed to see the signs. Clarisse had a serious boyfriend. She would have to have a serious talk with Clarisse. Her daughter (was it possible?) could be having sex, and her mother—so involved with her own lover—hadn't seen the signs, hadn't talked to her about the awful responsibility. Lidia put her hand to her heart as she thought of Clarisse leaving her childhood behind.

"I see," said Lidia tentatively, hoping not to reveal too much about her concerns. "Well, I'm happy for you, really—and I hope we can talk more—soon—and you can tell me more about Duncan."

"*Derek*, Mom. His first name is *Derek*. And where's Polly?" asked Clarisse as she looked around for the resident sage and advisor.

————◉————

After Jena and Chloe left, Polly joined the Raven women in the living room whereupon Clarisse immediately asked, "You took off the second you heard the news. Don't you approve, Polly . . . of Derek?"

"So, it's Derek, is it? Nice name." Polly considered whether it was wise to speak, and then without too much more thought, weighed in. "Look—since you've asked—I had sincerely hoped you would make it through high school without a serious relationship. I wasn't so worried about Carly—she seems quite focused, but—and I'm speaking candidly here, Clarisse—so stop me . . ." Polly paused, giving Clarisse a chance to tell her to mind her own business, but Clarisse instead looked down and softly said, "Go on."

"I've worried about you because you are so open—to people and to life—and sometimes others, boys, take advantage of that." Polly, who had squeezed in between Carly and Clarisse on the sofa when she came into the room, reached for Clarisse's hand. "Do you remember when I came back from Bali, I gave you the necklace of Saraswati, the goddess of knowledge? I wanted her for you as a reminder of your fine mind and my hope that you would be spending the next so many years developing it along with your very real musical gifts."

Clarisse let her hand remain in Polly's, but she drew a breath and held it before protesting. "But Polly," she began, "Why can't I do both? I can still be focused and have a boyfriend. I'm not so scatterbrained, am I? Is that what you think?"

"No, of course not. I don't know, I shouldn't, it's not my place to . . ."

"Not true. I asked you. Next to Mom, you're the one—my go-to goddess."

"That's good. I like that, 'go-to goddess.' I don't think I've ever been called that before." After a little mood-lightening laughter, Polly let go of Clarisse's hand and folded her own two in her lap. "Okay. Let's leave it, then. You know my concerns, and I'm being told you have things under control. So I will of course take you at your word."

"Just a minute," said Lidia. "If the time is right, I'd like to talk about something else, about intimacy . . ."

At this, Carly sighed deeply enough to convey exasperation to all within earshot. She waited until it was clear her audience had taken notice before saying, "I don't think we have to go there. Isn't it sort of, you know, personal?"

Lidia turned to Clarisse. "Is that what you think?" Clarisse shrugged her shoulders and did not make eye contact.

"Have I waited too long to have this conversation? Are you both now to be completely on your own in matters of sex?"

Carly was the first to answer. "Mom, you're forgetting something. We've had the discussion—when we were younger. It was just hypothetical then; now it's real, but those conversations, they're still with us. Aren't they, Clarisse?"

Carly nodded at Clarisse, as if to encourage her to speak up.

"Yes. Mom, look, you don't have to worry. First, Derek and I, we're not, you know, 'intimate'—yet. It doesn't mean we won't be, ever. I have feelings when I'm with him that I've never had before—but if we do decide to . . . it's you I'll come to. It's you I'll want to talk to."

Lidia had been lightly perched on the ottoman of the club chair, and she now rose immediately and pulled Clarisse up to fold her in her arms. "That's all I can ask, Clarisse. That's all any mother can ask." When they parted and sat back down, Lidia took a tissue from her sweater pocket to wipe her eyes.

"So let's see," said Polly, having taken in the whole scene with some satisfaction, "so far we've decided that first you have a dreamy boyfriend, and next we know he won't keep you from your studies, and that finally you're not having sex. I'd say this has been a successful chat. When do we meet him?"

"Soon," answered Clarisse. "Very soon, I promise."

———————●———————

After the little group broke up, Lidia knocked on Carly's door. She was grateful to her daughter for helping her and Clarisse make their way through a delicate topic. She also wanted to be sure Carly was really okay with things—with her sister having a boyfriend, a serious boyfriend. The twins had always been so close, and Lidia wondered if Carly would begin to feel left out when she and her sister were no longer spending so much of their free time together.

"It's not just the two of you now," she said, sitting on Carly's bed. "She won't always be there to go places, to talk about things. She'll be spending more time with Derek."

Carly, who had been lying down reading, put her book aside and sat up, hugging her knees to her chest. "I know, Mom. It's true, I guess, but you don't have to worry about us. Clarisse and I, we don't even have to talk—I know how she feels even when she's miles away. If we don't talk for a while, we both know we'll catch up when we can. We'll always be together, even when we're not." Looking up at her mother, she asked, "Does that make sense?"

Lidia stroked Carly's long dark hair, putting the strands that had fallen forward back behind her ears. "Yes, darling, it does, but only because I've raised you two, and I've seen the twin thing up close."

"Right, like the time I was coughing, you asked me my symptoms, and gave me medicine, but it was actually Carly who had the flu?"

"Something like that."

"Mom, you know, I also have friends. It's not like I depend so much on Clarisse for everything. I have a social life—I have Chloe . . ."

"I know you do. I know you two are very close."

Carly flung her legs over the side of the bed and sat up next to Lidia. "We've decided something. I hope you'll be okay with it. Chloe and I have decided that no matter what schools we get into, we'll pick the one that takes us both. So if I get Amherst, let's say—which is pretty high on my list—but the only one we both get into together is UMass, we'll go to UMass so we can be roommates."

Lidia's first reaction was to tell Carly all the reasons why she thought this was not such a good idea. She caught herself stiffening, her lips pursing, but then in a flash she envisioned Carly, ever sensitive to her mother's moods, withdrawing. Thinking to herself that it had been a good day, why ruin it, she took a deep breath, exhaled, and relaxed.

"You two have been friends forever. It must be hard to think of being separated." Lidia put her hands on her thighs and stood. "So I guess you'll have some decisions to make before too long."

"Yeah," said Carly. "Another heavy family discussion to look forward to. Don't worry—nothing happens without you."

At the door, Lidia turned to Carly and smiled. "How did I get so lucky?"

Later that night, after the dinner things had been put away and the girls had gone to bed, Lidia stood at the library door, wondering if she should disturb Polly, who was at the computer busily checking her accounts. Polly turned toward Lidia, apparently sensing her presence. "What is it, dear?"

"I need a drink. You?"

"Hmm. Brandy would settle nicely now. Yes, I believe I would."

"Here or in the living room?"

"How about here? The fire's already burning."

"Great." Lidia began pouring their drinks. "It's downright cozy in here."

"I know—I don't often indulge in heating up this behemoth of a room, but it is winter." Polly moved to the leather couch, sat, and fluffed up several pillows behind her. "I thought you'd be checking out your mother's address book by now."

Lidia handed Polly a crystal snifter and sat beside her. "I will, later. I just realized I needed to spend some time with the girls tonight—and to relax with you for a bit."

"Quite a night, wasn't it? You know, Lidia, I do believe Clarisse will be fine. She's a very sensible girl."

Lidia told Polly about Carly's decision to room with Chloe at college. "Those two have been together since grade school. I guess Chloe is almost as close to Carly as a sister."

Polly looked down at her drink, swirling the amber liquid, watching it reflect in the intricate cuts of the crystal. "I'm not certain they've sorted out all their feelings for each other. They're close, they love each other, certainly, and thinking of being separated is difficult—very difficult."

In the back of Lidia's mind, a muffled voice was raising a question she couldn't quite hear. She let it go, feeling the warmth of the brandy relieve all her cares for a while.

As the effects of the brandy began to wane, Lidia said goodnight and made her way upstairs. She closed the door to her room and opened the closet. She bent down to pull open the drawer of her portable filing cabinet. Under D she found *Documents—Mom*. It had once been a much thicker file filled with banking statements, records of paid bills, and insurance claims. Now all that remained were the obit notice, the cemetery plot information, her mother's death certificate, and her old address book. Lidia pulled it out. An artifact of years past, its yellow daisies against an orange background brought back instant memories. The book had remained for years on the kitchen counter directly under the wall telephone, its avocado green cord always twisted in various untamable coils. Lidia sat on the floor and began looking for names and addresses of her parents' old friends.

By the time she had finally completed the *Zs*, she had found six names that looked promising—all of them in either Queens or on Long Island and all with addresses and phone numbers. She put tabs on the pages with the names she had underlined and put the book on the night table by the bed. Her last thoughts before falling asleep were of Clarisse and Derek and of Carly and Chloe.

By noon the next day, sitting in the living room, her mother's address book on the sofa beside her, Lidia was disconnecting from the fifth number either not in working order or no longer belonging to anyone her parents might have known. *Only one more to go,* she said to herself. It had been a long shot, thinking anyone would still be at the same number or even still alive. As she picked up the address book again, she consoled herself. *There's always Google,* she thought, as she pressed the last digit of the number for Maria and Enrico Nardini into her cell phone.

"Hello?"

Lidia felt her heart jump. "Yes—hello. Is there a Maria or an Enrico Nardini at home?"

Long pause, then, "Who's calling?"

"I'm Lidia Raven, the daughter of Rudy and Giovanna. They were friends with the Nardinis—a long time ago." The woman who had answered did not sound elderly. The Nardinis would be in their eighties, Lidia figured. "I'm sorry. I don't even know if I have the right number. Is this the Nardini residence?"

"Yes, it is—and Maria is my mother. I'm Lana. Hang on a minute." Lidia could hear muffled voices in the background. The woman had obviously put her hand over the receiver. In a few seconds, she heard the rumbling sound of the phone passing, not easily, from one person to another. Then she heard the clunk of something metal, an earring, possibly.

"Hullo? I'm Maria. Who's this?"

In the course of a five-minute conversation, Lidia learned that Maria and her husband had revered her grandfather—"He was a very generous man. The whole family in Ravenna, good people," she said—and that Maria had been close to Lidia's mother. "But we lost touch. Over the years. It's hard to keep up with old friends," Maria had said, somewhat uncomfortably, Lidia thought, especially when she told Maria both her parents were now dead. "All gone," Maria said. "All of them, all gone. That's what happens. You live, and everyone else dies. What good is it, living a long time?"

"I'm sorry if the news about my parents upset you," said Lidia.

"It's okay," said Maria softly, quickly changing the subject. "Tell me about what you do."

Lidia stammered, not wanting to get into details about her life, for fear it would be too much for Maria to grasp in a brief conversation, given recent events—out of work, divorce, plane crash—certainly not that, not yet.

"My girls, I have twins," she said.

After a few minutes about a subject that seemed to lift Maria's spirits, she said she was putting Lana back on.

Lidia heard a muffled voice as Maria handed over the receiver.

"She gets tired quickly," said Lana. "But please, won't you come for a visit? It would do her good to see you. Just hearing from you has cheered her up."

They agreed that Lidia would make the trip to the Nardini home in Franklin Square, Long Island, the next day.

"She's changed since her illness," Lana said of her mother. "She was an elegant, educated woman, but you won't see that, unfortunately."

———————— ◆ ————————

Maria Nardini was eighty-five. She was a delicate woman whose face was miraculously unwrinkled. This was not easy to detect at first because her smooth complexion, under several layers of makeup, was all but hidden. In fact, with the combination of large black glasses, heavy gold hoop earrings, and a multi-colored rather thick headband covering most of her still dark hair, her actual face was a mere suggestion. Lidia had a fleeting thought of a very petite, near-sighted gypsy fortuneteller—sort of like the glass encased ones at a penny arcade.

"So you're Rudy and Gina's little girl," Maria said as they sat down in the living room, Maria, with Lana's help, in a straight-back chair with a cushion for her back. She motioned Lidia to the sofa across from her, a coffee table between them.

"I remember you. I do. You weren't happy. To be with us. Always looking for kids." Maria laughed softly, as though the effort it took might hurt her. "Am I right, Lidia?"

Maria had had a stroke a year ago, making movement difficult, and while her speech was largely unaffected, Lidia had the distinct impression that Maria wanted to say much more than she was able to. Maria may have been under assault from her mounting years, but she had been a vibrant woman once—that was evident.

"Here I am at the beach. With your mother," Maria said, pointing to a small black-and-white photo in the album she had asked Lana to take from the top shelf of the bookcase. "We look pretty good, don't we? In our bathing suits. I can't do that anymore. Parade around like that. Or go for a swim. Lana pushes me on the boardwalk. When the weather is nice."

Lana was a tall woman, as imposing as her mother was slight. She'd introduced herself and her mother to Lidia when she arrived, but then, after they were seated, she took a chair to the other side of the room, perhaps to be unobtrusive, though Lidia wasn't sure why.

"I'm here if you need me, Mama, but this is your visit," she said.

Lidia knew that Lana was hoping her arrival would be good medicine for her mother and didn't want to do or say anything to interfere with Lana's hopes.

The small room was full of dark, heavy furniture that had come from Ravenna when Maria's mother and father emigrated in the early 1920s. "We had money then. You can tell by all this furniture— can't you? Things weren't so bad—back home. In Italy. My father wanted to make it in America. He didn't want to be under his father's thumb anymore. He was strong—my father." She carefully took a sip of the coffee Lana had made for them. "Things were good for a while. We had a big house overlooking the water. It's all gone now." Lidia watched as Maria methodically put her cup on the silver tray lying securely on her lap and then precisely wiped her mouth on a neatly pressed linen napkin, dabbing one side and then the other.

"Poppa did okay again after a while. He worked hard, and we weren't poor." Lidia was eager to get back to her own family, but she didn't want to interrupt Maria, who seemed to have grown a few inches taller as she sat in her chair reminiscing. Lidia believed her patience would pay off in the end, and so she listened for whatever nugget of information would be revealed as Maria continued telling her stories.

———◗▬———

Stuck in traffic on the way home, Lidia thought to look toward the New York harbor while she was stopped on the Throggs Neck Bridge. She had one hand on her forehead, shielding her eyes from the afternoon sun. When she was a little girl on the way to the beach with her family, she'd always looked for the Statue of Liberty from the bridge. For a brief moment in the bright sunlight, she imagined seeing the family Chevy going by. Squinting, she could see her grandfather driving, talking to her from the front seat, "She's there, Lidia—Lady Liberty—who let us into America." Lidia never saw the lady, but she had always looked. She turned now to the road ahead to see the traffic had lifted, as had her spirits when she discovered during her visit with Maria that her grandfather had known the young woman whose picture was in the locket.

Just as Lidia had been losing hope that her trip to Long Island would help to answer any of her questions, Maria—freely associating—had blurted out, "Your great grandfather, Rodolfo, he knew many powerful men in Ravenna." She spoke of the family's success, how her great grandfather had risen to prominence. The conversation had taken the turn Lidia was waiting for. Wanting desperately to know about the picture, Lidia took the envelope with the necklace out of her bag. When Maria paused to take another sip of coffee, Lidia asked, "Do you know who this is?" The miracle Lidia had longed for began to unfold. "That's Angelica," Maria said.

Lidia's greatest hope—that all the mysteries surrounding Tina and her family would soon be solved—was not to be. She was, however, humbly beginning to accept her fate. It was as if she was wandering in a very large house with many rooms, and for every door she walked through, another was waiting.

"But who's Angelica," asked Polly that evening after dinner. Carly and Clarisse, also eager to know, both said, "Wait for us," disappearing into the kitchen to finish cleaning up the dinner things and loading the dishwasher. When they emerged a few minutes later, the foursome settled into the living room to hear the rest of Lidia's story. "Maria said Nonno rarely spoke of his family back in Italy, but she knew Angelica was my grandfather's brother's wife . . . it's complicated."

"So . . ." began Carly, pondering this news. "That means Angelica is your aunt—your great aunt."

"Exactly. I knew of her, but I never met her or my great uncle Paolo. He was my grandfather's older brother."

"So at least that part of the mystery is solved, then," said Polly.

"Well, not exactly. Maria said there was *uno scandalo*, apparently some big scandal involving Angelica, but she either didn't know what it was or she wouldn't tell me."

"Why wouldn't she tell you? It must've been like a hundred years ago or something," said Clarisse. "Seems silly."

"Yes and no," said Polly. "Silly by today's standards, but in those days scandals were spoken of *sotto voce*. Everyone might have known about it, but it wasn't broadcast. Not like today, for heaven sake, where everybody has to tell everything. All this baring of souls . . . it was unheard of. Good people just didn't do it."

"What could it have been, then?" Carly asked.

"The usual, probably—the sad tale of a 'fallen woman.' That's what it's always about, anything involving a woman—it's always about sex," said Clarisse.

"I don't know," said Lidia. "But I thought I'd give it some time. Maybe Maria will get over her unwillingness to talk—and I really don't know how much she knows."

———————◉———————

Over the next two weeks, Lidia tried to keep her mind off Harry's absence. She had not seen or talked to him since the morning he had left her standing in his shirt at his house. She knew he would call her if he could, and that's what worried her. Why couldn't he call? She busied herself staying in touch with the Nardinis. She called regularly and had gone back out to the Island to meet Lana and Maria on the boardwalk. She had spent an afternoon walking with them and sitting in the sun. It did her heart good, Lana said, to see her mother happy. "You remind my mother of her best days—many of them spent right here. I'm so glad you came," she said, putting a hand over Lidia's as Lidia pushed Maria's wheelchair toward the parking lot on their way back to the car.

Lidia wasn't learning anything new about Angelica, but she enjoyed hearing the enthusiasm in Maria's voice when they talked, and the sparkle in her eyes when she saw Lidia at the beach. Lidia had no choice but to accept Maria's silence around Angelica. And so she waited patiently. She believed that one day she would take her into her confidence and tell her Angelica's story.

Back at 10 Apple Way, Lidia began to throw herself into the choices she faced as rebuilding gathered momentum. There were moldings to select, fixtures, cabinets, doors, hinges, doorknobs—no decision was too small. Lidia looked through dozens of books to select sinks and tubs and dozens more in preparation for the day when paint would be applied and wallpaper would be hung. "I never would've had time for this when I was working," she said in exasperation to no one in particular on the day she finally decided on a pale yellow paper with delicate delphiniums for the master bath. Her total absorption in these countless details made it less likely that Lidia would focus on her unanswered questions—or on the absence of Harry. She thought about the night he had said they needed to talk—seriously. At first he had allayed her fears that *serious* meant *bad,* but as the days wore on, with no word, doubt was creeping in and curling up, making itself a constant companion in Harry's absence. Two weeks became three. A long time not to hear from him.

Added to this was the bliss apparent in Polly's smile and cheery countenance whenever she was in earshot of the name *Rocco,* uttered frequently since Lidia spoke with him daily about one decision or another. Ever since Polly had called Rocco, they had been inseparable.

The picture of them Rocco had taken at the tavern in Westport on their first "date" was now Polly's screensaver. Lidia found the suddenness of Polly's total infatuation difficult to accept. Polly was so levelheaded, so even-keeled, but she had given herself so completely to the possibility of a new love in her life, Lidia could only marvel at her daring. When Lidia had asked Polly if it were possible she was "rushing into things," Polly said in return, "How much time you do think I have left to spend thinking about it?" It wasn't that Lidia resented Polly's near giddiness these days, it was rather that she missed her own—with Harry.

On the day Lidia was in the store selecting wallpaper, Harry had called and left a message on her cell phone, but not recognizing the number, she hadn't picked up. Later, going through her messages, she heard Harry's voice. "How could I be so stupid?" she said. "Of course he was calling from a different phone." He never used his cell phone on the job; too risky, he had told her, not explaining why. Hearing his voice, she cursed herself for not answering.

"Lidia, I'm . . . sorry. I'm away on business and couldn't call. I told you I'd be tied up for a while and . . . I can't talk about it . . . but I hope you can . . ." He stopped abruptly as though something had distracted him. "Look. I've got to go . . ." he said, and he hung up. Lidia let the phone slip back into her bag. Doubt had a new companion: fear. What was going on? Was he in danger? He had hung up so abruptly, Lidia pictured someone hovering over him, putting a gun to his head. She put these dark thoughts out of her mind, but still she had never felt so helpless. There was no one to call at his office to find out where he was—it was the FBI, for heaven's sake. He was "away on business," he had said. Lidia had to laugh. *Not like any business I've ever known,* she said to herself. No, Harry was out there somewhere pursuing whatever threat needed pursuing, and he couldn't tell her about it. The wallpaper with the delphiniums began to recede in importance, no longer capable of bringing even a modicum of satisfaction.

Polly, when she wasn't preoccupied, was a comfort. "You've got to have faith that he's part of a professional team and that they know what they're doing. The FBI doesn't take stupid chances. They're trained professionals and Harry's one of them—a skilled, competent man who knows how to do his job." These words did help in the light of day, but at three o'clock in the morning—the hour at which Lidia now woke routinely—Doubt and Fear were who stayed with her, keeping vigil. They were a lonely threesome.

And so it was, by day Lidia let herself be consumed with the business of getting on, caring for the girls, working on selections for the new house—even looking up old friends from work and testing the waters of reemployment. She was in the midst of registering with an online networking site when Lana called. Lidia was reluctant to get her hopes up, but there it was. Lana had called, out of the blue.

"I have something you may be interested in knowing," Lana said.

The something, it turned out, was the name of someone who knew Angelica, who knew her well, in fact: her daughter, Teresa.

Teresa, thought Lidia. *Is her namesake Byron's Teresa?*

After the call, Lidia was frantic to talk to Polly. Was she out walking? Lidia paced back and forth in the living room. She looked out the dining room window. She moved to the library and looked out the window several times more before returning to the living room. She finally noticed that Opal was in none of her usual spots napping in the sun. *Well, that explains it—she's walking with Opal,* Lidia surmised. More pacing. Finally, she heard Polly in the mudroom. Lidia met her there before Polly had a chance to take off her coat and boots, before she had a chance to take the leash from Opal's collar.

"We were just walking out on the point. I hope we weren't too long," Polly said, putting her boots under the bench and hanging up her coat. "I wasn't expecting a welcoming party. What is it?" Polly refreshed Opal's water dish and walked into the kitchen with Lidia on her heels.

As Polly began to put water on for tea, Lidia said, "It's Lana. She called me a while ago, when you were out. She and Maria were keeping something from me after all."

Polly stopped what she was doing and sat at the table as Lidia proceeded to fill her in on the details of her conversation with Lana. "It's complicated. I hardly know where to begin . . ."

Angelica, the lovely young mystery woman whose likeness was preserved in the painting in the locket had had a daughter, Teresa. Lidia paused before telling Polly the rest. Teresa, it turned out, lived in Dayton, Ohio. Centerville, where the Walters live, to be exact. When Lidia first heard this, the effect on her had been so powerful, she could see nothing but a vast white sky, and then slowly the image of a Piper Cherokee emerged—coming straight at her. The possible connection between her and Tina was becoming more and more real, the likelihood of a random accident culminating in the loss of her home, less and less probable.

Hearing this news, Polly blurted out, "Oh my, that's a blow, isn't it? I mean, if we jump to conclusions, which we shouldn't." But then she continued, "On the other hand, Clarisse may have been right—a family scandal—about sex. It's always about sex, she said. So let's see . . . Angelica was married to Paolo, your grandfather's brother."

Lidia took a deep breath. "Yes . . . that's right."

"So her daughter, this Teresa, would be your father's cousin."

"Right again."

Then Polly said, "And if—"

"I think I know where this is going." Lidia held her breath.

"I might as well say it then. If Teresa is, she may be, Tina's real mother, then Tina would be your second cousin."

"Yes," said Lidia, exhaling.

"No wonder you're looking a little pale. Can't I get you anything?

"No . . . I'm just feeling a little weird. Especially when I think . . . if I let myself think that it was no coincidence, Tina's flying into my house."

"But still, Lidia, it makes no sense, why she would do that."

"I know it makes no sense, but I have to find out for sure about her. I can't just speculate. And to find out the truth about Tina, I have to find out about Teresa."

Polly then asked Lidia about the rest of her conversation with Lana.

"It was so strange. She said it was Maria's decision—that they had to tell me about Teresa. Maria had become quite fond of me, Lana said. My phone calls and visits had lifted some of the gloom since her illness. But it seemed that was about all they wanted to or could tell me. Lana did say that Maria had been in touch with Teresa for years. Apparently my parents stayed in touch with Teresa, too, but never mentioned her to me. They even saw her from time to time when I was in college. They all knew her. She even visited here when I was very young. Maria called Teresa when my mother died."

"She knew your mother died? I thought they were shocked when you told them about your parents on that first visit?"

"Yes, Lana was quite troubled by that, and once they got to know me better, they felt terrible about misleading me. Maria never lost touch with my parents either, like she told me. She was at my father's funeral, but that was so long ago, I don't remember her there at all. And by the time Mom died, Maria was already frail and couldn't go. It seems they kept all this from me because of Teresa. They didn't think they could tell me anything without her knowledge. But it's so strange, all this secrecy. I just don't get it."

"So Lana, with Maria's blessing, told you about Teresa, but why?"

"Here's the strangest thing of all. Teresa called Maria when she read in the papers about Tina and the crash."

"Oh dear, now that's a smoking gun."

"Yes, and that's where the information stops."

"Meaning that's all they knew to tell you, or that's all they wanted to tell you?"

"Apparently all they felt they could tell me. They felt the rest was up to Teresa. And she said she would talk to me."

Polly reached across the table and put her hand on Lidia's. "What will you do now?" she asked.

"I'm going to Dayton, I guess, to meet Teresa. It's funny, though, isn't it? Remember when Harry had to convince me to face my fears? And now it looks like I'll be tracking down more of this family saga— but this time without him."

"Of course, I remember. Harry's been a great help to you—and he will be again. I'm sure of it."

And so it was settled. During winter break, Lidia would go to Dayton while the twins went to Vermont with Owen and Robert to Robert's ski house. Owen was elated by the progress he was making with his daughters. This was a first, the girls joining their father on a trip with him and his partner. The girls were less ecstatic, but they were willing to go. This was a big step, one Lidia would have mulled over—testing it out—to see if she were happy or reluctant to give up this last hold she had over Owen. Would have mulled it over, that is, had she not been so preoccupied with the unknowns swirling around her. Like where was Harry? And what would come of this proposed meeting with Teresa? She told herself, finally, it was a good thing that the twins were going with their father and Robert—and then she returned to her own world of cares.

Polly would hold down the fort, as she put it, looking after Opal while Lidia was gone. It did seem, Lidia had noticed somewhat sadly, that Opal was quite smitten with Polly and the attention she lavished on her, always at the ready with a treat and a scratch behind the ears. "Opal is great company, and besides, I also have Rocco," Polly said happily. "I'll be fine. Makes me wonder, though, what did I do before all of you came into my life?"

What Lidia Learned

*V*oicemails to Harry on the way to the airport:

#1: "I hope you're getting this, Harry. Just wanted to let you know, I'm going to Dayton. I'm chasing a lead—you'd be proud of me, Harry. I'm a woman obsessed."

#2: "Remember when we went to Dayton together? I'm hoping to get home tonight, but . . . last time, I was happy for the bad weather . . . that kept us, overnight."

#3 (from the plane): "Okay, Harry—I have to turn off my phone, we're about to take off."

After leaving this last message, Lidia looked to see if by chance she had missed an attempt by Harry to reach her. Nothing. Lidia clicked her phone off and let it slide into the bottom of her bag before stowing it under the seat in front of her as she had been instructed. Lidia seemed unaware as a hefty businessman wedged himself into the seat next to her. She was staring at her bag as though the phone, now off, were holding Harry hostage. She imagined him trying to reach her and not getting through. She looked out the window to see the airport and White Plains receding beneath her. This was the same morning flight she had taken with Harry just a few short months ago. So much had changed since then. They had become so close, so intimate. Lidia, trying to shake the dark mood that had descended, began thumbing through the inflight magazine. After the second ad showing a couple in each other's arms, Lidia closed it with an emphasis, causing her seatmate to turn her way. Lidia looked out the window again, not wanting to strike up a conversation. The plane had ascended above the clouds. It was a lovely day, but all Lidia could think about was Harry and their first time together that night in Dayton.

There was so much more between them now than just the physical attraction they shared. That part of it, though, was a marvel to Lidia, who thought she would never feel such passion again. There was a genuine connection between them. That was why this silence, this separation, was doubly hard to take. She had finally let herself give in to this possibility—that Harry would be a part of her life for a long time; for the rest of her life—she had finally come to wish for it. And now this vacuum. She couldn't doubt him, not now. Of course Polly was right—she had to have faith. Harry hadn't abandoned her. He was for all intents and purposes incommunicado—and he would surface. She just had to be patient. And he had to be safe, she prayed. *Please keep him safe.*

As soon as Lidia walked into the terminal at the Dayton airport, she was reminded what day it was. Hastily assembled kiosks displaying single red roses in plastic tubes suspended from metal holders lined the walkways, each with an attendant vying for the attention of potential takers passing by. In one there were bright red helium-filled balloons, one of which had escaped, bumping against the ceiling like a nodding head. "Yes," it was saying, "get something now before it's too late." In another, heart-shaped boxes of chocolate candy were stacked precariously on a narrow counter. In a gift shop, women wearing tailored suits under their coats were busily picking out cards. Men carrying briefcases had boxes of candy tucked under one arm. Were they flying to meet the recipients of these tokens of love, or were they coming home from business trips, hoping to have something to give tonight at dinner? Lidia observed them all, reminded that she didn't have a valentine to give to Harry, and he would not have one for her. She buttoned up her coat and tossed her hair back as she made her way to the car rental counter.

She was meeting Teresa at an Italian restaurant south of the airport. When she arrived at the address, Main Street in Centerville, she pulled into a parking space in front of the building and was dismayed to see that the restaurant was closed. She was fumbling around in her bag for her phone when the front door opened to reveal an elderly woman with long white hair pulled back in a neat bun. The woman was tall and slightly bent, wearing a grey cardigan sweater over a black wool skirt. She motioned Lidia to come in. As she turned to go back inside, Lidia made note of the woman's dark stockings and low-heeled shoes, adding the final touch to her unassuming appearance.

Lidia entered the restaurant and followed the woman, who extended her hand and introduced herself as Teresa—DiRavenna. "I'm sorry for the confusion," she said. "The restaurant will not open until later, but the owner is a good friend and said we could meet here. I am afraid my apartment would not be suitable." Teresa held fast to Lidia's hand, until she realized what she was doing and released it. "Forgive me, but you look so much like . . . you remind me of someone very close to me."

"Oh?" said Lidia, sensing Teresa was alluding to Tina, but when Teresa didn't say anything more, Lidia decided to let it go. There would be time for that conversation, Lidia thought. After all, that's why she was here, to find out what Teresa could or would tell her about Tina. The two of them moved toward the tables.

Lidia slid into a long banquette near the entrance. Teresa sat in a chair across from her, a long table covered in white linen separating them. The sun shone through the windows and the beveled glass of the front door, making the water goblets, gold-trimmed plates, and silverware glisten. The abundant sunlight also shone on Teresa's face, revealing careworn eyes, the skin around them lined. Deeper lines framed her mouth and downturned lips. Not a happy woman, Lidia surmised, but her reserve aside, Lidia thought she saw a family resemblance in her height, the shape of her eyes and nose. Teresa was speaking about the restaurant's owners, a husband and wife from Tuscany, and Lidia began to pick up on traces of an accent in her voice.

"I'm sorry I couldn't invite you to my home," Teresa said again.

Sensing she felt awkward about the restaurant rendezvous, Lidia wanted to put her at ease. "This is a lovely place to meet. I'm just glad you had the time and could see me. This is fine, really," she said.

"Tell me about you," said Teresa.

Lidia told her a little about herself and her girls, but she soon guided the conversation to Lana and Maria.

"I'm so happy to have found them," said Lidia.

"No more than they are about you. Lana has told me what a tonic you have been for her mother."

After two glasses of Barolo brought to the table compliments of the owner, Regina, Teresa and Lidia agreed they had better eat something. Regina explained that the chef had prepared a special dish for them, fettuccine ragù alla bolognese. She poured another glass of wine when the main dish arrived. Helplessly yielding to the effects of the Barolo and the scent emanating from the steamy ragù before her, Lidia was beginning to forget the purpose of the visit—but then Teresa began her story. "My mother was a Gamba Ghiselli," she said.

Lidia could see Teresa's mouth moving, but the words were out of synch, echoing in her head after they were spoken. She asked Teresa to repeat what she had said. She put her hands to her temples. Now she knew without doubt what until now she had only suspected— that she was related, through her great uncle's marriage to Angelica, to the Gamba Ghisellis. So this was it. The pieces of this intricate puzzle were going to come together.

"They were a very important family in Ravenna," said Teresa. My mother was the youngest. Her sister made a good marriage, and Grandpa expected the same of my mother, but Mama had a wild streak. Today we would say she was independent, that she had a mind of her own, but her times were different. Her father, Grandpa, was the mayor at that time, a man of business—with power. And yet he could not control his daughter."

Teresa swirled the wine in her glass and then put it down. She touched the end of the table with both her hands. "You can imagine, when she said one day that she was in love with a common laborer, what Grandpa did." Teresa laughed softly to herself. "He nearly threw her out of his house. But she wouldn't give the boy up, and soon rumors began to spread—in shops, cafés, all over town. When Grandpa learned of the gossip, he was furious, but it was more than that. He was afraid no prosperous young man would have her. Eventually, he put her in a convent. He was ready to declare her dead to the family. That would have been the end of it, but Papa had always loved my mother, and he was heartsick that she had been sent away. He was jealous of the young man she loved, but he couldn't bear it that she was gone. His brother saw a solution. But first I should tell you something."

Lidia's heart began to pound, not sure what was coming.

"We are related."

Lidia let out a sigh of relief. Now they could address everything between them in the open. Apparently, Teresa was ready to let all the old barriers fall away and all the old secrets be told.

"Frankly," she replied, "all I know so far is what I've been able to search out. I know there was a connection between my family and the Gamba Ghisellis of Ravenna. And the locket with the picture of Angelica came to be in my grandfather's things, but the rest is speculation. And then there's the accident, the crash into my house . . ."

Teresa put up a hand to stop her, with a look of great sadness. "Please, not yet."

Lidia reached into her bag and pulled out a small package of tissues, handing one to Teresa. "I'm so sorry. I didn't mean to upset you."

"I know," Teresa said, wiping her eyes. "You've been very troubled too. A terrible thing happened to you and your family. And you've been very kind to my dear friend, Maria. It's time you knew the whole story, but we must start at the beginning."

Teresa started by putting the family puzzle together for Lidia. "Your great-grandfather, the first Rodolfo, and my grandfather, Pietro. Let us start there."

As Teresa spoke, Lidia remembered her discovery of the debt that

was somehow owed to the Gamba Ghisellis. Perhaps now the nature
of that relationship was to be revealed.

"My grandfather was revered in Ravenna for many reasons—land
reclamation was one, for example. He was able to make good soil
from useless marshes—in spite of those who said he couldn't do it.
Then he opened a hospital when there was a cholera epidemic. And
he was a great hero to the workers because he tried to improve their
lives, even though many of the owners liked things the way they
were." Teresa came to life talking of her grandfather, but she did not
hesitate to give credit to others who may have deserved it. "And in all
this," she continued, "his helper was Rodolfo, your great-grandfather.
They were great friends. Some said Rodolfo was the true architect of
what Grandpa had achieved. Rodolfo was a smart man," Teresa said,
pointing a finger to her temple. "And so was your grandpa, the young
Rodolfo. He was the one who saw a solution to the Angelica problem.
He had a plan that would not only make his brother happy, but could
also help all the DiRavennas. So he went to his father with his idea."

Before explaining about the "idea," Teresa looked at Lidia and
frowned. "My grandfather Pietro was loved as a savior of the workers,
but a common laborer would never do for his daughter. You see the
folly in this—or hypocrisy? But I shouldn't speak ill of the dead . . ."
She looked into her wine glass. It was as though she had to give voice
to other truths needing to be reconciled. Great men were, after all,
human and not God.

"The older Rodolfo liked what his son proposed and went to
Pietro with the idea. If Pietro agreed, Paolo, my father, would marry
Angelica and restore her honor. You see, because of the rumors,
my mother's reputation had been ruined. That is why she was sent
away. Ordinarily, such an idea would have been unthinkable, but
these were not ordinary times. Grandpa had no choice but to think
about it. Your great grandfather was a respectable man—but his
fortune was nothing in comparison to the Gambas. Grandpa also
knew, though, that his daughter had no prospects with the powerful families he wanted for her. And while he was very angry with

his daughter, he also knew she couldn't stay forever at the convent. She would either ruin their serenity or they would break her. You see, Pietro loved his daughter still, in spite of his anger, and he knew this plan for a respectable marriage would save her from a miserable life. So—he agreed to the marriage. Of course, Mama's feelings were of no importance to anyone but my father. He knew Mama loved the common boy, and he knew her heart was broken. He insisted they give her time to come to love him. At first, Mama resisted. She knew my father loved her, but she was not ready. He would have to win her love, and eventually, he did—by wearing her down with his devotion. By the time they were married, she had come to truly love my father. These were the stories she used to tell me when I was a girl. I loved hearing her tell me how happy they were together. And they remained that way, until death separated them."

Teresa smiled, and Lidia paused to consider this story—so appropriate on Valentine's Day. A high-spirited young woman won by the relentless pursuit of the man who loved her. Where could you find such love today?

"They had three boys and, finally, me," said Teresa. "My brothers were good sons, but I inherited my mother's wild streak, I think, and when I was young and foolish, I fell in love with a boy my father would never approve of. So, you see, history does repeat itself. We were still aristocratic in our ways. There were good marriages or there were unacceptable ones. When I wouldn't stop seeing the boy, my mother came to my room, sat on my bed, and told me her story. She said Papa was going to send me to the same convent that had taken her in when she was young and reckless. She said I would go there in the morning if I didn't change my mind."

Teresa's heart began to sink into her memories. "I will never understand why my father was so harsh. After all that my mother had endured, and yet he had no sympathy for me. When Mama shut the door to my room, I packed a bag and sneaked out the window and met the boy. We ran away."

Lidia didn't know what to say. Teresa's own story was going by in a torrent of words, revealing what in its day must have been a terrible family scandal. Lidia couldn't imagine this regal, elegant woman at the heart of it.

Teresa said, "It seems hard to believe, I don't know myself how I did this, but in time, the boy and I saved our money and sailed to America. We settled in New York, where we landed. He worked in the tunnels and on the bridges of the city, and for a time I sewed for a tailor. Then the boy left me. Just like that, he was gone, and I was alone."

Teresa gave no reason for the sudden breakup, and Lidia didn't ask, but she saw that Teresa's memories caused her great pain, perhaps explaining why she was not lingering on her words. Lidia sat with her hands in her lap, not knowing what to say.

"I went from job to job, from boy to boy, and when I got in trouble, a friend told me about her sister who was a nun at a home for girls in Ohio. That is where I went and where I gave up my baby—to the nuns who found a home for her. I had ruined my life," Teresa said, reaching for another tissue, catching tears as they were about to fall. "And there was no Uncle Rodolfo with a plan to save me. Mama sent me money—to her dying day she did this. I think Papa knew. I wanted to go home, but Papa wouldn't let me." Teresa turned her face away and said almost inaudibly, "My father disowned me."

"How terrible for you," said Lidia. "To be so alone and having to give up your baby."

Teresa crumbled the tissue in her hand and looked into Lidia's eyes. "I had to give her up, but I knew who she was. My baby was Tina."

And there they were—the words Lidia had come to hear. And now she had to know for certain they were true. "But how could you know that?" asked Lidia. "How could you be sure your baby was Tina—how did you find her after you gave her up?"

"I stayed on at the home and worked for the nuns for years. It was not hard for me to find the adoption information. I never gave her up, not in my heart. I watched her grow. Later I worked at her school. I saw how smart she was. She was always reading." Teresa laughed. Lidia watched as Teresa's face brightened remembering this.

"Always books about flying. Mama's sister married a famous flyer. I wanted to tell Tina, so she would know about him, so she could know about her family. One day when she was in the library, I talked to her. I told her about a famous Italian flyer who knew the Wright brothers. I could tell she liked the story. She studied books about the Wright brothers and about Mario then . . ."

It was all coming together. Teresa's aunt was the Emmy, or Amalia, Lidia had read about—who was married to Mario Calderara. Lidia had to let this sink in—that it was Teresa who had nurtured Tina's love of flying with stories of her family, of her aunt's famous husband—and of his connection with the Wright brothers. Lidia sat back against the cushioned seat, remembering Tina's room, not far from here—the books, her model planes. The sun had risen away from the windows so that the light was no longer streaming into the room, and Teresa's face was in shadows. Her voice, though audible, was sad and tired. Lidia felt great sympathy for this cousin who had watched her daughter grow, never able to tell her who her mother really was. To confirm this terrible truth, Lidia asked, "And so Tina never knew who you were?"

"I never told her, not until years later."

Lidia was not sure she had heard correctly—had Tina known Teresa was her true mother? She asked, "Tina knew you were her . . ."

"I told her when she was grown. She had known me for so many years. I used to meet her at this restaurant, on days like this, when it was closed. We would drink espresso, and she would tell me her dreams, how she wanted to fly and fly only, how life made it difficult to follow your dreams. I told her who I was, hoping it would cheer her, to know she was connected to Mario. But it didn't seem to please her at all. I was never sure she believed me, but I think she did. Maybe she always knew. She was curious to know what I had to tell her, but she never embraced me as her mother."

"Why do you think that was?" asked Lidia.

"She wanted Mario's blood in her veins, I think—our family did not interest her." Teresa frowned, a memory flittering by. "She used to quote from little books she carried with her the last few times I saw her. She would say, 'The only true law is that which leads to freedom.' I remember that one. Another was, 'I have slipped the,' what was it? 'the bonds of Earth.' I didn't know what she meant. It scared me when she said these things. She seemed disconnected from . . . the life she should have been living—with friends, a boyfriend—she seemed so alone. It's funny, isn't it? That I would remember those quotes. I don't know them, but I remember them."

"I know them," said Lidia, putting a hand on Teresa's across the table. Lidia remembered that Tina had underlined these passages in her diary. "They're from *Jonathan Livingston Seagull*—and a poem by a famous aviator. 'High Flight,' it's called."

Teresa smiled. "That sounds like Tina."

"What more did you tell her about her family, about us?"

"I told her I had family in Connecticut, that there were DiRavennas in Connecticut."

"So she knew about us, about my side of the family," said Lidia, half-hoping she had heard wrong.

"Lidia, Maria told me you did not know that your family stayed in touch with me. Your grandfather tried to get my father to take me back. He would not—your parents knew this. They knew it broke my mother's heart. Your mother and father were very good to me when my parents died. They wanted me to leave here—to go to Connecticut—but I would never leave Tina. At first, before she was born, I wanted nothing more than to go home, but that changed. Your parents were family to me, so I told Tina about them."

Lidia hardly knew what to say, knowing words could change nothing. "I'm so sorry—for all your losses, Teresa."

Teresa smiled. "Thank you, Lidia," she said. "You are a good woman. I hope you are happy in your life." The two sat for a time quietly, hardly aware that their pasta dishes and wine glasses had been replaced with espresso cups and plates of homemade biscotti. Stirring sugar into her cup, Teresa seemed more at ease, wanting to talk more about all that had transpired. "My grandfather Pietro's father was the brother of Teresa Gamba Ghiselli, who was the lover of Lord Byron."

"Yes, I know of her," said Lidia. "I have spent many hours reading about her—and her memoir."

"You see, you knew you were of our family," said Teresa.

"I had my suspicions," said Lidia. "Now I know for sure."

"I was named after her, the other Teresa. I, too, have been unhappy in love, but there is a great difference between us. Her father never stopped loving her. He embraced her and her lover. Even Grandpa forgave my mother, but my father could never forgive me. I have two great sorrows—that I could not have my daughter and that my father never forgave me."

There was nothing Lidia could say in the face of such regret. She knew she was doing all she could do. She was listening.

"But I have learned something in this life," Teresa said. "Never give up on those you love." This seemed enough to have learned and to have shared on this day set aside for lovers, Lidia thought to herself as the two sat and continued to talk over a second cup of coffee. Teresa told Lidia she didn't know Tina had taken off that day in October for North Carolina, but when she heard the news about a plane that had crashed into a house in Connecticut, her heart stopped. She was sure it was Tina—and of course, it was. Lidia spent the rest of her time with Teresa, sharing in her grief. The loss of Tina was an open wound.

The sun had already set as Lidia and Teresa said their good-byes with promises to stay in touch. Lidia would just make her early evening flight if she didn't hit traffic. At the first red light she thought of something Teresa had said—that Tina had wanted Mario's blood in her veins—the same words Tina had written in her diary. Then Lidia remembered the Walters—and their grief. She thought of Teresa sitting at the table in the restaurant, crying. *They could be a comfort to each other,* Lidia thought, wondering how she could make that happen. Before she left the restaurant, she had told Teresa about Tina's diary—a mistake she realized after she said it. Teresa wanted to read it, but Lidia made up some excuse, knowing she couldn't give it to her—not without the Walters' knowledge. She had never mentioned the Walters by name, but surely Teresa knew who they were. The light changed. Maybe the diary held the key to getting Teresa and the Walters together, Lidia thought as she headed north toward the airport.

On the way home, above the clouds, Lidia relived her afternoon with Teresa. *What is to be done with all that I now know?* she wondered. Then she realized. There was nothing to be done. She would never know why she had done it—why Tina had chosen to end her life in the second story of Lidia's house. Lidia would never know why Tina would choose to endanger innocent people. Lidia would never know what to make of it, finally, but the real tragedy was Tina's. This she knew. Lidia looked out the window to see the lights of the White Plains airport coming into view. *My girls, thank God, were not harmed. I'm still here. I'll get my house back. My losses were just things, not people. Am I finding peace at last?*

Storms on the Horizon

*T*he day began gloriously—a beautiful February morning imitating spring—warm and sunny. The night before, after Lidia had unpacked, taken a hot bath, and thrown a plush robe over her pajamas, she and Polly had stayed up talking. Sitting near the fireplace in the living room, Lidia shared with her friend all she had learned and all the emotions she had felt on her trip to Dayton, the strongest of which was her sympathy for Teresa's suffering. Polly took it all in, no doubt reliving her own time of great sorrow. "Mothers who live with this burden are a sad lot, Lidia. Not a day goes by that I don't think of my Kate," she said.

Lidia was able to lighten Polly's mood when she revealed her emerging sense of acceptance—in spite of all her fears and misgivings since the accident.

"Keats called it 'negative capability'—being able to live with uncertainty," Polly said. "What were his words? Let me see, I used to know this. He said, capable of being in uncertainty or doubt without reaching after fact and reason, without an irritable reaching after fact and reason. Isn't that lovely, an 'irritable reaching'?" Polly seemed quite pleased to be able to haul out this wisdom. "And the wording—it's rather perfect. He says 'being' in doubt, not 'having' or 'considering' it, but capable of *being* in doubt. That's extraordinary—quite Zen, actually. And that's where you have arrived, isn't it? No longer needing facts and rational explanation—you're just able to accept the mystery. And it is a mystery, dear. I'm afraid you'll never know what drove that poor child to do what she did, or if she did indeed do it intentionally."

After they parted for the night, Lidia slept soundly, not worried about Tina, Harry, the twins, or Owen.

And now this glorious morning seemed to conform to Lidia's new positive outlook.

Lidia walked into the kitchen to find Polly already up and brewing the morning coffee. "Ah, Lidia. There you are. A few questions I forgot to ask last night," she said, pulling the milk out of the refrigerator. "Did you ask Teresa about the loan mentioned in the papers?"

Polly was always like this—wide awake in the morning, not needing a shot of caffeine to get her started. Lidia, on the other hand, needed time to work up to the day, and coffee was what got the gears going. Polly picked up right where they had left off, as though a night's sleep and Lidia's morning grogginess were not separating them. "Loan," Lidia said, sitting down at the table. When the word failed to ignite a memory, she asked, "What loan?"

Polly put a full mug of coffee in front of her and sat down across the table.

"Sorry, dear. I shouldn't be starting in on this so early. I've been up for hours, and I've been thinking about one of our conversations a while back. There was a man mentioned in the newspaper article about your grandfather, alluding to a loan. You remember. The money supposedly made it possible for your great grandfather to start his own business."

This jogged Lidia's memory. "Yes—I did ask about it," said Lidia. "At first I couldn't remember the man's name, other than he had been a Gamba Ghiselli, and I knew it wasn't Pietro. Teresa said something about my grandfather, about how he thought the marriage to Angelica would be good not only for Paolo, but for the whole family."

"So there was a *quid pro quo*?"

"Something like that, I guess. When I asked Teresa if she knew about a loan that had been made, she said right away, 'Ruggero made it.'"

"Yes, that was the name. Who was he?"

"Pietro's brother. And apparently he made the loan to my great grandfather so it would not appear that Pietro had paid Rodolfo for taking Angelica off his hands. Teresa didn't know if my great grandfather had asked for the money, or if Pietro arranged for the loan to be made out of gratitude for everything Rodolfo had done. That seems more likely, I think."

"Yes," said Polly. "From all we've learned about them, I can't see Rodolfo asking, and I can't see Pietro ignoring this man who had been such a loyal friend and partner. What a great story. You're lucky, you know. Not many of us get to have this window onto the past opened for us in this way. And you deserve a lot of credit for seeing this through. Well done, my dear," Polly said, raising her coffee cup.

"Thank you, Polly. I am rather proud of myself," said Lidia, reflecting on how much had changed since those days when she had wanted to pull the covers over her head every time she thought about the plane and its pilot. Harry had helped her to face the truth, of course. And now she had. Thoughts of Harry were on the verge of overtaking her when Polly interrupted her reverie. "There is one other thing. Do you mind if I press on? I'm sorry, I guess I can be a nuisance in the morning."

Lidia laughed. "You're spry in the morning, I'll admit, but of course, you can go on, Polly. I'm all yours."

"I think we understand how you might share a resemblance to Tina—but how to explain the resemblance to Byron's Teresa and to Angelica? They're not related to you, except through marriage."

Lidia, elbow on the table, let her hand rest on her chin and thought about this for a moment. "I know—that's a good question. I guess it's just coincidence. I don't know. Another part of the mystery. But it sure added to the drama, didn't it?" Lidia raised her coffee cup to Polly and laughed, satisfied with her newfound ability to be in doubt.

Lidia and Polly discussed their plans for the day—Lidia would go to the tile and stone showroom in Stamford for her master bath selections; Polly to the library for her Adopt-a-Shelf volunteer work.

"This afternoon, come hell or high water, I'm walking to the point with Opal. Will you come, too?" Polly asked.

Lidia wasn't sure how long it would take her to look at the displays and to pore over the catalogs, so she made no promises. "Don't wait for me," she said, looking down at Opal, who stretched out by Polly's feet under the table. "You and Opal are quite the pair these days. I'm not sure I'll be missed."

On her way to Stamford, pressing buttons to find a good radio station, Lidia paused when she heard the weather come on. Dropping temperatures and thunderstorms were predicted for the afternoon. Lidia was wearing only a light jacket and hadn't thought to bring an umbrella. The sun was so bright when she exited I-95 toward the showroom, it was difficult to believe a forecast of storms. She thought to call Polly, but just then a Navigator pulled in front of her, forcing Lidia to slam on the brakes. "God, I hate those monstrosities," she said aloud.

It was quite late by the time Lidia left the showroom. The shower stall, she had decided, would be pale yellow imported titles with hand-painted fish in a deep blue. Additional tiles with gold sunbursts would accent the fish, a design which Lidia felt created a subtle old world effect she found pleasing. When she saw the computer-generated rendering, she was reminded of tiles one might find in a villa on the Adriatic, one that Teresa and Byron might have rented. She wondered what Harry would think, whether he would like her choices.

Then it was on to the flooring. After some consideration, Lidia decided against the tile she had first thought would do nicely, thinking later that stone might be best, but then she thought maybe wood, until finally she shook her head and gave up for the day. The whole enterprise had taken far longer than she had anticipated, so she was alarmed when she walked outside to find rain being driven sideways by the howling wind, and the storefront awnings being whipped nearly off their frames. She drew her jacket close to her body and made a dash for the car. The temperature had dropped at least ten degrees, just as predicted. Lidia turned on the heat and headed home.

She was gripped by panic when she turned into the driveway and saw a patrol car and an ambulance blocking the way. "Carly, Clarisse," she said out loud. But the girls were skiing with their dad and Robert in Vermont, not Greenwich where there hadn't been a single flake of new snow. She parked the car hastily and ran into the house. There was no one there. From the kitchen, she heard men's voices outside and Opal barking frantically. Lidia ran to the mudroom door—in the direction of the commotion. Outside she saw two policemen, two ambulance attendants, and Rocco beside a gurney. Opal was in a state that could only be described as hysteria. Lidia began running toward them as though she had left herself standing by the door. "Polly!" she screamed, approaching the gurney.

———————◆———————

That afternoon, just as she had planned, Polly attached Opal's leash to her collar, and the two had walked out of the house and onto the road until they'd eventually come to the path leading to the point. Polly had noticed clouds gathering, but the day was still mild, and so beyond admiring the background of dark clouds in the distance juxtaposed against the brilliant blue sky in the foreground, Polly gave the weather little thought. Instead she turned her attention to the calm sea—unusually still for winter, she noted—and to what she distinctly recognized as crocus shoots poking up on both sides of the path. "Seems early," she said. Opal, walking ahead, turned to look at Polly. "It's okay, Opal," said Polly. "I'm just admiring signs of things to come. Spring. We'll be out here much more in the next few weeks."

When they got to the largest outcropping of rocks, forming a jetty out into the Sound, Polly leaned down and unclasped the leash. Opal immediately started running in small circles on the brown grass in front of them, looking in Polly's direction as she widened her circles.

"Oh, I know what you want," Polly said, picking up a stick and throwing it in Opal's direction. Opal, who was not always particularly interested in a game of fetch, preferring usually to pause and chew once she had pounced on her prey, was today happy to run and retrieve repeatedly, much to Polly's amusement.

"Good girl, Opal," said Polly, picking up the stick for the eighth or ninth time. "But I've got to stretch my back a minute." Pushing the palms of her hands into her back and extending her spine, she turned in the direction of the sea to see waves forming. It was then she noticed that the wind had picked up and that clouds were moving rapidly in their direction.

"Looks like a storm is brewing," said Polly, turning in Opal's direction. "We've been playing so hard, we haven't even noticed the weather. We probably better head home, girl," she said, reattaching the leash. "But a little rain never hurt anyone, now did it?" As they began walking, the wind intensified and a light mist of rain turned to large pelting drops, soaking Polly and Opal as they quickened their pace. "It must be a microburst, Opal," said Polly loudly over the din. "We'd better hurry," she said, breaking into a jog. Just then, there was a crack of thunder and soon a bolt of lightning. "That's pretty close," Polly said, lowering her head and drawing in her shoulders. As they approached the property of the estate, she cut off the road toward the oaks and birches leading straight to the house. Opal dug in her heels, not sure about this change in direction. "It's a short cut," shouted Polly. "C'mon, girl." Opal relented and they continued through the trees.

Thunder rang out and shook the woods. Polly cringed in response. *Biblical cataclysm,* she thought, *would be like this.* Then immediately, a blinding flash of lightning, an explosion. Polly thought a fog had descended; was it smoke?

———◆———

As Rocco walked quickly toward the ambulance, holding Polly's hand, he looked up and heard Lidia's cry. "She's alive," he called to her, his shoulders quaking as he broke down with this utterance of thankfulness. Lidia threw her arms around him, and then without another word, they continued in haste to their destination. Rocco and Lidia, not allowed in the ambulance, followed instead as quickly as the law allowed in Rocco's truck. Opal, back in the house, sat at attention behind the closed mudroom door, where she would remain for several hours.

In the waiting room at Greenwich Hospital, Lidia went to the cafeteria to fetch two cups of coffee for her and Rocco. Lidia sat down next to him in one of the blue cushioned chairs in front of a square coffee table covered with magazines. The spacious well-lit room was arranged in similar clusters of tables and chairs. Handing Rocco a cup, Lidia looked out one of the large windows framing the room to see trees still being tossed by the wind and rain pelting the glass. Rocco began to fill Lidia in on the details of how he had found Polly.

He told her how he had let himself in when Polly didn't answer. Getting concerned, he was relieved when he heard Opal barking, thinking they were both returning from a walk. He went to the mudroom to let them in, ready to chastise Polly, ready to say, "What were you thinking, out in this?" But instead, looking down at Opal, soaked and shivering, muddied leash trailing behind, he only uttered, "Where the hell is Polly?"

Opal backed away from the door and began barking. She ran a few paces toward the trees, then turned to look at Rocco, still standing by the door. She ran back, then turned again toward the trees, barking furiously. This time Rocco ran after her.

He found Polly right where Opal led him. He tore at the branches in an effort to free Polly. There were no heavy limbs covering her, Rocco noted thankfully. He pulled out his phone and dialed 911. He searched Polly for signs of life. He leaned over and gently put an ear to her chest. He took off his jacket and covered her. Within minutes an ambulance and squad car arrived. Rocco and Opal were pushed aside as the two paramedics checked Polly for vital signs.

"I was just praying she was alive, Lidia. All I could do was watch. I never felt so helpless in my life."

Lidia put a hand on Rocco's shoulder as he put this head in his hands. He pulled a handkerchief out of his pants pocket and wiped his nose.

"I guess you can tell I'm pretty stuck on her, huh?" he said, trying to lighten the moment.

"Yes, Rocco. And I guess it's no secret that she's pretty stuck on you," she replied, patting his shoulder before taking her hand away.

They had been there for over an hour and there was still no word. It was near dark. For the moment at least, they were the only two in the room. Since Rocco and Lidia had arrived, one high school boy had come in with what appeared to be a sports injury and one elderly man had been taken in immediately to be treated for cardiac arrest. Lidia stirred her coffee with a wooden stirrer, trying to dissolve the powdered milk.

"It's my fault," she said, almost inaudibly.

"No, Lidia. You can't blame yourself. Why? How could it be your fault?"

Lidia cleared her throat and raised her voice a little, still looking into her coffee. "I heard the forecast this morning, when I left the house, and I knew Polly was planning to take Opal to the point. I meant to call her, but I was too busy with my own stuff and I got distracted. How could I be so selfish?"

Rocco put his cup down on the table in front of them and turned to face her. "Lidia, look at me. This is not your fault. It's not anyone's fault, for Chrissake. A falling tree is not your fault. Besides," he said, sitting back. "She still would've gone—even if you had called her. You know I'm right. She's pretty strong-willed."

Lidia laughed. "That's true, I'll give you that," she said.

The doors to the ER opened, and a young doctor with dark hair pulled back in a loose bun, wearing a black skirt and grey sweater under her open white coat, came down the hallway toward them, her black pumps tapping the floor as she walked.

Introducing herself as Dr. Pandit, she looked at her chart and said, "I'm afraid I don't have your names. You're with Mrs. Niven, but you're not family, is that right?"

"That's right," said Lidia.

"Does she have family—next of kin?"

Lidia's knees wobbled. She reached for Rocco, who grabbed her waist.

"Oh no, I'm sorry—it's not that," the doctor said, seeing Lidia's distress. "We need some information. There are a few gaps in her medical history."

"I see," said Lidia, gathering her strength. "She has a daughter, Kate. But they're not . . . Polly, Mrs. Niven, is not in touch with her."

Seeming to be satisfied with Lidia's answer, Dr. Pandit began an explanation of Polly's condition, but all that registered with Lidia was that Polly was alive. Rocco let go of Lidia's waist. She heard him sigh with relief. They'd both been implementing the same strategy—trying to talk to pass the time, forcing themselves not to think about Polly behind closed doors.

Dr. Pandit explained that Polly was in a coma, and that the next few days would be crucial to her recovery. "She has a few slight fractures, nothing serious, but she took a severe blow to the head. And given her age . . . well, time will tell . . ."

"She has a head injury? Could there be brain damage?" asked Lidia, no longer comforted by the news that her friend had not died.

"No, and we should not jump to conclusions, Mrs. Raven. Mrs. Niven has a 'head injury,' not 'brain damage.' A big difference—but even with that, I must say again, it is too early to have a prognosis—for the time being."

Lidia was speechless. Before leaving them, Dr. Pandit added, "Please don't give up hope. I've seen patients fully recover when everyone least expected it. Her age doesn't preclude a similar type of recovery. Be patient."

"Patient. Yes, doctor. Thank you."

Knowing there was nothing they could do, Rocco and Lidia

decided to take turns waiting. Rocco went back to Polly's to check in on Opal. Lidia stayed and called Owen at the ski house, knowing she needed to break the news to the girls.

"They need to hear it from you, Lidia, to know she's okay. That's the main thing. She's alive. Just tell them what the doctor told you." Lidia found Owen's words comforting, and the conversation with both Carly and Clarisse had gone reasonably well, but when Owen returned on the line, Lidia could hear them crying in the background.

Owen said they would leave for home first thing in the morning. "As soon as we know the roads up here are passable," he had assured her.

Her heart ached with sorrow, and she wanted nothing more, other than Polly's miraculous recovery, than for the girls to be with her, so she could hold them and tell them everything would be okay. Maybe she could even convince herself a little. When she felt she could talk without crying, she called Harry—and left another message. Rocco returned a few hours later. Polly had been transferred to intensive care, and Lidia and Rocco spent the night in the waiting room around the corner from Polly's room.

The next morning was clear and sunny, belying what had occurred the afternoon before, with the exception of the fallen trees and branches strewn over lawns and roads all over town. The morning news shows were producing a steady stream of eye-witness accounts— cars and houses with roofs caved in by falling trees—and reports of power outages with newscaster warnings to stay away from downed power lines. Lidia was numbly watching the TV in the waiting area, too weary to wash or to eat. She had just sent Rocco home, and when he protested, she assured him she would go herself when he returned. She was waiting for word that she could see Polly.

By mid-morning, Lidia was mindlessly turning magazine pages when the head critical care nurse tapped her on the shoulder and told her she could go in. Lidia followed her down a long corridor, each step they took echoing loudly on the shiny tile floor. Entering Polly's room, Lidia wiped tears from her eyes as she gazed down at her friend, so small and fragile under her sheet and light blanket, tubes extending from her arms, and a pulsing machine keeping time with her heart, which was thankfully still beating.

"Oh Polly," said Lidia.

"She's resting peacefully. No pain," the nurse said.

If only Lidia could be sure. She reached for Polly's hand. It was warm but limp—and so pale. Lidia gave it a gentle squeeze, but there was no response.

"Polly," she said, "I know you're going to be okay. I'm so sure of it. And we'll be back to our talks and our outings before you know it." She looked around for the chair. Finding it behind her, she slid it toward her and sat down next to the bed, grasping Polly's hand in hers again.

"It's just that . . . I think all this is my fault. I knew the weather was going to change. I heard it on the news—that a storm was coming. And I knew you and Opal were going to the beach. I should've called and warned you." Lidia lowered her head and cried. She couldn't be sure, but she thought she felt a slight tightening in Polly's grip. She held her breath and waited for some sign, but there was nothing. Lidia wanted to believe her friend had sent her a signal saying it was all right, that she was going to pull through this. But there was nothing, nothing real, and so Lidia, disappointed, remained at Polly's bedside, silent.

Rocco came at ten to relieve her, and after her nightlong vigil, Lidia went back to Polly's to shower, rest, and wait for the girls. Opal was at the door when she arrived, and Lidia knelt down to pet her. "You saved her, Opal. Do you know that?" Opal nuzzled Lidia, and when she stood to go upstairs, Opal followed. After showering, Lidia lay down and closed her eyes, but she couldn't sleep, not even a short nap. Instead she lay staring at the ceiling, Opal lying on the floor beside her, paws outstretched, head on paws. She wasn't sleeping either.

Lidia felt a wave of great sorrow. "She's going to die," she said. She was giving in to the worst possible conclusion. She couldn't help it, this reaction to fear. She heard Polly's voice in her heard. *He who foresees calamities lives them twice over.* It was a favorite quote of hers. One she hauled out every time Lidia dwelled on the worst possible outcome of whatever worry she was harboring at the time. "That's the truth of it," she had said. "Why waste your time worrying? What good can come of it? There are only two outcomes, both bad. Either the terrible thing doesn't happen, and you've wasted all that precious time, or it does happen, and now you have to live it all over again. I tell you, it isn't worth it."

If the worst does happen, Lidia thought, *my God, how will I bear it?*

It took her several terrible minutes to answer her own question. *You will bear it, Lidia. That's what people do. They endure, and so will you.* Then Lidia decided that she was going to spend these days doing exactly what Polly would want her to. She told herself, *If I have to live with her loss, I'll not begin that suffering now. There must be some good I can do. I will not spend this time worrying.*

She heard the front door open. "Mom? We're home," said Carly. "Are you upstairs?" Clarisse asked. She heard them running up to her, and soon she was in the arms of her two girls. After hugs all around, the three then went down to help Owen, who was bringing in the last of the girls' luggage and ski equipment.

"How is she?" he asked, putting down a boot bag.

"Only time will tell, Owen, but she's still here," Lidia said, welcoming Owen's comforting arm around her shoulder.

———◆———

The next few days were spent visiting the hospital and waiting for some signs of hope. Owen and Robert joined Rocco and the Raven women in their vigil until winter weather returned, bringing in a blizzard that kept the waiting party indoors at the Niven estate. Mercifully, the power stayed on, and everyone participated in preparing meals and cleaning up. It was the sort of gathering Polly would have relished. Realizing this, Lidia could almost feel Polly's regret for her own absence. *I wish you were here, too,* she said to herself, retreating to the library, where a fire and Brahms helped her to feel close to her missing friend. She busied herself with searches at Polly's computer, taking breaks to pull down the Byron volumes and to reread some of Polly's favorite lines.

It was dusk of the fourth day after the accident before Lidia realized the blizzard had passed. Carly knocked on the door and stuck her head in to tell her mother that she had called the hospital and visiting hours would be back to normal that night. Seeing Lidia's imploring gaze, Carly added, "Sorry, Mom. There's still no change, but she's holding her own." Lidia put out her arms, and Carly met her embrace. "Still want to be alone?" she asked. Lidia nodded, yes. "Just a little longer." Carly nodded and left the room, closing the door behind her.

Lidia resumed her reading, not sure how much time had passed before she heard a light tap and saw the door begin to open.

"'She walks in beauty like the night.' I'm sorry. It's the only poetry I know by heart, but I think it fits."

"Harry!" said Lidia, dropping the book to rush toward him.

And then they were in each other's arms, Lidia crying, a mix of emotions impossible to sort. Great sorrow, relief, and yes, joy. In this most difficult of times, joy. Lidia sobbed and Harry stroked her hair as she cried into his chest. He gently rocked her in his arms and told her it was okay, that everything would be okay. It was okay, thought Lidia. Okay to be comforted. It was okay to give in to tears of joy and of sorrow—and to hold onto hope.

For the next half hour, the two reunited lovers were left in solitude. Behind the closed library doors, Harry was deeply sorry for his long absence, but it was unavoidable, he explained. He told Lidia how each of her messages, left unanswered by necessity, was a wound that could not be healed. He tried to ignore them, but it was impossible. And then the last one, about Polly. No longer able to bear the weight of it, Harry asked for emergency leave from the case he was on. "As close to a family emergency as I can possibly have," he had said. The case was close to wrapping up anyway. There was enough cover to complete the work, he had assured his boss. And then, the decision— yes. Yes, Harry could leave the job to his colleagues. He was free to go.

Lidia was only half-listening to what he was saying, attentive only to the sound of his voice, the warmth of his hands on hers, and mostly to the depth of his blue eyes. How she had missed falling into his gaze. And now he was here. He drew her close and held her breasts, kissed her with a deepening urgency, making it difficult to find restraint. It would be so easy to fall back onto the enveloping leather couch and give in to their need for one another, but they did not.

Pulling apart, the two walked out of the library to meet the others, who were dividing up for the drive to the hospital. Rocco left first, alone in his truck. Lidia asked that the girls drive with Owen and Robert. "The roads may be icy," she had said aloud, sounding a cautionary note. "Sorry," she said. "I guess I'm just a little nervous about any more accidents in this family." *But lightning doesn't strike twice,* she told herself, thinking of the calamity that had befallen Polly. *Then again, it can, and it does,* she thought, knowing that there was no protection from life's random acts.

In the car, Lidia looked over at Harry as he drove, serious but calm, a wonderful calm. She breathed deeply, gathering strength from his presence. She wasn't imagining him. He was there. She put a hand on his thigh. He covered her hand with his and tightened his grip. They rode in silence to the hospital.

———●———

"The longer it takes for her to revive, the worse, and the harder it is to expect . . ." Dr. Pandit measured her words. "But a full recovery is still possible."

"You're losing hope?" asked Lidia.

"Let's try not to do that, but we must be prepared as well," she said. "Her daughter. Have you been in touch?"

Lidia shook her head. The doctor's words sounded loudly in the waiting room.

"Can we see her?" asked Harry. Dr. Pandit nodded, and they all took turns visiting her room. Even Owen wanted to go in and see her. "If you think it's all right, Lidia, I'd like to see her. She's been so great to all of us, you and the girls of course, but also to Robert and to me. What do you think?"

"She would want to see you, Owen. She's one of your biggest fans, yours and Robert's."

Lidia and Harry were last to go in. Light-headed at the sight of Polly, Lidia reached for Harry and held fast to his arm. If anything, Polly had become a mere suggestion of who she once was, more ephemeral with each passing day, the light blanket covering her seeming to float above the tiny figure lying beneath. Was this what it was like? Was this death, this diminishment of the physical body as well as of the spark, the spirit inside?

Harry sat by the bed and began talking. He called the fragile form under the thin cover Sleeping Beauty and told her it was time to wake up, that her prince, Rocco, was waiting for her, that his kiss would be all she needed to be restored. He told her about all the wonderful things waiting for her— spring then summer and picnics at the beach, tea and sunshine on the porch with the Ravens and her rescuer, Opal. He told her that plans and preparations for the twins—graduation, then college—could not go on without her. She was needed and must wake up from her long nap.

Lidia watched Harry as he lovingly implored Polly to rejoin the world. How easily he had shifted into this gentle cajoling manner, she thought, feeling closer to him with each word, but she was beginning to think it would take a miracle to rouse Polly. She forced herself to cling to the picture of the future Harry was drawing, that one day soon Polly would return to them and be happier than she ever thought she could be. Rocco was indeed waiting for her, as were they all—and perhaps one other person would join the vigil. Lidia held fast to this vision.

——————●——————

It was with great hope the next time, a few days later, that Lidia walked into the Greenwich Hospital Critical Care unit. A little more than a week had passed since the storm had taken Polly down. Lidia and a new visitor walked into Polly's room.

"There's someone here to see you, Polly." With these words Lidia stepped back, allowing Kate to come forward. She looked at Lidia with uncertainty.

"Just talk to her. Just let her hear the sound of your voice. And then say whatever is on your mind."

Lidia walked softly out of the room, leaving Kate to find her way. She had brought her to Polly because chances were slim that Polly would recover and Kate was her next of kin, but regardless of what she had told Kate to get her there, she believed her friend would hear Kate, would know her daughter had come home to her. And this, she believed, would bring Polly back.

Lidia had made a decision to find Kate that first day after the accident, when she determined she would not give in to her doubts and fears. She had then spent her evenings, when she was not at the hospital, at Polly's computer entering keywords of what she knew. She searched the Oregon white pages for Kate Cramer, using Polly's maiden name. But of course, she found nothing. Then she tried a random search of Oregon forest rangers. When that yielded nothing, she tried searching local newspaper archives. Miraculously, in the *Central Oregonian,* she found an article about a ranger who visited the local schools with her mascot, a horned owl named Wiccan that she had rescued from a fire the year before. "Prineville Reservoir Park Ranger Kate Parsons, instructing her audience: 'Tell Mom and Dad that the family campfire has to be completely out before leaving the campsite.'"

Lidia had stared at the photo, enlarging it until she lost focus, trying to get as close a look at Polly's daughter as she could. She was about Lidia's age, in uniform and wearing a wide-brim hat. Lidia could see long straight blonde bangs almost covering but not dimming her piercing eyes. That was her. No question.

From there it was a challenge, but eventually, Lidia was able to contact Kate through Oregon's Parks and Recreation Department. Who could ignore a plea like this one? Kate almost did, but once Lidia was able to actually talk to her, Kate relented. She admitted to Lidia that she had thought about her mother often over the past few years. She remembered how she had rejected Polly and had grown to regret it. She was afraid to get in touch with her, ashamed of her behavior and not sure she could face the mother she had ignored. Lidia assured Kate that Polly would embrace her with open arms if she got the chance. The news of Polly's coma hit Kate hard, but Lidia convinced her to come—to see her mother before it was too late.

When Kate emerged from Polly's room, she all but fell into Lidia's waiting arms. "If only she could have heard me," she said. "I didn't know I had so much to tell her." Kate pulled away and took a tissue from her pocket. "Thank you, Lidia," she said, drying her eyes. "I've thought about seeing her again for a long time. If only it weren't like this."

Lidia put an arm around Kate. "We can't give up hope." Lidia didn't press this point, but she was sure that somehow Kate's words hadn't been uttered in vain. She felt a rush of certainty from head to toe she could not explain. "You're here now. That means so much," she offered. Kate smiled, and the two walked out of the hospital into the late afternoon sun.

Changes!

*L*idia was on the deck looking out over the orchard. There would be a record-breaking crop in the fall, a bountiful harvest of Renettes, making her the fourth generation of harvesters in her family, since the orchard—all ten acres—was hers. Was it possible? And yet, this new reality was but one of many nearly unbelievable events that had occurred. It was August, and so much had transpired since that day in October, almost a year ago, when Tina's plane had crashed into her house and changed everything. Lidia could pinch herself, feel the sting, and still not believe it.

She, Lidia Raven, was in the midst of preparations to market bushels of apples and apple wine made according to her family's ancient recipe. On the day she had descended into the basement of her home on Apple Way, the same day the letters and the locket were found, Lidia had also found among her grandfather's papers the original sketch of the logo for the family business—and the recipe for her great grandfather's apple wine.

As the colors of the day began to soften, Lidia glanced down at her watch. It was six, and she was preparing dinner. A large tray of homemade lasagna was bubbling in the oven, and a glass bowl of green salad was chilling in the refrigerator. There would be seven places to set at the dining room table.

Lidia opened the long top drawer on the mahogany breakfront and paused before taking out a meticulously pressed embroidered white linen tablecloth. Lidia recalled the telephone conversation she had had with Lana when she first told Lidia that Maria wanted her to have the china cabinet and tablecloth. Lidia had been both shocked and deeply touched.

"My mother is still so sorry she misled you when you came to her with questions about your family. This is her way of making up for it. Please take it," Lana had said.

When Lidia tried to object, Lana said, "You saw how full our house is. We're not going to miss one piece of furniture, honestly."

Lidia remembered all the antiques in their home that had come from Italy. She tried once more to say no, but relented, not wanting to hurt Maria's feelings. On the day the van arrived and the movers placed the piece in the dining room, Lidia vowed that the fine linen tablecloth in the top drawer would be reserved for only the most important of family occasions.

Although this dinner would be a gathering of those closest to her, Lidia had not billed it as anything special, but to her it would be a celebration of many important events. It seemed to Lidia that only wondrous things had followed the accident on Apple Way—beginning with Harry, then the unraveling of her family's secrets, her deepening friendship with Polly, and the miracle of the day back in March when Dr. Pandit had phoned telling her to return to the hospital at once.

As soon as Lidia had put down the phone that day, she raced up the staircase at Polly's to rouse Kate, who had retreated to the guest room for a nap between hospital visits. Knocking on the door and then entering, Lidia touched Kate's shoulder gently to wake her. Kate pushed back her bangs and looked up at Lidia, who was struck by the similarity of mother and daughter. It was as if a younger version of Polly were staring up at her, dazed and confused.

"What is it, Lidia?" Kate asked as she rose to her elbows.

"It's the hospital. We have to get back right away. I don't know what's happened, but I'll wait for you downstairs." Lidia rushed to the mudroom to pick up the car keys and her jacket before going to the garage to wait for Kate in the car. In a few minutes, Kate was opening the door to slide into the passenger side.

Dr. Pandit met them at the entrance to Polly's room. She wasn't smiling, but her face was bright. Standing in front of them, she reached toward the two women, taking first Lidia's and then Kate's hand, holding on tightly before letting go.

"Lidia, you should go in first and wait a few minutes before telling her about Kate. We don't want to shock her." Without saying another word, she stepped aside, letting Lidia enter.

"These bones may be old, but it will take more than a spindly, sick tree to do me in," said Polly, sitting up in her bed, wearing the pink bed jacket Lidia had brought in one day after finding it in Polly's lingerie chest.

After a joyful reunion, Lidia gently told Polly that one of her prayers had been answered. Without missing a beat, Polly said, "Yes, I know you've brought Kate to me, haven't you, Lidia, dear. Is she here?"

"But how did you know?"

"At first I thought I must've dreamt it, but then I knew it was true. That she had truly been here. It was Kate, and you, and Rocco—all of you brought me back.

It was as if Polly had climbed back into the body that had all but faded away.

Then another reunion began, this time with Kate bending in tears to kiss the face of the mother so long lost to her but now returned. After a few brief moments, Dr. Pandit entered, motioning Lidia and Kate to join her outside Polly's room. "She needs her rest," she told them as the critical care nurse brushed past, entering the room to adjust the machines monitoring her newly conscious patient.

"It's just as I explained, Mrs. Raven. Sometimes when we least expect it, patients recover from comas. Against the odds, they recover. I'm so happy for you, both," she said turning her attention to Kate. "At first, I have to admit, when I saw you, my thought was, 'Good. The daughter is here. She will be able to say goodbye,' but now look. Now you have your mother back."

"How is this possible?" asked Lidia. "She seems like her old self. She's so feisty and full of life. Just yesterday, she was . . ."

"Near death? Yes. It was a distinct possibility, but she wanted to live.

Her will brought her back. Her condition has completely reversed, as far as we can tell. She is scoring at the highest levels on all our scales. Her scans are normal for a woman at least ten or fifteen years younger. What can I say? She just woke up. It's rare to see this kind of recovery. I will say, it was in her favor that her condition did not persist longer than it did. She's been here for two weeks, and it's good she is coming out of it now. Congratulations," Dr. Pandit told them. "I'll be back to check on her in a little while. We are, of course, monitoring her closely."

"When will she be able to come home?" asked Lidia.

Here, Dr. Pandit stopped making notes on her chart and brought her arms to her side. She looked directly at Lidia. "Let me just say, Mrs. Raven, that her reversal was spontaneous and that this is most unusual. Because recovery is so rare, I can give you no guarantees. We are in uncharted waters. When I say we have to monitor her closely—I don't want to alarm you—it's to be sure there isn't a relapse. So even if she continues to improve, we will want her here for a while longer—and then she will go to rehab for a time. She must gain back her strength. It's March; if all goes well, I will release her in two weeks. Then several more weeks in rehab. I can't make you any promises. I'm afraid some patience is called for. But now, go, and enjoy the mother and friend who has been returned to you."

When Dr. Pandit left them, Kate and Lidia walked back into the room to take their places on either side of Polly's bed. Lidia's optimism was unshaken by what she had just been told. She looked at Kate, pushing aside a few wisps of Polly's hair. Lidia was sure Kate, too, would remain hopeful.

Polly's progress continued to be steady. Lidia was sure it was because she had heard Kate's voice the day she first walked into the room, that she had known Kate was there, and it was indeed Polly's indomitable will that had brought her back to them. Polly went from the critical care unit to a rehabilitation center and was not released to go home until mid-April. During the intervening weeks, Kate, who'd taken a leave of absence from the park, was by her side through all of it. When Polly sat up on the edge of the bed for the first time, Kate was there. When Polly took her first steps with a walker, it was Kate who held her steady. When Polly took her first unaided steps, her journey ended in Kate's arms.

These weeks were a time of physical healing to be sure, but more, it was a time of great emotional healing for both mother and daughter. Rocco, always in the wings when he wasn't working, watched the evolution of their relationship with patience, knowing how much Kate's return meant to Polly. But next to Kate, it was Rocco Polly longed for. And knowing this, Lidia gave this threesome room to nurture their still-growing bonds. *It's all about what is best for Polly,* thought Lidia, who would do anything for her friend, including keeping her distance when necessary.

The day Rocco drove Polly home, Lidia and Kate were waiting for them at the end of the driveway. When the car pulled up, both women ran to them as the nurse rolled the wheelchair up. Polly embraced them each and held out her hand to the caregiver, but waved away the chair. Lidia's smile faded when she saw that Polly had been crying as she tried to tuck the tissue in the pocket of her sweater before anyone saw.

"Is everything all right, Polly?" Lidia asked, putting an arm around her as they walked toward the house, Kate on her other side.

Rocco, walking behind said, "She cried as soon as she saw the daffodils and tulips all along the driveway. You sure did a great job, with all the planting, Lidia."

"I had a lot of help," said Lidia, looking over at Kate. "It seems Kate's picked up a thing or two about gardening out there in Oregon."

"These are tears of joy, my dears," said Polly. "The profusion of spring colors, the dazzling yellow of the forsythia, all the of colors of yet more tulips. You can't possibly imagine what it has done for my soul to see all this beauty."

Flanking the house were trees in full bud, apple, cherry, and pear. It was as though a grand orchestra had begun an overture as soon Polly approached the property, just as Lidia and Kate had planned.

Spring followed Polly into the house, filled with flowers from friends and well-wishers, all of whom had been following the story of the lady hit by a tree but who had miraculously awakened from her coma. The drapes were all pulled back and light flooded the house. A cool breeze from the open sun porch doors brought the fragrance of nearby roses to the living room, where Polly sat to take it all in and where Opal, after licking Polly's hand, curled up at her feet. Polly leaned down to scratch her behind the ears. "Thank you, old friend," she whispered. Then, looking around her, she said, "My home. I'm home at last."

Over the course of the following weeks, after Polly's return, there were many adjustments—not all of them Polly's. It was with surprise that Lidia heard her friend say, over the protests of the nurse, that she wanted to return to her bedroom upstairs rather than to sleep downstairs in the room she had been occupying since Jean Paul's death. A few days later, Lidia shook her head in disbelief when Polly accepted a call from Claudia Dobbs, who wanted to interview her for an article in the *Hartford Courant*.

"I guess it's the new me," said Polly when Lidia reminded her that she had sworn off reporters years ago. "After all those lectures I gave you about letting go and accepting life on its own terms, I've come to realize I've been a bit of a fraud, harboring resentments and clinging to grief. Nothing like a near-death experience to help you clear away the cobwebs," Polly said, fluffing the pillows behind her head.

Lidia pulled open the drapes of the master bedroom suite, letting the morning sun pour in while Polly chatted away. She had been talking a lot, non-stop in fact, since her return home, and much of what she said alluded to her "near-death experience."

"I'm just happy to be alive," she said at the end of every conversation, especially after the complaining ones detailing life's petty annoyances. "Aren't we lucky to have such problems?" she would say, and then, "I'm just happy to be alive."

———●——

Thinking back on Polly's springtime recovery and homecoming, Lidia smiled as she opened the oven to check on the lasagna, which was cooking nicely for her dinner party. Another five minutes. Then she went back to the dining room to finish setting the table. She worked out the seating logistics in her mind, determining to sit at the head of the table so that Kate and Rocco could each sit next to Polly. Lidia glanced over at the two gifts she had wrapped and placed on the breakfront. She hoped Polly and Kate would like the framed picture she had duplicated for each of them.

One April afternoon when a golden light had filled the sun porch at Polly's, Lidia had snapped a picture of mother and daughter holding hands and in deep conversation. They looked so attentive to one another, as though they had had a long history of compelling talks. Kate had just explained to Polly that she would be returning to her life in Oregon, but that there would be trips to see her mother, as often as possible. Lidia's heart had gone out to Polly, who she knew would struggle with the separation after all she'd been through. Lidia could empathize, thinking of how the twins would be leaving soon.

Lidia looked away from the two gifts and down at the table, visually mapping out the placements of her two girls next to her. Her grown daughters, soon to be on their own.

———————◆———————

It wasn't too many days after Polly's miraculous recovery that the last of the twins' acceptance letters had arrived. Carly and Clarisse stayed in their rooms that afternoon, talking, starting in Clarisse's, then moving to Carly's. After dinner, they had returned to Clarisse's room for more talk. They emerged later that night.

"Mom," they both called out, looking for Lidia. When she stuck her head out from the kitchen, they said, again in unison, "We've decided," Carly adding, "but we want your advice first." This was twin-speak for: We know what we want, and we hope you'll go along with it. Lidia had motioned them into the kitchen, where the three had taken their places at Polly's kitchen t table.

Clarisse went first. "I thought I wanted Brown—that's where Derek will be—but then I got to thinking, why not seize the day and go where I really want to go?"

"Someplace where you can get a good education, I hope," said Lidia.

"Yes—and that won't cut off any options about grad school later . . . Look Mom, what do I love more than anything?"

"Making your mother happy?"

"Besides that."

Feeling a little exasperated, Lidia stared at her daughter. "Clarisse, I really can't play games with you right now. Something's telling me you're about to join a Mexican dance troupe instead of going to college, so out with it," said Lidia, her heart pounding.

"Okay," said Clarisse. "It's not so bad, really. What I really love more than anything is music. You know that. Polly knows that. Look, I never take off the necklace she brought me from Bali, remember?" she said, pulling open the top of her blouse to show the goddess Saraswati dangling from the fourteen-carat gold chain around her neck.

"Of course, I remember. I also remember Polly telling you to develop your mind as well as your talent for music."

"And I told her I could do both, and I can. Mom, I want to go to Berklee in Boston. I've been accepted."

Lidia felt a surge of motherly pride, remembering the audition and how Clarisse had shone that day; how happy she had seemed to Lidia, like a fire had been lit from within. "Why did you think I wouldn't want this for you?"

Clarisse sat silent for a moment. "Well, I just . . . I thought you wanted me to hit the academics hard—and pursue music on the side."

"Darling—am I so demanding? Don't you think I want you to pursue your dreams?" Then smiling, she added, "And you'll get a little space from Derek—I'm thinking this is good news!"

"Mom," said Clarisse.

"Okay, okay—Derek's fine, and so is your decision. Berklee it is! How wonderful, darling."

Clarisse and Lidia got up from the table and hugged each other. Out of the corner of her eye, Lidia saw Carly watching them, looking pensive.

"Well," said Lidia, sitting down again. "What about you, Carl? What do you have to tell me?"

Carly ran a forefinger over one of the whorls in the oak tabletop. When she looked up, she said, "I'm kinda tired. It can wait till morning." She rose and left the room. "What on earth?" asked Lidia, turning to Clarisse for an answer.

Clarisse then rose as well. "Me, too, Mom. I've got to get some sleep."

"What just a minute, Clarisse," said Lidia, reaching across the table, grabbing her daughter by the wrist before she could turn to go. "What's going on?"

Clarisse stood still, not answering. Then she said, "Mom, you know it's Carl you've got to talk to." She put her hand on top of her mother's and said, "You'll be okay with it, just like me, you'll be okay with what she tells you about her decision—and why she made it." She patted her mother's hand. "You've always understood. You're our rock." Clarisse gave Lidia a kiss on the top of her head. "Good night, Mom," she said and left the room.

Lidia sat for a moment alone, feeling more the child than the mother, more the innocent left in the dark while her two wise daughters went on with the business of knowing. Lidia's impulse was to run up the stairs to Carly's room, but she resisted. *No, I'll wait till morning,* she thought. *If Carl wanted to tell me now, she would've. There's a reason she's putting me off, so I'll wait. Patience.* She had learned it while waiting for Harry and then for Polly to come back to her. And they did. Both of them. Lidia resolved to give Carly her space.

The following morning, Lidia took advantage of the clear, bright light filling the sun porch and sat down to read the newspaper. She jumped a little when she felt a tap on her shoulder. There stood Carly, still in her pajamas.

"Can you talk now?" she asked, settling in next to her mother on the wicker love seat. She pulled her knees up, resting her chin on one knee, her face hidden under the dark hair tumbling over her folded legs. She was running a forefinger along the edges of a freshly pedicured toenail when Lidia drew back one side of Carly's hair, placing it behind an ear.

"Okay, Carl. Out with it. What's up that's so difficult to talk about?"

Just then, a tiny chipmunk caught Lidia's attention. She saw it dart up and settle on the first stonewall that began several levels of terraces on the lawn leading down to the Sound. Carly looked up and out the windows enclosing the sun porch, too. For a moment, Lidia and Carly were silent. The chipmunk sat up and nibbled on some nugget it had nudged from between the stones. Lidia made note of its coat shining in the sun, the stripes running from the tip of its nose, down along its sides, and ending where its tail made an *S* over its spine. She had a fleeting image of its miniscule heart and lungs working furiously within, protected by tiny ribs no bigger than matchsticks.

Carly was the first to speak. "It's complicated, Mom," she said.

Just as Lidia turned to give Carly her full attention, the chipmunk scampered from the wall away from view.

"Then just start from the beginning, Carl. There's no rush," said Lidia.

"Okay, but I'll start with my decision and work backward." She put her bare feet on the floor and darted over to the rocker across from her mother. There she sat cross-legged and began. "I've decided on Amherst . . ."

Before she could say another word, Lidia was up. "Oh, Carly. How fabulous. I know how much you wanted it. It was your first choice."

Before Lidia could hug her, Carly put up her hands. "I know, Mom. I knew you'd be happy . . ."

"So what's the problem, then?" Lidia said as she backed into her place on the loveseat.

"I almost decided on U Mass."

Lidia looked at Carly blankly.

"Because that's where Chloe is going."

Lidia continued staring at her daughter, waiting for an explanation.

"We were going to be roommates."

"Yes, I know. You told me you would do that if you didn't both get into the same school, but now you've decided on Amherst. U Mass would've been a good back-up plan, but this is better."

"It wasn't going to be my back-up plan." Carly paused and stared at Lidia before continuing, as though she were carefully considering her next words. "That was going to be the plan. Chloe's and mine, Mom."

Lidia, confused, was about to speak—to declare her stupidity—but instead, Polly's words came back to her. *They love each other,* she had said, of Carly and Chloe. *It will be hard for them to be separated.* In a flash, Lidia grasped what her daughter was trying to tell her. She wanted to respond, to say something, but she remained silent, not wanting the first words out of her mouth to be the wrong ones. Meanwhile, she realized that Carly was trying to gauge her reaction, waiting to see how Lidia would respond. All she could do was smile at her daughter. It was a smile to let Carly know that she had understood and that it was all right, her decision, her reason for it—all of it was all right. She wanted to grab her daughter up into her arms, but before she could do or say anything, Carly spoke.

"It's like Clarisse, Mom. How she decided not to go with Derek. I decided I needed time right now—to find out who I am and what I want. Chloe, too. Everything started moving so fast."

"Darling," said Lidia, rising again and kneeling in front of Carly and opening her arms to her. This time, Carly accepted the embrace, and Lidia held tight to her girl. "Whatever decision you make, or have made, I know it will be right for you—and for Chloe. You are both such thoughtful, intelligent young women."

"We didn't know, Mom. We didn't know our own feelings. We've been together for such a long time, and then suddenly there was this need for one another." Carly began to cry, head in hands, crying, sobbing. "And Dad. I was so unforgiving. I was such a hypocrite."

Still holding her daughter, Lidia began to cry too. "It was my fault. I nurtured my anger for such a long time. And I knew I was bringing you and Clarisse into it."

After some time, the two drew apart, Lidia rising to pull one, then two, three, four tissues from the box on the windowsill, handing two to Carly.

"But the important thing is that Chloe and I know we have to give each other room, to meet new friends, to see how we really feel. And I think we're both okay with that decision. We'll see, you know," she said, dabbing her eyes, then blowing her nose. "We just have to give it time. And you know, Mom, Polly knew all along. Don't be hurt, but I talked to her first. She also said you of all people would understand because there isn't a thing I could say that you wouldn't understand, and she was right."

The two were locked in an embrace when Clarisse came down the stairs looking for them. Lidia caught the smile on her face when she saw them. "Thank God that's over," she said.

Lidia, in the middle of this happy moment, was aware of a slight pang of regret—that Carly had gone to Polly first—but she quickly let it go, glad her friend had been there to comfort her daughter. Really there, not just emotionally, but bodily—alive and well. Lidia said a silent thank you to whomever might be willing to accept her cosmic gratefulness. And then she completely and finally for all time forgave Owen for the pain he had caused. Now she had to be sure to help Carly and Clarisse make their peace as well.

————————◉————————

The doorbell rang, bringing Lidia back to the present. She quickly took the lasagna from the oven and ran to open the door.

Polly entered the great room ahead of Kate and Rocco and twirled around with her arms outstretched. "I love it," she beamed, Opal made circles around her feet. "Hello, old girl," said Polly, kneeling to give her a scratch behind the ears.

This was Polly's first time in the new house—not the house on Apple Way, which Lidia had put on the market the day her offer on the house and orchard in East Lyme had been accepted. She had thought she would never leave her restored family home in Greenwich—the architect and Rocco had done a superb job. In the end, though, the future came calling, ushering in a new beginning, one that didn't leave behind her heritage, but instead one, she would come to see, that delivered her to her destiny.

When her old colleague Delia Larson had called to tell Lidia about a job in the city, her heart had begun to race. There was a spot in wealth management in UBS's New York office, and Delia wanted to recommend Lidia for the position. "What do you think, Lidia? Want to go for it?" Lidia's first inclination had been to act quickly. She knew all too well how high the stakes were and how tough the competition was in these lean times. But for a reason she didn't quite understand, she didn't go for it. "Think about it?" asked an incredulous Delia. Lidia promised she would, knowing full well the consequences of failure to act. "Opportunities like this don't come along every day, you know that," Delia had implored as they ended their conversation.

And think about it she did—about her working life, her clients and colleagues, her designer suits from Neiman Marcus, her Jimmy Choos from Saks, all that had gone up in smoke, figuratively, when the bottom fell out of the banking industry, and literally, when Tina's plane flew into her house. Maybe it had been a sign. Did she want, after all, to return to that world? As she pondered these and more questions, something happened, something as random as a stranger bumping into you on the street and then continuing on her way. Some would call it random, but Lidia would come to see it differently.

That very afternoon after Delia's call, a pop-up for real estate offerings flashed across her computer screen while she sat browsing online. The one that caught her eye was for an apple orchard in New York. She started aimlessly surfing for orchards for sale—in Connecticut—and that was where she found the listing for the orchard in East Lyme. Thinking back on it, Lidia was surprised at the speed at which it had all happened—as though it was meant to be. The night in May, still at Polly's, before the closing, she woke up promptly at three in the morning, agonizing over her decision. Had she acted too impetuously? Sleep was fitful, dreams rampant. In the morning she called Harry, who assured her that the new house, the orchard, and her dream of a new life were all good things.

The next day at the closing, the seller and former owner shook her hand and wished her luck. "Happy, darling?" asked, Harry, who had gone with her to the closing.

"I am now," said Lidia, knowing she would never think twice about her decision, with Harry by her side.

———◆———

Polly and Rocco and Kate took their seats on the couch looking out the large plate glass windows framing the orchard and hills of East Lyme in the distance. Lidia served them cheddar with apple splices and apple wine while they waited for the others to arrive. "A little heavy on the apple motif, I know," said Lidia, "but it's fitting, don't you think? For the first official dinner party at the East Lyme address?"

Polly's full glass sat on the table untouched. "You're going to have a hard time enjoying our little happy hour if you don't stop holding hands," Lidia said, laughing, when Polly held up both hands to show that each one was respectively linked—one to Rocco's hand and the other to Kate's. She quickly let go and lifted her glass and picked up an apple slice.

"I didn't even realize what I was doing. I hold onto Kate to convince myself she's really here, I guess," she said, glancing at Kate, who was nearing the end of one of her frequent visits to see her mother. Polly put her glass on the table again and fumbled to find a napkin for the apple, all the while looking at Rocco. "And I guess I do the same for you," she said to him, tears welling up. "I can't believe my good fortune. Rocco and Kate, with me, here, at the new home of my best friend. Not so long ago I was alone, and now look." She clasped hands with both again and looked up at Lidia. "It's true what they say about one door closing and another opening. One could get a little overwhelmed, no?" Another errant tear began to fall. "There, see, I can't help myself."

"Now you'll have to let go to wipe your eyes," said Lidia, handing Polly another cocktail napkin.

It was hard to grasp all the changes that had occurred. On this, Lidia had to agree. Here it was, the end of summer, ebbing August light casting a golden glow over the great room and its occupants in this chateau-like home in East Lyme, a home Lidia never would have dreamed of owning a few short months ago, but since April—when Polly was released from rehab—it was as if the gods had determined nothing would be the same for those who had been living or seeking shelter under the gabled roof of the Niven Estate in Old Greenwich. Lidia looked at the antique cut diamond in the platinum setting, remembering when Harry had given it to her.

———————◆———————

Soon after the closing, Harry reminded her of the "serious talk" he had wanted to have.

"Remember that Sunday morning when I sent you home in a cab—and then you didn't hear from me again? Well, for awhile anyway?"

"Yes, I seem to remember that."

"Well, that talk that we never got to have, maybe we could have it now," he had said.

Harry told Lidia he had wanted to talk to her as soon as he had taken leave from the Bureau, but Polly was the first priority. Then, when she recovered, Lidia had found the house and orchard, and Harry once again decided to wait.

"When you found the orchard, I couldn't talk to you because I didn't want to complicate things. The most important thing was for you to buy the property—to do what you truly wanted to do."

But when Harry was sure the time was right, he didn't hesitate.

With tears in his eyes, he had told her that his sister Jo had saved the diamond ring for him since the day his adoptive mother had died. She told Jo she had always wanted Harry to have it. "Maybe one day he'll look back on us, your father and me, and accept us as his parents. I know he doesn't now," she had said. "That changed everything," Harry had told Lidia, and with that he put away the old ghosts that had haunted him. Lidia said yes immediately, her heart pounding with joy, certain this was the right thing. And with her answer, Harry had slipped the ring on her finger.

And now in the new living room in East Lyme, here they were, Lidia, with Rocco, Polly, and Kate, waiting for Harry and the girls on this August evening—the first time they had all been together in Lidia and Harry's new home.

Our home, Harry's and mine, thought Lidia.

Harry came in first, apologizing for being shoeless. "I had to leave my boots outside, too much muck and dirt from the orchard," he told his guests. "Give me a minute to clean up."

"He goes out there every evening after work to check on how the apples are coming. I think his next career will be superintendent of the orchard, he's so enamored with it," said Lidia proudly. When she had told him her plan to sell the house on Apple Way to buy the orchard, he had lifted her off her feet and twirled her around until she was reeling from the thrill of it all. And now here they were, Harry, their own place, plans, and hearts full of hope.

Just as Harry joined them in the great room, Clarisee and Carly arrived. They greeted everyone and asked if there was anything to drink other than apple wine, apple juice, or apple cider.

"They're not quite as excited by the prospect of a house full of Raven Renettes as we are," Lidia explained. And with that the group made their way to the dining room for dinner.

Wedding Bells

*W*asting no time, as soon as Lidia had said yes to Harry's proposal, they set a date. By late June, Lidia was upstairs in her old room at Polly's, putting the finishing touches on her hair and makeup. Before sitting at the mirror, she turned on the TV, hoping the background noise would quiet her nerves. She half-listened to a news report about water on the moon.

"There is far more water on the moon than just about anyone thought, enough to sustain life one day perhaps," one announcer reported. "Water may be ubiquitous within the lunar interior," he said, quoting researchers, "but with life-sustaining water, the potential may be limitless. And it's been there all along."

Then suddenly, it hit her: the NASA probe crashed into a deep crater near the moon's south pole on the day Tina had crashed into her house on Apple Way. The probe had been on a mission to find water on the moon. She didn't know what it meant, getting married on the day they decided there's an ocean of water up there, but she hoped it was a good omen. She put Angelica's necklace over her head. *Something old, and borrowed,* she said to herself.

At that moment, the twins tapped gently and opened her door. "You look so beautiful, Mom," said Carly. "So beautiful," echoed Clarisse.

"It's time to come downstairs," said Carly. "Dad's waiting."

Owen stood at the foot of the stairs. "You look prettier than I've ever seen you," he said, ready to escort his ex-wife, the mother of his children, outside and down the steps to the first terrace, where Harry was waiting for her. Determined to be in the present, Lidia

was intensely aware of the significance of this moment, Owen leading her to her new life with Harry. *One door closes and another opens,*
she repeated to herself.

She let go of Owen's arm to meet Harry under a canopy of pink
and white peonies. She took in the moment, the look on Harry's face
as she took his arm, the warmth of his hand as he pulled her to him
more tightly. The minister spoke of the vows they were about to take
as Lidia looked out at the sparkling sunlight on the Sound. *I must be
dreaming,* she thought.

"I do," she heard herself say as Harry slipped the simple platinum
band on her finger.

After the vows and after Harry kissed the bride, the couple stood
together under the tent to welcome their guests. Everyone present
agreed it had been a beautiful ceremony. Harry raised his champagne
glass and said the bride was the most beautiful he had ever seen. Lidia
blushed and said everyone and everything was particularly beautiful
on this very special day. She thanked Harry for being on duty that
day On Apple Way when he had told her she was trespassing on her
own property. And then in a quick but heartfelt litany, she thanked
Polly for the wedding venue and for so much more. She thanked the
twins for their love and understanding and for their good hearts.

Then she turned to Owen. "We brought two very special souls into
this world, Owen. So thank you for being there for those years we
spent raising them." Owen, standing next to Robert, the girls by his
side, raised his glass in Lidia's direction, and with his free hand, he
blew her a kiss.

During the reception, as the newlyweds began making their rounds
of the tables under the tent Polly had insisted on, Lidia couldn't help
but be overcome. She had to keep reminding herself to "breathe and
be present," as Polly had instructed her. "You don't want to miss one
of the happiest days of your life. Be sure to take it in, all of it."

As they approached the first table, Lidia reached for the locket,
pulling it up over her head and into her hand. She and Harry then
greeted Maria Nardini, looking quite a bit sprier in her bright pink

dress than she had the last time Lidia had seen her. Her daughter, Lana, stood to shake Lidia's hand as Lidia drew her in for a hug.

Then Lidia turned to Teresa DiRavenna, reaching for her hand and placing in her palm Angelica's locket. "I know your mother would want you to have it," she said. When they embraced, Teresa whispered into her ear, "You've already done so much. Thank you for the Walters, and for the diary." Lidia assured Teresa it had been a joy to have played a small part in her friendship with the Walters. In her heart, though, Lidia took pride in that accomplishment. Soon after her trip to Dayton to meet with Teresa, Lidia had been on the phone with the Walters, explaining all she had uncovered about Tina's adoption. Lidia had been right, that Teresa knew about the Walters, but they did not know she was Tina's mother. Lidia had been instrumental in getting them together. The friendship among the three proved comforting to each of them, and soon a deep friendship developed. After Lidia had returned the diary to the Walters, Mrs. Walters delivered it to Teresa herself.

Lidia then turned to Mrs. Walters, who said with tears in her eyes, "It was so good of you to invite us. Cal wanted to come, but his health . . . you understand."

"Please send him my love," said Lidia. "And here's Harry, you remember Harry."

Lidia took this moment to look in Polly's direction and to breathe mindfully. As she did, Polly saw her and smiled.

As the evening wore on, Lidia and Harry spent time with Jo and the boys, with Robert and Owen, and, of course, with Polly and Rocco, and Clarisse and Carly, Chloe and Derek and Jen, along with all the friends and acquaintances who had touched their lives. It had been an afternoon and evening to cherish.

That night, as Lidia and Harry changed and packed, getting ready for a few days in Bermuda, Harry turned on the TV for the weather report. The reports about the water on the moon were still topping the headlines.

"The water, not immediately accessible, is incorporated in the rocky interior of the moon, according to the report. Most scientists now believe the moon was formed when a Mars-sized object hit the Earth four and a half billion years ago, knocking off material that compacted to form the moon, beginning a process leading to the formation of water molecules . . .

"We can now finally begin to consider the implications and the origin of water in the interior of the moon."

Later, after one last embrace, Harry kissed Lidia gently on her shoulder. "Good night, Mrs. Caligan."

Lidia smiled. "I like that," she said, turning on her side and pressing against him.

The implications of water on the moon, thought Lidia, drifting off to sleep. *It had been there all along. Just waiting to be discovered.* Like so much in life.

Apples of the Moon

*H*arry and Lidia were sitting in the great room of their home in East Lyme when Harry got up to put another log on the fire. "Our first fire of the season," he said. Lidia was reminded that it was October already, almost exactly a year after the plane crash that had changed everything.

Harry sat down on the sofa next to Lidia and picked up his book. Then, turning to her, he said, "I've got another one for you."

"Another what?" asked Lidia.

"Another poem. I told you I was going to learn a poem—or part of one by lots of poets—every day or every week at least, ever since we found out how much we owe to the late, great Lord Byron. So here's the latest."

Lidia, smiling at her husband-turned-poet, listened—and watched—as he cleared his throat and, after a few tentative lines, seemed to find a steady and sure voice.

> *"Though I am old with wondering*
> *Through hollow lands and hilly lands,*
> *I will find out where she has gone,*
> *And kiss her lips and take her hands;*
> *And walk among long dappled grass,*
> *And pluck till time and times are done*
> *The silver apples of the moon,*
> *The golden apples of the sun."*

"It's beautiful, Harry," said Lidia, struck by his earnestness. "I love it. Let's do it."

"Yeats, William Butler. I meant to say that at the start. Do what?"

"What it says. Say the last line again, from 'pluck.'"

"And pluck till time and times are done/The silver apples of the moon,/The golden apples of the sun."

"Yes, that. Let's do that, until time is done."

That night, after finally pulling away from one another to sleep, Lidia lay in the silver light of the harvest moon streaming into their bedroom window. Soon Harry fell asleep, and Lidia, listening to his rhythmic breathing, began to think of what he had said earlier about Byron. He had been right. They owed a lot to Byron—and to Polly of course—and her first editions.

Upon Polly's return home from the rehab center in April, she'd gained strength rapidly, and soon her attention had turned once more to her finances. Before long she was found again at her desk in the library, lamenting the state of the economy in general and her finances in particular. One day she had remarked to Lidia and Kate that she needed to consider her first editions. Maybe it was time to sell.

"How much do you think you could get on eBay?" Kate asked.

"Well, dear, probably not as much as I could get from a UK dealer. So many of my books are by British authors, and they would naturally be more appreciated in their native land, I do believe. Take my Byron collection, for example. I have so many leather-bound firsts—they must be worth something—if they haven't moldered away by now. I really haven't kept them as I should have all these years."

That was when she went over to the stacks and began pulling down her Byrons. In *Don Juan*, the volume Lidia had been reading the day Harry returned to her in the library, Polly noticed a sheet of paper peering out over the top.

"Look at this," she said, holding the sheet up to the light.

"Yes, it fell out the day I was reading it. I tucked it back in when I put the book away. Why?" asked Lidia.

At first, Polly explained, she thought it must have been

hers—she often made notes and stuck them in the pages of her favorite books—but looking at the thin, yellowed page now, in the light, it looked different. It was not in her hand, and it looked old, very old.

"I think this may have been written by Lord Byron," she had said that bright spring day.

And so it had been, in his own hand. Not a page of Polly's notes at all, it was a letter written by Byron to a friend.

After the sale to a London bookseller, the company advertised the letter for $15,000. It had been written to a Captain John Hay in 1822, thanking him for the gift of a wild boar, the spoils of a rather lavish hunt. When Byron moved to Pisa in 1821 to join the Shelleys and Teresa, Hay had become a part of their circle, but the Pisan idyll was to end badly, beginning with the death of Byron's daughter and then with Shelley's drowning. All so ill-fated, Lidia had remarked at the time of the sale, remembering her discoveries about the star-crossed lovers, Teresa and Byron.

As it turned out, the letter, which went for the full asking price, was the least of the lot. Polly had regretfully (but fortunately) sold all of it, including *The Giaour*, which had fetched the most, going for $50,000. It too had signed sheets by Byron within its pages.

"I thought I had read each volume thoroughly, turning each page, but I guess I was remiss in my perusal, thankfully remiss," said Polly when the final sale yielded enough to refurbish the Niven estate, to secure her future, and to offer a loan to her friend, which made it possible for Lidia to augment the funds required to close on the property of her dreams in East Lyme.

"But I hung on to the *Don Juan*," Polly had said. "That one I'll never sell."

———————◉———————

With her head full of the poetry Harry had read earlier, and of Byron and his first editions, lying there beside Harry, Lidia thought of yet another poem, one that would never make any-one's fortune.

Could I without regret . . .
tip my wings to one I never met
before I ventured to be free?

The last lines of Tina's poem. When she'd first read them, she had been sure they signaled Tina's intent to crash into her house. Now she saw it another way.

In this new version of events, Tina, knowing she had family in Connecticut, had intended to tip her wings to the relatives she had never met, to acknowledge them. Then—as was her intention from the start—she would turn not toward North Carolina, but instead, she would head out to sea—to be free. But she miscalculated, hor-ribly miscalculated. It had been a suicide, there was no escaping that (the empty gas tank was proof—Tina was an experienced pilot, after all), but she had never meant to hurt anyone else.

Lidia turned toward Harry, to wake him, to tell him of her new certainty, but she did not. She chose instead to lie beside him, letting the moon bathe them together in its silver light.

End Notes

*T*he main characters and events of *Water on the Moon* are fictional, as is the DiRavenna family. The Gamba Ghisellis portrayed in these pages, however, are from an actual illustrious family of Ravenna, Italy. Count Ruggero Gamba, 1770–1846, was the father of Teresa, 1801–1873, who was in love with the poet George Gordon Byron. One of Teresa's brothers, Ippolito, 1806–1890, was the father of Pietro, 1849–1903, who was the father of Amalia, who married Mario Calderara, 1879–1944, the famous aviator and friend of the Wright brothers. Pietro Gamba was a revered statesman and an acknowledged benefactor in the City of Ravenna, but he was not the father of Angelica, a fictionalized character, who in the book is the sister of Amalia. I have, in creating characters related to them, taken liberties with the history of the Gamba Ghiselli family, meaning in the process to cast no shadow on their true and noble history.

The information that Lidia finds about the family while searching online can be found at www.calderara.com.

The Byron letter written to Teresa that Lidia also finds in her search is from Byron's selected letters, August 25, 1819. It, too, is readily available online, as is Teresa's memoir, *My Recollections of Lord Byron and Those of Eye-Witnesses of his Life.*

For them all, this: *requiescant in pace.*

Acknowledgments

I would like to thank She Writes Press for providing a wonderfully supportive community for women writers. My special thanks to Brooke Warner for her guidance, her warmth, and for her always insightful suggestions. Most of all, my thanks for her unfailing encouragement.

About the Author

photo © Steve Rubin

*J*ean P. Moore began her professional life as an English teacher, later becoming a telecommunications executive. She and her husband, Steve, and Sly, their black Lab, divide their time between Greenwich, Connecticut and the Berkshires in Massachusetts, where Jean teaches yoga in the summers. Jean's work has appeared in literary journals, newspapers, and magazines. *Water on the Moon* is her first novel.

SELECTED TITLES FROM SHE WRITES PRESS

*She Writes Press is an independent publishing company
founded to serve women writers everywhere.
Visit us at www.shewritespress.com.*

Watchdogs by Patricia Watts.
$16.95, 978-1-938314-34-6

When journalist Julia Wilkes returns to the town where her career got its start, she is forced to face some old ghosts—and some new enemies.

Clear Lake by Nan Fink Gefen
$16.95, 978-1-938314-40-7

When psychotherapist Rebecca Lev's father dies under suspicious circumstances, she becomes obsessed with discovering what happened to him.

In the Shadow of Lies: An Oliver Wright Mystery Novel by M. A. Adler
$16.95, 978-1-938314-82-7

As World War II comes to a close, homicide detective Oliver Wright returns home—only to find himself caught up in the investigation of a complicated murder case rife with racial tensions.

Fire & Water by Betsy Graziani Fasbinder
$16.95, 978-1-938314-14-8

Kate Murphy has always played by the rules—but when she meets charismatic artist Jake Bloom, she's forced to navigate the treacherous territory of passionate love, friendship, and family devotion.

Shanghai Love by Layne Wong
$16.95, 978-1-938314-18-6

The enthralling story of an unlikely romance between a Chinese herbalist and a Jewish refugee in Shanghai during World War II.

Trinity Stones by LG O'Connor
$18.95, 978-1-938314-84-1

On her 27th birthday, New York investment banker Cara Collins learns that she is one of twelve chosen ones prophesied to lead a final battle between the forces of good and evil.

CPSIA information can be obtained at www.ICGtesting.com
Printed in the USA
BVOW03s0908060614

355630BV00001B/1/P

9 781938 314612